A GLEAMING SHARD OF GLASS

A Gleaming Shard of Glass

A GLEAMING SHARD OF GLASS

SOWON KIM

to those who are fighting
and to those who have won the fight

PROLOGUE

The young girl knew she was soon going to die.

Did she care? Not a chance.

Lying on the cold floor and staring at the old, white ceiling, the chilling wind from the open front door blew at her hair. The air caressed her face forcefully, as if to warn her of what was about to happen. But again, she didn't care about her death. She swatted her curly hair away, sighing.

There were so many things the young girl regretted about her life. She regretted running away so carelessly 102 days ago, so without thought. But what was done was done. There was no turning back.

"Boring," she grumbled, standing. A sense of relaxation spread through the girl's torso as she stretched her arms. "Let's just get this over with." Her feet pounded on the wooden floor, creating a symphony of intense creaks. She hoped to attract savage animals. The animals that would get rid of her and her life.

The young girl glanced at the floor, where several shards of glass were scattered about. She had always told herself that they came from the three broken light bulbs above, but she had never been sure. Just an assumption.

The moonlight glinted off a shard, making a chuckle escape her dry lips. For whatever reason, the gleam filled her with hope.

She hoped that someday, someone would be brave enough to change society. Something she'd never dared to do, no matter how great the desire had been.

The girl glanced to the purple, wallpapered wall to her left, and the large crack adorning it. She hoped that someday, a runaway like herself would find this abandoned cottage and read the entries in her notebook. The notebook that held her deepest secrets. Those secrets might activate in the reader the desire she herself had—to make change in the world. Those secrets might also confuse the reader, and they might ignore her writings, but one always had to be optimistic, right?

The young girl heard a growl from perhaps a couple of feet behind, followed by a creak from the front door, and that moment, she knew it was all over.

But the possibility of her notebook living on, of someone reading it, was enough to plaster a smile onto her face as the animal tackled her down.

PART ONE
WHEN THE GLASS IS STRICKEN

1

TO FEAR AND TO QUESTION

TWO YEARS LATER

The possibility of losing her human rights was the least of Grecia Rivera's concerns. But this time, she wasn't going to fall into a black hole of fear. This time, she was determined to have a normal day.

Grecia stood in the back corner of the grand auditorium. She kept her eyes peeled for her friends, although she knew they weren't going to arrive any time soon. She had arrived early; thirty-two minutes early, to be exact.

With trembling lips, Grecia watched as children and teenagers of all kinds—blonde, freckled, short, short-haired, long-haired—sat on whatever seat they liked with careless smiles on their faces.

No, not careless. Naïve.

Grecia ran a hand through her straight, obsidian-black hair and sighed. Waiting for your friends, and looking around a place you've been to, like, a million times. How fun!

The auditorium was perhaps the largest place in her school. A black, metallic stage covered half of the room. Once could have wrongly said that the thousands of seats were identical to those in a cinema. However, these were unable to be folded and were much softer, their texture like that of an animal's fur. The red of the seats, walls, and floors gave it a regal tone, as if the existence of the place itself were as important as the person speaking. Curtains hung from the ceiling, not lengthy enough to make contact with the audience, but enough to make a statement.

When someone has nothing to do except look around, random thoughts are inevitable. Soon enough, after about five minutes of waiting, Grecia's brain slipped into a nebula of dread. She had been determined to not get sucked into it, but deep down, she had known this would happen.

Everything is going to be okay. Everything is going to be okay. Everything is *okay.*

But *was* everything okay? If so, why would her lips be going powder-white, her teeth digging into them? Why would she be standing in the corner of the auditorium with her eyes closed, head down?

Besides, today was the city-wide Regulation Day. Today was the day she hated the most. Today, her brain would be examined, and if her level of intelligence wasn't up to par for children her age—if she failed the test—her human rights would be stripped away. She'd be considered no more than a creature.

And again, that wasn't even the greatest of her concerns.

If only the—

No. I'm not even going to think about its name.

Everything is going to be okay.

Grecia sat on a red velvet seat and faced the stage in front of her, followed by her friends Cayenne and Liam. By now the auditorium was packed with chattering. She took off her leather jacket, revealing a blue tie-dye shirt, and tied her jacket around her waist.

"Sheesh, what took so long?" Grecia crossed her arms and leaned against the back of her seat. "Liam, were you eating?"

"As always," Liam said, stifling a giggle.

Grecia smiled. "No wonder there are cookie crumbs under your chin."

"Wait, really?"

Liam swept a finger around his chin. The cookie crumbs fell off, one after another. "Aw," he said. "I wanted to eat them."

Cayenne turned, staring at him with wide eyes. "Ew. If these were the ancient times, those cookie crumbs would have had a ton of germs!"

Liam patted her shoulder. "But these aren't the ancient times, madam."

"Well, you sure sound like someone from the ancient times."

Cayenne's and Liam's laughter filled the air, making Grecia's ears tingle. There wasn't anything she loved more than seeing her loved ones happy. Or even seeing a stranger happy, for that matter.

"Now, shush," said Cayenne. "The speech will start soon. We could be punished if we talk too loudly once it—"

The words halted at the tip of her tongue as Mayor Neville's footsteps echoed through the room.

Although he was meters away, the mayor's piercing gaze sliced through Grecia. His presence was the only thing necessary to make everyone shrink. Even his footsteps' echoes radiated power. It almost felt as if there were a thunderstorm, the wind slashing through the buildings and trees outside.

Grecia gulped.

"Welcome everyone, to this brand-new day, July first. Welcome to Regulation Day!" said the mayor with a booming voice. "I am truly honored to be speaking with the future of our dear city, Nepenthe. Most of you will play an important role in our society." He paused, eyeing the audience. "But not all of you."

A chill climbed up her spine.

If only it wasn't forbidden for parents to teach their kids about Nepenthe's educational system in fear of misinformation. Then Mayor Neville wouldn't have to explain the same exact points every Regulation Day for the clueless eight-year-olds attending their first Regulation Day. Then Grecia wouldn't have to hear his disturbing speech every six months.

"But let's not talk about that for now. I shall start explaining how Nepenthe is such a grand place. How it has managed to flourish so grandiosely as just a city. Not even a country." Mayor Neville paused for dramatic effect. "What is so distinguished about Nepenthe is our education system. The education system you're going through right now is the most faultless in what lies on the planet Earth. Every child learns the basics of all subjects until the first day of the year in which they turn eight years old, when they choose what Sector they want to study in. This happens in an event we denominate *The Settling*. Their choice is based on the subject they truly enjoy. The subject they are actually talented in. Everyone in the Kinetic Sector, raise your hands! Now, everyone in the Musical Sector, your turn! Linguistic Sector! Mathematical Sector! Artistic Sector!"

Grecia's hands went up at the name of her own Sector, the Artistic Sector, as well as Liam's and Cayenne's hands. The three of them had met after choosing to enter the Artistic Sector six years ago, and they had been inseparable ever since.

"Artistic Sector equals best Sector," Liam whispered, shrugging.

Though her raised arm showed enthusiasm, Grecia cringed at the childish words of the mayor. He surely didn't know that what he thought was energizing the crowd, was, in reality, a group of cringey phrases and way too dramatic pauses.

"Why waste a student's time with activities they aren't talented in, things they don't really care about, when we could take out all the potential they have in their areas of true talent?" Mayor Neville continued. "Talent is precious. It cannot, under any circumstance, be wasted, and neither can potential. When students turn eighteen, they stop studying and taking Exétasis. After leaving their respective Sectors, they serve Nepenthe for three years through volunteer work before becoming independent citizens with bright lives up ahead of them. "

A wave of enthusiastic nods went through the audience, but Grecia's head didn't budge.

"But there are two types of...*special* people, who don't exactly fit into this education system. Let's start with the positive ones." Mayor Neville coughed into the microphone, nagging the attention of all those who had been drifting into boredom. "Some children are gifted with multiple talents. Perhaps they excel equally in both sports, math, music, and language. So, what happens to them? Are they forced to choose between all those possible Sectors they could be in? Quite the opposite, actually. Those special few are the students we encourage to apply for the extremely exclusive Governmental Sector. The only Sector that requires an application. If accepted, the multi-talented children will unlock an honorable future serving Nepenthe as a teacher at this very school, or as a worker in the Nepenthe Governmental Sector. The best part is that you may apply to the Governmental Sector at any age and at any time of the year—not only at the age of eight, when choosing a Sector.

"But we must also talk about the other side of the spectrum...when a student is completely talentless."

Oh no. The thing Grecia was afraid of, the thing she dreaded so much...it was coming.

"These talentless *creatures,* whose intelligence is not up to par," Mayor Neville said, "ruin society. They use our resources when in the future, they won't even contribute to Nepenthe, which is why they're such a waste. This is why each first day of January and July, all students from ages eight to seventeen take the Exétasi, a test to spot the creatures among us. Because we strive for a better future. We strive for a place without inequality, without hunger nor war. This is why the creatures we spot during Regulation Day are sent to Alcatraz, and everyone knows how much of a horrible place that is, considering its namesake."

Everywhere Grecia looked in the audience, she could only find smiling and grinning faces that enjoyed hearing such a horrifying speech. Grecia took a shaky breath, closing her eyes. How could she be the only one who hated hearing all of this?

"Now, to end this speech, we shall see the faces of those who failed the Exétasi on the last Regulation Day, so that each one of you can be reminded that even the most normal-looking people can be creatures."

Grecia, horrified, wrapped her finger around her ears to block out the cheers and applause around her.

No. He was right. These creatures didn't deserve to live here. Right? She gripped her ears even harder.

A hologram with a blue hue lit up the front of the stage, displaying the faces of those who had been sent to Alcatraz six months ago. Unlike the holograms in sci-fi movies from ancient times, looking at this one was equivalent to watching a movie on a high-definition display.

There were no more than five creatures, which was a relief for Grecia.

Only five.

Their memories had already been erased. Not only memories of moments, but memories about the way to talk, to write, and even to walk. In Alcatraz, they were now like newborn babies without caring parents to care for them. No food, unless the waste the Nepenthe workers threw into the terrible place could be considered nourishment.

The creatures had once been children, just like her…

Don't think about it. Grecia shook her head. *Nepenthe always does the right thing.*

2
THE EMOTION

Grecia struggled to keep her eyes open and bit her lips to seep her distress into them.

For her, the scene wasn't a show, because it made her fear appear in front of her.

Or, better said, it made it surge inside of her.

Eight months.

For eight months, Grecia had been fearing the day of the Exétasi, because it was on Regulation Days when this strange emotion would burst.

But why would she be afraid of an emotion? Weren't emotions part of human nature?

Well, what if it wasn't even *natural* for her to feel it?

She started feeling it at a young age. Back then, the impact had been close to nothing. A mere tickle. Nothing to worry about. It gradually started growing, however, and only eight months ago, the touch that the emotion had been had turned into a punch.

It wasn't anything like joy, or confusion, or regret. Grecia didn't know what it was. And that was what terrified her. Perhaps the emotion was actually something having to do with growing up, or perhaps it was girl stuff. But if it really was part of a natural process, why did it burst only on Regulation Days?

She couldn't reach out to anyone. She didn't want to be seen as crazy.

Grecia took a deep breath, keeping her head straight. The emotion rushed through her veins, making her heart race. Her muscles tightened, and it took every ounce of her willpower to not yell, to not punch the seat in front of her.

Why did it have to surge out of her whenever she saw a banishment taking place?

The hologram twitched when it zoomed in, showing the creatures' faces. One of them barely looked nine...

No. This wasn't cruel in any way. Nepenthe was always in the right. Was it?

Another reason she hated the days of the Exétasi. Everything felt wrong, regardless of the fact that banishment was for the good of humanity.

The holograms ended so quickly. Either that, or Grecia's head was too fuzzy, loaded with so many thoughts. As shown in the holograms, the creatures were carried into the boat, and it sped through the water toward Alcatraz.

When the illumination in the room disappeared, Grecia unclenched her fingers. The nail marks were more than visible.

"You're sweating." Cayenne pointed out. Grecia took some time to realize she was talking about her.

"Uh, it's warm in here," Grecia said with an awkward smile. "Sheesh. Guess it's just me though."

Noise packed the room again as if nothing had happened. People continued their casual conversations, making the Auditorium seem more like a cafeteria.

"Ahem..." The director coughed into his microphone. Silence fell over the room. "Now, for the Exétasi. Each one of you will go to your Sector's respective area, where you'll be tested."

Everyone inside the room stood from their seats, eager to get this over with. They scurried out of the Auditorium and flooded the corridors the same way pigeons would gather for treats.

"See ya, losers," Liam said as he and Cayenne joined the crowd.

Grecia went in last. The students walked about like soldiers, not one person bumping against another. It was as if they had all once been a part of the Spartan military.

School was the only place in Nepenthe with an architecture similar to ones of the Ancient Times. The walls were the color of a banana without its peel. Every fifteen meters or so, there was a thick, gray archway on the right wall, which led to a classroom. The marble ceiling, which had been curved outward like a dome, towered fifteen meters above her. It was filled with the best paintings from the best students of the Artistic Sector. She could find all types of styles—surrealism, cubism, abstract—and they all held a certain spark of uniqueness. Grecia knew that remaking these paintings would be impossible.

She wished that someday, a painting of hers would be added to the school's art collection. But that could wait. She still had six years until her graduation at the age of eighteen. After that she'd be obligated to work for three years in the service industry like every other citizen of Nepenthe. Some options for required service included cleaning streets or serving in a cafeteria, which didn't at all excite Grecia. But after completing those three years of service, she'd have all the free time in the world to paint something remarkable for this ceiling.

As Grecia daydreamed, her head hit someone's back, making her take a step backward. The person halted and spun to face her.

"You should be more careful," the boy said. He was tall with ruffled blonde hair. "You have probably ruined the whole crowd's pace." His voice was tinted with an elegant accent, which meant he was definitely from the Linguistic Sector.

"Well, pardon me, Your Majesty," Grecia said, trying to imitate his accent. She rolled her eyes as dozens of people rushed between them. She was about to walk away, but then she caught his gaze.

Her posture stiffened.

His eyes glinted with misery.

It was the type of misery that would leave Grecia unsettled for the rest of the day.

So many questions raced through her mind.What had the blonde boy gone through to look so afflicted?

The emotion made Grecia's head burn with rage Why was she asking herself such a question? The answer was obvious. Nepenthe had caused the boy's misery. Their glorious city literally sent children to their deaths. Indirectly, but it was still death, nonetheless.

Grecia snapped out of her flaming thoughts. What? Of course not. Nepenthe had always been perfect, and it would stay perfect until the end of time.

Grecia sat on a metallic chair, comfortable bands holding her hands and feet still. A white, spherical object hung above her head.

"You're Grecia Rivera, Artistic Sector, age twelve, and citizen number 32, 789. Am I correct?" said the woman sitting next to her.

Grecia nodded.

"Allow me to check your status."

The woman pulled a bracelet out of her bag, which sat on a

white table next to her, and placed it on Grecia's wrist with a *click*. "Until now, you have had twenty four examinations, all of them negative for *creature*. I see that your neurons are extremely connected. Some of the most connected I've seen among twelve-year-olds in the Artistic Sector."

Only people who worked for the government possessed the bracelet. It could recognize each citizen of Nepenthe, their examination results, and other personal details. It was kind of like a barcode scanner, but for Nepenthe citizens.

The woman continued speaking about Grecia's past test results as Grecia stared at the ceiling, doing anything but listening.

"And…that's it," the woman said. "I'm sure you'll get negative results this time too."

"Okay," Grecia said. "I'm ready."

"Alright. Eric, ready the machine." The woman's face had remained the same throughout their entire conversation, which unnerved Grecia. She shuddered.

Before Grecia knew it, an engine-like sound started running, and the ball that had once been hanging above her opened into claws and covered her head.

Her impatience caused her to count in her mind. The Exétasi always ended when she reached six. *One, two, three, four…*

A red light blinded her, and Grecia frowned. During her past examinations, there had never been a red light.

"You're done," the woman said. "You can go home now. Like always, the results will be sent to your house tomorrow morning." The same serious, robotic face.

Grecia sat there, paralyzed. Red dots swam through her vision, and she blinked to dissipate them. What had the red light meant?

Had she...failed?

No, it wasn't that. It was probably just part of a new procedure for the Exétasi.

"Thanks a lot." Grecia put on a genuine smile. She was one of the best artists of her age, after all. Teachers would always point that out. In art contests, she would always be the youngest among the top three, the other two always at least four years older than her. There was no way she could have failed the Exétasi. Of course, it was part of a new procedure.

She skipped down the room and through the hall, oblivious to the dirty looks she received from the people she had accidentally bumped into.

Phew, Grecia thought as she halted in front of the school's gates. She wouldn't be bothered by that stressful emotion until the next Regulation Day.

She pushed the metallic doors with a *clang* and stepped outside.

"Grecia!" Cayenne called from a few feet away. She wore black leggings and had a purple jacket tied around her hips. "What took you so long?"

"Well, guess it was my turn to be late." Grecia smirked as she trotted towards her friends, and of course, a lunch full of burgers and French fries.

"Hey, kids. Long time no see."

As the trio entered the McDouglas Burgers Shop, the owner, Mr. McDouglas (wow, incredible) greeted them with delight.

"Good afternoon," Cayenne said. Liam and Grecia repeated her greeting.

The restaurant only consisted of a grand room with walls made of glass. A few dozen round tables were neatly ordered to make enough space for the workers to move around. On each table lay a tablet for customers to place orders. Sprouting from the ceiling were tubes that both sucked out the empty plates and brought the customers' food.

Seemingly, Mr. McDouglas had been waiting for them.

"How'd it go?" he asked. His stout body, along with the long mustache running along his upper lip, usually weren't signs of a kind person for Grecia, but Mr. McDouglas was an exception.

"It went pretty alright I suppose," Liam said, waving at him with a warm smile. "Two Big Sets, please."

The trio sat at the nearest table. The Big Set was a combo of two burgers, a box of French fries, and two milkshakes, which was perfect for them, considering how Cayenne hated hamburgers.

"Noted." Mr. McDouglas tinkered with the keyboard on the tablet. "One with a strawberry milkshake, and the other with a cookies and cream milkshake without the cream on top, or have your tastes changed?"

Grecia could say that man knew her better than most of her friends. The three of them went to his restaurant so often that Mr. McDouglas knew every detail of their orders. Cookies and cream, Grecia's favorite flavor, had hypnotized her with its sweet and milky flavor two years ago, although she found the cream on top obnoxious. As for the strawberry milkshake—that was Liam's. For whatever reason, Cayenne would always drink water.

Liam fished a few coins and bills from his pocket and threw them inside the tube. It slurped the money into it, a *whoosh* filling the air around Grecia.

"You guys have grown so much," Mr. McDouglas said. "I remember when you first came here. Was it three years ago?"

"Four," Cayenne said.

"Right." The man wiped the sweat on his forehead with a small towel, which immediately sucked the moisture from his skin. In a blink, his forehead was as dry as coal. Nepenthe scientists were more than genius when it came to creating innovative tools.

"I remember when I was in the Cuisine Sector," he continued. "Gosh. That was so long ago. Anyway, I loved the Regulation Days."

Liam gazed at the entrance to the kitchen, eagerly awaiting the food. "It's cool," he said with a quick nod. Grecia could tell that he meant what he'd said, despite not paying much attention.

"Yeah," Cayenne agreed. "I mean, it's great to see our government in action."

"Yeah..." Grecia said with a nervous and dry laugh. "Right."

"Going to Alcatraz," Mr. McDouglas said with a sigh. "Poor creatures."

"At least it's better than the outside world. Well, at least according to Mayor Neville. And there's really no reason we should doubt *that*." Cayenne shrugged and stared out the window.

Liam eyeballed the tube hovering above them, his fingers tapping on the table with impatience. He grumbled in frustration and scratched his head. Luckily for him, the tube gently dropped their orders onto the table after Liam's eleventh tap.

"Finally," he exclaimed, patting his tummy. "Time to feed this little stomach."

Mr. McDouglas left them, their conversation simmered off, and Grecia and Liam started eating their lunch.

Grecia weakly grabbed a handful of fries and tossed them into her mouth, one by one.

But she didn't feel the crunchy fries sliding down her throat. The milkshake didn't refresh her. Not even the burger's flavor was enough to snatch her attention.

They didn't mean it. There was no possibility that Cayenne, Liam, and Mr. McDouglas actually enjoyed seeing the creatures get sent to Alcatraz.

But Grecia had heard it. All of it. How lightly they took the banishments, with no pity whatsoever in their voices, after ironically having said the word *poor.*

"What were we talking about?" Liam asked, making Grecia wince.

"The Exétasi, I think." Cayenne blew bubbles into her cup of water with a straw. She was drawing something on the table, using a French fry as a brush and the ketchup as paint.

Food used as artificial objects.

Well, they *were* artificial objects. Artificial, edible objects. Since animals had been removed from Nepenthe, scientists had come up with a way to make food with the same flavors and nutrients as meat. Even though plants and fruits weren't banned, they *were* genetically altered to be tastier and healthier.

"Right." Liam glanced at a drop of ketchup that had fallen onto his green sweater. "Am I the only one who thinks the ceremony is a waste of time?"

Grecia's hopes rose. A little bit, at least.

"I mean," he continued, "the ceremonies are getting old. We just listen to the Mayor's speech for the billionth time and see some people who don't deserve to live here get banished. They aren't even people anyway. They're animals. Why have a whole display just for them? We'd save so much time diving into testing right off the bat."

"It's whatever. I don't really mind the ceremony" Cayenne said. "You're just being impatient again."

Why were they talking about Regulation Day as if it were a birthday party they didn't enjoy going to?

That strange emotion filled her lungs once again, and Grecia gasped.

Why was she feeling it right now? It was supposed to leave her alone after the Exétasi!

Grecia's heart thumped so fast she thought it would jump out of her chest at any moment.

"I need to leave."

Grecia's chair screeched against the floor as she pushed it aside. She stormed out of the restaurant with thundering footsteps, not bothering to explain her sudden outburst to Cayenne and Liam.

Grecia only moved. She walked with no destination in mind. Every footfall was a new flare of wrath, and with every ragged breath, the roaring in her veins strengthened.

Why is the emotion so much stronger this year? This is the first time I've ever physically panicked and let it control me. There must be a reason.

After a few minutes, she sat on the cement sidewalk and wrapped her arms around her knees, panting.

The center of Nepenthe consisted of the city's school, some markets and shops, and political buildings. For a twelve-year-old, there wasn't much to see here. There were only fancy, modern buildings with artificial plants on their roofs and posters that read *SALE* or *50% DISCOUNT*. Perhaps the only store that Grecia found interesting was her mother's clothing shop, *Veronica & Co.*

Nepenthe sure did have an interesting structure though, its borders forming the shape of a hexagon. The city's architecture had been based on beehives, so even houses were shaped as hexagons, nicely stacked next to each other. There were six rows of houses shooting out of the border's vertices, and they all ended in front of Nepenthe's center, where Grecia was currently ubicated. The space between the rows were utilized as roads for vehicle transportation, and there were also smooth, metallic sidewalks beside them.

After catching her breath, Grecia stood up from the sidewalk with a sigh and continued on her walk.

Her eyes caught the NGC building, officially called the Nepenthe Governmental Center building, which towered above with such magnificence that only a few decades ago, a building similar to it would have been impossible to construct. It was one of the only buildings in Nepenthe that wasn't shaped like a hexagon. Instead, it looked like a thick string made of glass that hung from the clouds and had been twisted into knots. Artificial plants hung from the ceiling, draped along the glass like vines.

It was in the NGC where the creatures who failed the Exétasi were held for around two hours before getting sent to Alcatraz. It was also where governmental workers, officials and Nepenthe's mayor worked.

She wanted to curse that darn building so bad.

Grecia continued until she reached The Nepenthe Grand Park. It was the only park in the city, but that didn't undervalue its name.

It was a vast area of emerald green with pathways of cement surrounding it like an anaconda. Birds—robotic ones—hovered above, and the trees had been genetically modified to stand only a foot tall. Scientists had considered trees a dangerous threat to children who might fall from the branches and break their bones, even if the doctors could heal them in what could be as short as five minutes.

Grecia didn't stop. The anger that flared in her eyes was a fire burning away all the voices inside of her. The multiple voices that contradicted each other. She didn't care about them anymore.

From the corner of her eye, Grecia caught a more-than-usual scene. A mother ordering her son to do something, and the little boy immediately complying to her orders.

Typical Nepenthe obedience. Stupid Nepenthe obedience. She bet that if her teachers ordered her whole class to throw themselves off a hundred-floor building, they would comply. Because the older ones were *always* right. Well, they were, but…

Her steps were consistent for quite some time. She passed restaurants, shops, and eventually, rows and more rows of houses. She kept taking quick strides until an unexpected scenery towered in front of her.

The walls. The borders of Nepenthe. Transparent enough for Grecia to see the huge orange and red trees behind them, but not enough to perceive each detail.

Outside, it was autumn. Inside, seasons were fictitious.

I hate Nepenthe.

The thought was a fire—a fire that burned her skin. She hated her home city. She was sick of it. It was all so wrong. How could she be the only one to see that? Those kids being sent to Alcatraz had once had a family. Friends. They had plans for next week. And they were still considered creatures who didn't deserve to live here?

You're crazy, another side of her countered. *They don't do anything to help society. They deserve it.*

But this time, those whispers were nothing but annoyances. Her belief was now as firm as a hundred-year-old tree, rooted to the ground.

Grecia lifted her head, and her eyes took hold of the light pouring upon Nepenthe. Though blurry, the sun was visible through Nepenthe's borders. However, the heat didn't come from it, but from the sophisticated weather control system the scientists had made a few decades ago. Thanks to the control system, there were no droughts, no blizzards, and so on. The same perfect weather every day. The inconsistencies of the coming of seasons' due dates, caused by what people called *climate change,* didn't exist in Nepenthe as well, as the

temperature and humidity were even throughout all periods of the year.

Well, that's kinda nice...

She shook her head and faced the transparent walls once again.

Grecia could run away right now. She could cross through the wall, and it would all be over. She was sure that, on the other side, there was freedom. She was *sure* of it. The Exétasi didn't exist there, so she wouldn't feel the emotion in the Outside. Running would definitely set her free.

Freedom had been Grecia's ultimate goal ever since she'd learned the word. It tasted so sweet every time she spoke it.

There were only two things she knew about freedom. First, its definition, and second, that she hadn't achieved true freedom. Yet.

Should I run away?

Yes, of course there were going to be consequences. Everyone knew how it worked, leaving Nepenthe. It wasn't prohibited or anything of sorts—anyone could leave. But while living in such a *perfect* city, who would even think of it? Besides, as everyone said, the Outside was dangerous. Nature in its truest form, as they called it. Diseases, wild animals, and brutal death. But some people chose to cross the borders instead of getting banished to Alcatraz, even if that meant returning to Nepenthe would never be an option. The walls could detect anyone returning to the city, and if they happened to detect someone, that person would black out and immediately be taken to Alcatraz.

Strange, because even the government thought the Outside was worse.

Perhaps it was because the Outside was a place only for things worse than creatures—rebels.

Rebel was a synonym for monsters in Nepenthe, not even creatures. Monsters. Though until now, there had never been any rebel attacks in Nepenthe history, the thought of someone directly trying to sabotage the government's plans was horrifying.

So horrifying that the government had a plan for each worst-case scenario, even with the diminutive odds of a rebellion even happening in the first place.

Death for Nepenthe's enemies, as some people said. At least, that's what Grecia had been taught.

Death for the rebels.

Despite all these horrifying things people said about what was beyond the walls, Grecia knew that freedom awaited her there. Or maybe she simply hated Nepenthe more than she feared the Outside.

Maybe she should cross the border now. Why should she not? After all, the walls were only a few feet away from her. Grecia dug her gray sneakers into the ground, preparing for the run that would decide the rest of her life.

She could easily run away right this moment. Crossing the walls would be easy—they were like a waterfall that surrounded Nepenthe, just that they weren't made of water. A hologram of sorts. It would only take a few steps.

But was she really prepared to make such a choice? Was she ready to risk everything? What if this was the wrong decision?

What if, after running away, she missed what she had left behind?

Grecia gulped. She tightened her limbs once again, but this time, it didn't last. A sigh escaped her lips.

She'd come back later. She'd know when she was mentally prepared enough to run away. She'd know when it was the right time.

As long as she was with the people she loved…

As long as she didn't need to make big decisions that would change her life forever…

And as long as her actions didn't affect Veronica, and everyone that mattered to her…

Freedom could wait.

3
THE CURSED WORDS ON THE GRAVE

When Grecia's hand moved over the canvas—her fingers wrapped around a brush—it was almost like her mind was directing her movements without a thought. Instinctively, the brush moved to the right spots, displaying the foggy thoughts in her mind on the blank fabric.

She had a certain inclination to canvases. Sketchbooks were obnoxious because they couldn't be used again after all the pages were given a painting. On the other hand, canvases could be reused over and over, needing only a splash of white paint above the previous artwork. In fact, as Grecia moved her brush, countless drawings lay on the canvas, covered in ivory pigment.

Once, a teacher told Grecia that in the world of art, one sees reflections of their own mind, the way they think. But there was something else there too. She didn't know what, and perhaps she had always imagined it, but when Grecia painted, she felt closer to sanity, and it gave her peace she couldn't find in any other way.

She opened her eyes, bit her lips, and lay her eyes on the painting

The tone of it was muted and silent, a style reminiscent of Monet, an artist from beyond ancient times. Each stroke resembled a reflection in a rippled puddle. But as she soaked in all the details, her heart stopped.

On the canvas, the five kids who had been banished earlier today were sitting on the planet Earth, legs crossed. They were all holding hands, and their grins were wide enough to reach their ears. The space around them was a gala of diverse colors, from the obnoxious neon orange to the calming grayish blue. Maybe that was how life worked. It would have its obnoxious and calming moments. It would have different colors.

Grecia had painted the banished kids surrounded by life and sitting on life. The life they never had the chance to live.

Satisfied, but also saddened by the thought, Grecia set the canvas on her desk to let it dry just in time for dinner.

"Yum," Grecia said, propelling herself from the wall. She sat at the dining table in a swift movement. "Sheesh. It smells like heaven."

The living room wasn't anything luxurious—a round room with white walls and a white floor. No objects except for the dining table, its papaya-colored surface like a highlighted line in a page full of text. Six corridors shot from the living room, each one directing to another part of the house. For instance, the bathroom, Grecia's room, or the kitchen.

Spread throughout the light, orange surface was a variety of plates, from spaghetti to fried chicken. The food's scents lifted into the air and merged together, creating a fabulous smell that made Grecia's stomach grumble.

"Do you want some lettuce?" Veronica reached out her hand to the other side of the table and rubbed her daughter's back. "I also have banana milk."

"What about a cookies and cream milkshake?" Grecia

smirked at her mother before plopping a spoonful of vegetables into her mouth.

Sometimes she wondered how such a small amount of Veronica's looks had been passed down to her. If a stranger had looked at the two of them, they would have never guessed they were daughter and mother. Veronica's skin was light; Grecia's was tanned. Veronica's eyes were blue; Grecia's were brown. Veronica's hair was brown; Grecia's was black.

Her mother was wearing a plain, gray t-shirt, accompanied by a navy jacket as well as turquoise slip-on shoes. The blue skirt she was wearing reached her shins.

Grecia smiled. "I like your outfit. Looks nice."

Veronica beamed at her. "Why, thank you."

Silence filled the room as Grecia chomped on her food. After such an unsatisfying lunchtime, she was determined to gobble up everything her stomach could digest. Spoonful after spoonful, the plates started emptying.

"Can we eat barbecue tomorrow?" Grecia asked.

Veronica chuckled, crossing her arms. "Oh, come on. You should eat more things that connect you to your heritage. Because your dad's great grandma was what people used to call Mexican, you are part Mexican. I better make *quesadillas* tomorrow."

Grecia's neck stiffened at the word *dad*. She might as well have been stabbed—her whole body became still, and not a single muscle tensed, though razor blades poked her heart. "Can we, uh, not talk about this?" Her voice, muffled because of her full mouth, came out as a squeak.

"What, about your heritage?" Veronica cocked her head with a grim expression.

"No. About my...dad." Saying the word aloud left a weird taste in her mouth. A...sour, unpleasant taste.

"Grecia, you should get over this. I know it's hard, but you can't keep avoiding family conversations." She crossed her arms, and an electrifying, spiky tension ubicated itself between the two.

Grecia stopped chewing and gulped all the vegetables down. "Why can't it?" she muttered. "Do you think it's easy to just get over the fact that your dad is dead when he shouldn't? *Nobody* in Nepenthe dies unnaturally. But he did. And even the reason is unknown. So now, I'll ask you again, why can't I avoid the so-called family conversations?"

Veronica frowned, and the sparkle of gentleness that had once resided in her eyes vanished. "Grecia, you don't understand."

"*You* don't understand! You got to meet your dad!"

Veronica closed her eyes in a dangerous manner, her breaths intensifying and her chest heaving quicker than before.

This wasn't going to end well.

Before Grecia could intercede, her mother exploded.

"I'M DOING MY BEST, OKAY?" Veronica smashed her fist onto the table, making some of the plates vibrate.

Veronica's yell was so shrill that afterwards, Grecia could only stare at her. A warm tear rolled down Grecia's cheek, followed by dozens. But not one sound escaped her throat.

Regret scratched her mind. Regret of everything she had said during this conversation.

"I'm doing my best," Veronica continued, though now her voice was closer to a whisper. "I really am. I've seen and heard things you haven't, Grecia. I try to be as cheerful as possible, so that I don't spread my sadness to my own daughter. I guess that doesn't work." She spoke without spilling a single tear.

Grecia grabbed the edge of her tie-dye shirt and pulled it up to her face. The tears seeped into the polyester. "What do you mean?"

"I just want you to know that everything I do is for you." Veronica stood, walked around the round table, and wrapped her arms around Grecia.

After a moment of shock from her mother's sudden embrace, Grecia hugged her back.

"I'm so sorry I yelled," Veronica said, stroking her daughter's hair. Her fingers traced the young girl's face, from her coffee-brown eyes to her pointy nose. "Do you know that Dad would've loved you with all his heart? I bet he *does*, right this moment."

"But how?" Grecia asked, squirming away from Veronica. Light reflected from her tears. "He isn't even here with me. Or whatever."

Her mother's eyes had a sad look, but her mouth expressed warm happiness. "Some people live forever." She softly patted her daughter's chest. It took a while for Grecia to understand she was patting the very place in which her heart was positioned.

"I love you," Grecia said.

"I do, too," she replied.

Grecia thought back to the time she had visited her father's grave when she was five years old. The following words had been engraved into the tombstone:

My child will have my support and guidance in whatever they believe in. Forever and always.

And never in her life had they sounded so cursed.

4
A VERY NORMAL MORNING

"Grecia," Veronica mumbled. "We need to talk. Now."

It was the next morning, Saturday. Grecia rubbed her eyes before blinking and taking in her surroundings.

Her bedroom was half the size of the living room. It was painted completely white, with green and pink spots here and there. She lay in a sky-blue bed big enough for two people in the left corner of the room, with a clean window next to it. Her desk was to the right of her bed, and again, it was white. Yesterday's painting was still sitting on it.

Most importantly, a canvas (yes, another one) with colorful spots thrown around like confetti, stood on the other side of the room. Several old and wasted bowls were perched next to it like decorations.

"Grecia? Wake up, this has to be quick." If voices were colors, Veronica's would have been red at that point in time. Panic. Alarm.

Only then did Grecia spring to her small feet and snap her eyelids open. She kicked the bedcovers away and stood on wobbly feet.

Veronica was leaning against the doorway. She tip-toed over to Grecia, her troubled expression complemented with…were they tears?

She had been crying? What was so troubling that she had shed tears?

"Listen." Veronica towered above. She kissed Grecia's cheek, staring at her.

Grecia stared back.

"Oh gosh, it hurts to even think about," Veronica continued. After saying those words, she started trembling. Drops of liquid dripped from her face.

Tears. They really *were* tears.

A shadow formed around Grecia's eyebags. "M-Mom?" she stammered. "W-what's wrong? You're scaring me."

"Grecia," Veronica suddenly found the courage to say what she had to. To do what a real parent would do. She folded her fingers against the floor, readying her last cry. "The results came in the mail and. You—"

She took a deep breath.

"You failed the Exétasi."

The numbness that followed seemed to be everlasting, as if her nervous system had failed. The world around her dissolved, making her float without anything in mind. Grecia paused, trying to hold back the strange feelings rumbling inside her, but she couldn't.

No. It couldn't be true.

Please tell me it isn't true.

She hadn't failed, had she? This had to be a joke.

When Grecia glimpsed Veronica's devastated image, the sobs broke through.

Her fat, warm tears drizzled the cold floor below. It wasn't only a flood for whatever microbes there were, but also a flood for Grecia. A flood of desperation and confusion and panic.

It was all ruined. She wasn't even a human anymore.

Grecia leaned against a wall for support.

How hurt would Veronica be once she was gone? Cayenne? Liam? The rest of her friends?

With the result of a test, Grecia's life had turned upside down. It had changed.

The thought terrified her more than death.

"Why..." Grecia whimpered. "Why did I fail?" Common sense vanished from her, and the only thing left in her was desire. Desire to stay with Veronica. Desire to be able to go back in time, study harder, paint with more determination, acquire more calluses.

"Grecia," she whispered under her breath. When her mother had stepped to her side, Grecia had no idea. But she embraced her gently. Soft breath blew at her hair. "Calm down. I sort of knew you were going to fail the Exétasi. I knew it. Don't worry."

Grecia's train of thoughts came to a rest.

"What do you mean?" Grecia asked, rubbing away her tears. "What are you talking about?"

"Your father. He told me something." Veronica stroked her daughter's hair, sending flames of comfort to both of them. "This is something your father saw coming, though I don't know how."

Grecia blinked at least a few dozen times, trying to process the words she was hearing.

"Before he died...he told me that if we had a child, there was a possibility they would fail the Exétasi someday. I think he said it had something to do with the brain activity...in the amygdala. He didn't give me any more details. He made me promise that I would make her follow her own path. H-He made me promise I was going to do that when the right time came. I guess this is it. The right time."

By now, Grecia's tears had dried on her cheeks.

The woman's face darkened. A smile, somewhat forced, materialized on Veronica's face, making her look older and more exhausted than any average thirty-eight-year-old woman should have been. A more aggressive and piercing voice came out of her throat. "I don't know why he made me promise those things." This time, she exhaled, deflating the fury from her brain. "I guess you would understand why he did. This morning, I accepted the truth. Now it's your turn."

"But I still don't understand," Grecia murmured between sniffs. "Why did I fail the Exétasi?"

"I don't know," Veronica answered with a broken voice.

"But"—Grecia's own sobs went down her throat—"I'll have to leave you. And my friends."

What were Cayenne and Liam going to think later that day? In what ways would her life change?

"No, I'm not leaving," she said. "I'm staying here. I just can't go."

A familiar word echoed in Grecia's head.

Freedom.

What about freedom? What about it? She didn't care anymore.

An image popped into Grecia's head—the nine-year-old creature's peaceful face in yesterday's hologram, waiting to be taken to Alcatraz. No, not a creature. Girl. A child. Someone like her.

Grecia bit her lips. But…she'd have to leave everyone.

"Grecia…" Veronica sobbed once again. Her tears soaked Grecia's clothes, leaving a mark of her mother on them. Now, her clothes were stained with misery. "Even if you stay, you won't be a human. You'll be taken from me this afternoon. It's convenient for you. For me. Because as long as you're happy, as long as you're alive, even, I'll be happy with you."

Her words hit Grecia like a bullet to the heart. But not the kind of bullet that kills. The kind of bullet that shoots people into a new kind of consciousness.

After a wash of cold, she stepped from the shadows, feeling a new warmth to the day. She placed one hand on her mother's shoulder.

"I'll miss you. I swear I will. Don't forget you mean the world to me, will you?" Veronica said.

"I won't forget." Grecia let go of her lips, sniffing.

"Go, before you are taken."

Grecia stood steadily, tears blurring her vision, and gave Veronica one last glance.

After that, everything was a blur. Grecia didn't remember sobbing until she had no tears left to cry. She didn't remember running with a speed that could even match someone from the Kinetic Sector. She didn't remember the dust that coated her aching legs, or how her skin tickled when she crossed the border.

She had crossed it.

She had actually crossed it.

People gazed at the wild animal. "What a pity," they said.

For them, it was a fleeing animal that lacked common sense.

But for Grecia, she was a girl, running towards possible freedom.

Freedom. Freedom. Freedom. That word resonated inside Grecia's soul, a motivation to keep going.

Or perhaps a warning.

5
THE RUSTLE OF LEAVES

Grecia wasn't stopping for anything. Even with the unexpected, numbing cold, and the strange insects flying and buzzing around, she continued running.

The idea was rooted into her head. The greater the distance between her and Nepenthe, the closer to freedom she was. Her eyes stayed glued to the path in front of her while the forest passed in a blur of orange, yellow and red. *Autumn*, some people called it. Not even the unfamiliar hiss of the wind and the rustling of fallen leaves could distract her.

Only a day ago, she had stopped herself from running away, thinking up diverse excuses to stay in Nepenthe. Yet now, outside her home city, she was delighted.

Freedom. Freedom. Freedom.

The words thumped against her head like a heartbeat.

Freedom. Freedom. Freedom.

Every time her inner voice said it, Grecia wanted it more.

Freedom. Freedom. Freedom.

It was that word that kept her going, made her muscles function, made her brain conduct them. But one word came into her mind.

Mom. Mom. Mom.

Grecia's back hit the grass with all the elegance and charm of a rhinoceros, as she gulped a mouthful of dirt. Her legs shivered, and she felt as if they were fading away. But what caught her attention the most was a salty liquid trickling down her forehead.

Sweat. Strange. Only people from the Kinetic Sector got that.

"I…" she whispered. Now, what had once been utter determination was complete hopelessness, with guilt as a final touch. "I left Mom. And my friends."

"Because as long as you're happy, as long as you're alive, even, I'll be happy with you."

It was then that all pain came back to Grecia, that her brain picked up on it. Hunger, thirst, cold, absolute fatigue…and the bitter choice she had made. Guilt of leaving the person who had held her life up.

Grecia's sight fogged up, like what happens when one is wearing glasses in a humid place. But this time, it wasn't her tears. Throughout the Stygian space, her heartbeats and wheezes thundered, echoes ringing in her ears.

Would her father have wanted her to experience these things?

Perhaps the answer to that was an *absolutely not*. Or perhaps an *of course*.

Who knew?

In the darkness, wisps of fog cradled Grecia from the slicing cold. Wind blew at the dead leaves, whistling an eerie, spine-chilling song. Another sound overpowered the melody. Droplets of water plopped on the invisible ground in a constant rhythm.

Those were followed by the clicking of light footsteps, growing louder and louder. Closer and closer.

People?

The murky tendrils of fog tightened themselves around her and pulled her from the black, unconscious world.

The first thing Grecia saw as her eyes snapped open was the vague silhouette of a person looking down at her. Two, actually. But as her vision clarified, she found two girls staring at her. Grecia blinked several times to make sure she wasn't dreaming.

What? How?

"Oh, look, fancy girl woke up," one of the girls said.

Grecia was lying down, the two strangers standing above.

She tried to stand, but even bending her knee shot an ache through her body. The only thing she could do was glare at the girls in confusion.

They both had the shoulders of swimmers, the torso of wrestlers, and brown skin with a warm undertone. The girls' hair was a chaotic mess, reminiscent of a bird's nest.

Their clothes were all brown from ankle to neck. There was no brown in their shoes, however, because they didn't exist; the two girls were barefoot in the cold.

Grecia shifted her focus to her right. An enormous hole that reached the top overwhelmed her already tired brain. The light that poured in spilled on the ground, and through the hole she could see what looked like…trees.

A place with a giant hole, set in nature…

The description perfectly fit her conception of the word *cave*.

A yellow-brown tone coated the rocky top of the cave, which was textured with bumps of various sizes; same with the areas to the front and left of Grecia. Behind her, however, was nothing but a heap of boulders and stones of an odd, black tone, spotted with green.

Waking up to find yourself surrounded by strangers, in a place you had only seen in drawings—how unexpected was that?

And the strangest thing was that the girls looked *exactly the same*. No, they didn't look like the usual twins. They were simply the same person. The only difference Grecia could see between them was that one of them had a warmer glow to her smile, as well as two moles around her left eye, while the other one had some annoyance sprinkled into her frown.

Who were they? Why were they here, outside Nepenthe?

"Hey," the girl with the frown said. Her voice was Mariana Trench-deep, which didn't match her appearance. "Why are you so heavy? Carrying you here was a pain." What followed was silence, but she wasn't done. Soon after, she grabbed something out of a pocket from her pants and passed it to the girl with the moles.

Grecia didn't have enough energy to ask them who they were or what they were doing. The only sound that escaped from her throat was a weak grunt.

The strangest thing happened afterwards.

The girl with the moles touched Grecia's mouth.

What was she doing, and why?

Oh no.

She wasn't touching Grecia's mouth. She was *feeding her with her hands.*

Was the girl poisoning her? Trying to mess up with Grecia's tongue? Or her mouth? Dread climbed up Grecia's toes.

Surprisingly, an umami, delicate substance clashed with Grecia's tongue, making color return to her skin and lips. Even though the flavor was unpalatable to the point where she could have puked, it energized Grecia. She tried separating her lips to finally talk. Unfortunately, the annoyed-smile girl put her index finger on the rescued child's lips.

"Don't worry, it's just something we found in the river close by," she said, smirking.

Grecia's skin looked like it was going to turn pale again. She tried to open it once again, this time to protest, but the finger on her lips was a barrier for her vocal cords.

The annoyed girl snorted. "What? You've only eaten fancy food?"

Grecia tilted her head, her emotional state in the middle of confusion and anger.

"By the way, my name's Juniper," she added. "And this is my irritating twin, Sienna." She pointed at the girl with the moles and the warmer smile.

Sienna glared at Juniper.

"Yeah, I'm Sienna," she said. "We saw you running like crazy three days ago, so we thought you needed some help. That's why we brought you here."

Grecia would have only nodded if not for her quick brain. "Three days?" she exclaimed, pushing Juniper's finger aside. "What do you *mean*, three days?"

"Yeah. You were asleep for three days straight. Quite usual for someone's first day, actually," Sienna explained, scratching her nose with a finger and making it wiggle.

"What did I eat?" Grecia asked, pointing her finger at the twins accusingly.

Juniper was about to say something when Sienna glared at her. By now, it could be assumed that Juniper had been on the verge of saying something sarcastic.

"That's fish," Sienna said matter-of-factly.

"Yeah, and some fancy girl didn't even know that. That's what I call hypocrisy," Juniper retorted with a snort.

"For once, I agree with you." Sienna sighed, covering her face with dusty palms.

Grecia scowled at the twins. She sat up, but a bit *too* rapidly. As soon as her head lifted itself from the ground, she stumbled down in shock. Her limbs were noodles, her feet blanketed with spikes.

"Ugh," Grecia grunted once more. "Who *are* you people? What are you doing outside the walls, and why are you helping me? How are you—uh, alive? Also, who's Juniper and who's Sienna, again? I need to call an adult right now..."

The two twins glanced at each other, as if thinking, *not this again*.

"I thought you would realize this by now," said Juniper. "There are no adults here. Like, *duh*. You know that no adult in Nepenthe would escape. They've passed all the Exétasis, and the city is perfect, and yeah. You know what I'm talking about. There used to be one, though. He helped us survive. But he was kind of old and some things happened." She looked down, frowning. "Anyways, no adults here. Oh, and I'm Juniper. That's the extremely irritating Sienna."

Sienna slapped her twin on the cheek, and they both burst out in laughter.

Grecia shook her head and blinked. "Gosh," she complained. "I don't even know what's happening. Is this a dream or something? I can't believe I left my mother in Nepenthe."

The twins, clearly confused, gaped at Grecia. Their lips were pursed, and their smiles turned into frowns. An awkward silence separated them, and Grecia scratched her neck.

Soon after, Juniper burst into laughter.

"Oh my gosh." *Wheeze*. "So you're the type of kid who thinks their parents love them?" she hollered. "That's"—*wheeze*—"hilarious!"

Sienna buried her face in her arms, embarrassed. She turned to glance at Grecia.

"Sorry for her behavior. She's usually like this."

But Grecia wasn't listening. Her pupils wavered as she gulped.

"The reason I'm here is because my mom loved me. *Loves* me," Grecia said with confidence. "Don't assume things about me without really knowing me."

"Okay, we understand," Sienna said with an emphasis on the

we. "But first, let us take you to our home...." She paused. "You've never told us your name.

"M-my name's Grecia," she stammered.

"Age?"

"Twelve. You?"

Juniper snickered. "I bet she just escaped because of puberty and not because of valid reasons."

"We're sixteen, by the way." Sienna shot a look of warning to her twin. "I bet you're wondering how we ended up here. You see, it's a long story, so I think you should follow us. We'll take you to our home."

"Why should I trust you?" Grecia asked, arching her eyebrows.

"We're offering you food and a home here in the wild," Juniper said, exasperated. "Also, we're people who understand you. Kids like you. Cool, right? Now, let's go."

Grecia was pretty sure that by *home*, Sienna meant *dumpster* or *just a place where we eat and sleep.* However, when you've lost your mother and there are people offering you at least some shelter, you only have one choice.

Besides, a sentence had caught Grecia's attention.

Also, we're people who understand you.

Had they been referring to that strange emotion?

Looking at Grecia's face of worry, Juniper tried to cheer her up. As sarcastically as possible, of course.

"Calm down, you can trust us. Besides, our place smells like roses."

"Okay," Grecia responded, trying to remain courageous. Or at least somewhat unafraid. "But if I discover you were lying to me..."

"Let's go," said Juniper, standing up and cutting her off. "We have to go before night, or else some stupid wild animals like bears and wolves will try to hunt us down and eat us. How fun!"

Grecia had never thought of the Outside as beautiful.

They had been wrong. They had been completely wrong. This place was amazing. How could she even compare this to Nepenthe?

The cold, however, was unignorable, and the wind fiddled with Grecia's skin with its frosty fingers. She rubbed her arms and hands, trying to stay warm. The temperature wasn't the only unignorable thing, however.

The autumn forest shimmered with life around the trio, and the dead leaves gave satisfying crunches under their feet. The orange and red frosting of the ground fit well with the brown and thin trunks poking out of it. The sun shined through the thick cap of leafless branches above, spotting the ground with light. Twirling through the air, a pair of dry leaves grazed her nose before landing onto a patch of sunbeams.

While Grecia stumbled along the way, she grinned through chapped lips. Swallows sang in the canopy, and their chirps were oddly relaxing. It took a moment for Grecia to realize the swallows weren't robotic—that they had beating hearts inside of them.

This, Grecia thought, *is what I can call freedom.*

"Oh, look." Juniper smirked. "Fancy girl is pretending she's a princess. She thinks this forest is heaven. Don't you? Can't wait for you to realize some serious things."

By now, Grecia knew to ignore Juniper.

It wasn't long before Sienna and Juniper halted in front of an opening, about three feet tall and three feet long, on the left wall of what looked like an old fortress.

"This"—Juniper snorted (she sure did love snorting)—"is our home. I'm very sure you'll adore it. Like, a lot."

Juniper bent her knees and elbows to crawl through the

opening. Without a choice, Grecia followed behind Sienna and crawled into the unknown.

Juniper couldn't have been more wrong.

Inside the hole was a tunnel that curled away into infinite corridors and darkness, the light that showed the rough walls dwindling as it snaked away. Grecia's skin shuddered, and her brain started to defocus, searching for a way out.

Her knees were sore from having crawled for such a long time. Well, at least for more time than she had ever crawled. The fact that they seemingly weren't going to get to their feet in a long time, with still no change of environment, wasn't encouraging.

Also, this place was plain stinky.

It was the kind of smell that demanded attention. It smelt of old fried eggs and coffee, tinged with a cigarette that had come out of the trash can.

"Why does it smell so bad?" Grecia asked. "I don't even want to breathe right now." What could have been a sentence with an exclamation mark turned into a plain one, but only because Grecia was eager to breathe as little as possible.

"I can almost see you complaining," Juniper said, rolling her eyes. "I may as well call you Complaining Girl." A cruel, mocking laugh echoed through the corridors, making it sound like a whole crowd was making fun of Grecia.

"Juniper…" Although she couldn't see Sienna's expression, Grecia could imagine her scowl. One that resembled the gaze of a wolf, studying its prey for the right moment to attack.

"Fine. I'll only say, 'Nice things.'" Juniper grunted, but it wasn't long before she forgot what she herself had said a few seconds ago. "Welcome to the place of your dreams! "It's genuinely cool for me, but for you *fancy* kids who have parents, maybe not."

"She's joking." Sienna shook her head in a motherly way. "We'll be arriving soon, by the way." Her voice's volume lowered a considerable amount. "You'll uncover the reality of this tunnel."

The way she had spoken caught Grecia's attention. She could tell Sienna was hiding something. Grecia's crawl quickened, almost making her slip. It wasn't long before she recovered and steadied her pace.

"What do you mean?" Grecia asked in between pants.

"You'll discover soon enough," replied Sienna, biting her nails.

Grecia suppressed a grin.

You'll discover soon enough.

A phrase Veronica would say whenever she had a big surprise for her daughter. Oh, how bittersweet it felt, hearing those words.

Before Grecia knew it, her eyes became bloodshot.

She tried to control herself by holding her nose and covering her mouth. But tiny, warm drops of water started flooding out of her eyes. "Sheesh, w-what's with all these tears?" stammered Grecia, her voice unbalanced. She was sobbing with a throat that hadn't made contact with water for three days.

Juniper stared at the floor, clearly not knowing what to do with her. She opened her mouth, but nothing came out.

"We have a lot of things to work on," Sienna said, pressing her lips into a thin line.

They continued inching toward the surprise, centimeter by centimeter.

"We're close," said Sienna after a while. "There in about three minutes."

"Can we rest for a bit?" asked Grecia, letting go of a heavy breath. "I'm tired." That much was obvious; dark circles drooped from her eyelids, and her lips looked like a drought had plagued them.

"Oh my gosh, I'm so sorry." Sienna stopped and crossed her legs like a pretzel. "I forgot you were tired."

"But they're waiting for us," complained Juniper. "It's just three more minutes."

This time, Sienna ignored her. It must have not been normal for her twin to stay silent, because Juniper glared, clearly surprised.

"We'll rest for five minutes while Grecia catches her breath," announced Sienna. "We need this too."

"Yes, of course we do. Even if we do this thing every day and never get tired," grumbled her twin. "Obviously we need some rest."

While the two of them had a staring contest, Grecia breathed heavily. Her chest rose and fell as sweat trickled down her neck.

"Relax," said Juniper, rolling her eyes. "Breathing too heavily will make you feel more tired."

After a few minutes of rest, the three girls set off on their small journey again. They passed corridor through corridor, crawling step by step, until they arrived at a tiny door.

The door was so camouflaged into the tunnel's walls that, unless they were aware of its existence, anyone sitting there for hours, staring, wouldn't have noticed it.

"Welcome to Home," Juniper said. "Yes, we just call it Home. So creative, am I right?"

She carefully pushed the wood, and as it creaked, Grecia's mouth formed a circle.

The inside was incredible.

The walls and floor resembled sheets of blue glass. In the middle of the circular room stood a carton box the size of a piano bench, decorated with sprinkles of mud. There were two words written on it: *FOOD STORAGE.*

The best thing was that although the room didn't smell like roses, it didn't smell bad at all. There was no smell, which relieved Grecia.

Food, lots of space, and no unacceptable odor.

Grecia's eyes went wide in happiness.

She raced like an avalanche and tried opening the box of food, clawing at it. However, the lid was quite heavy for someone as small as her. She frowned, upset at the fact that she was much weaker than she'd thought.

A chill crawled up her spine. It wasn't long before Grecia noticed the uneasy rain of stares. She turned around to meet eyes with three other kids.

Their clothes were brown like Juniper and Sienna, although the tone varied from person to person—some lighter, others darker. They, too, were all barefoot. A boy walked up to her, hands hidden behind his back. His eyes, wide and unblinking in curiosity, locked with Grecia's.

"My name's Washington," he said as soon as he got close enough to their new companion. He extended his hand with a light smile, patiently waiting for Grecia to shake it. His dark skin, covered in sweat, glistened against the light coming from the torches on the walls. Almost nothing remained of his short, brown hair, as it had been cut into a short style. He appeared to be at least a year older than her, as he had to move his head fully downward to make eye contact

Grecia was glued to the ground. Apart from her quivering chin, the shock didn't let her muscles move. What was wrong? She was usually social, always the first to talk.

Was it possible that so many kids like Grecia existed? Kids that *perhaps* understood the strange emotion?

"Hi," she stuttered. Or at least tried to. What came out from her mouth was a whisper.

"Sorry, I didn't quite catch that. Can you say that again?" asked Washington, leaning closer.

"Hi," Grecia repeated. This time, her breath touched his face, but there were no audible words.

The boy shrugged his curiosity away, running at his fellow friends (cave mates?). Three pairs of eyes met Grecia's, watching her every move.

"Guys," Sienna called. "This is Grecia. She finally woke up." Inclining herself closer to Grecia, she whispered, "You have to present yourself."

Grecia nodded, shifting her weight from foot to foot. "I'm Grecia," she said. "A-and, um, I ran away three days ago." She paused, trying to fish out memories from the not-so-distant past. "I like painting and stuff related to that. I used to be from the Artistic Sector, and…yeah." Grecia finished off with the regalest word in linguistic history, as good as she was with words.

"I'm Maya," a girl standing next to Washington yelled. Grecia estimated that Maya was slightly taller than herself, therefore about her age.

The giggle that reached Grecia's ears, coming from Maya's lips, was an unstable one, as if something incredibly hilarious was going on. Which wasn't the case. Maya started doing jumping jacks, and then trotting about the room. Her blonde hair swished with her every movement. Her grin lightened up her face, which was covered with pale, acne-covered skin.

Grecia's eyes followed the strange girl, curious of what she might do next.

Maya's trot ended next to the box of food, in front of an object Grecia hadn't noticed before. A bowl. Its bright brown color made it look like it had been made in a factory. When Grecia looked closer, however, she could see tiny marks, coming from the construction of it. And of course, the strong, green smell made it clear that it was made from natural wood.

Maya grabbed it and lifted it, one inch at a time. As she did it, several swishes came from it, and reached Grecia's ears. The sound of…

Water.

She immediately ran toward Maya, her arms shaking from the thought of feeling water descend through her stomach and throat.

Please don't tell me it came from the forest, Grecia thought.

"It came from the river nearby," Maya said proudly. Grecia's lips parted open, but not wanting to show too much disappointment, she gulped and forced a grateful smile.

"Okay," Grecia said. "Okay. I'll drink it." With both hands, she grabbed the bowl, and her lips touched wood.

Surprisingly, it wasn't too bad. Not bad at all, actually, although it was tinged with an odd, salty flavor.

"That was *okay,*" Grecia thought aloud, grinning at Maya. She beamed back. "It feels different. The flavor and all."

A sudden drowsiness took over Grecia. A drowsiness that reminded her of how she'd fallen unconscious after escaping Nepenthe. This time, however, it was more enlightening than painful.

"Sleep," Sienna whispered comfortingly. "You've been running and walking for a long time without enough food and water. I'll wake you up when it's time and tell you the rules of Home."

Rules? Why were there rules outside Nepenthe?

She'd worry about that later. She was too tired to think anyway, and it wasn't long before Grecia, lying on the cold floor, was wrapped in profound sleep.

6
CARVING BY STONE

"First rule: you don't leave this place for the next two weeks, because you're new and could ruin the work. There's one exception, but we'll talk about it later. After the first week, you'll be an escort to help both Maya and Washington in their work. Then you'll work on your own until who-knows-when. Simple.

"Second rule: everyone here, except for the newbies, goes outside every day to collect food, water, and other things we need. Like wood. For the fires, you know.

"Third rule: on the last day of newbies' first week here, we have a sort of camping thing where we have fun. Enjoy."

Among the words Grecia would have wanted to hear in the morning, *rules* wasn't one of them. But at least the third one sounded fun.

"Any questions?" Sienna asked when she was finished with the rules. Her uplifted chin gave a glow of authority and pride. She sure did like being listened to.

It was time. Grecia had to make sure these people also felt the emotion. Well, Sienna kind of had said that yesterday. But just in case. However, first she'd have to ask the basic questions. She didn't want to stress the other girl out.

"How did you make this place?" Grecia asked. "Like, out of nature?"

"Oh," Sienna started, twisting her head to examine the place. "Actually, we didn't make it. Probably a sewer from ancient times, according to Juniper. She was from the Historical Sector back when she lived in Nepenthe."

Grecia nodded. "Do you have spare clothes?"

"No. We use the same clothes every day. And wash them when we work. Y'know, we mostly work in front of a lake."

"What kind of food do you eat?"

"We gather fruit from the trees. And fish. The fish is good."

"Where do I go when I want to go to the bathroom?"

"Near a tree."

"Ew."

"Any more questions?"

"Yes. How did I get here in the first place? Since I was asleep, I didn't see anything."

Sienna sighed in an amused tone. "You have lots of questions." She flicked something out of her hair, maybe some sand or flint. "Juniper and I were looking for fruit when we saw you run, trip, and pass out. Brought you here, but since you weren't waking up, we tried waking you up with cold water from the river."

Being woken up with cold water...Grecia shuddered.

"The water plan failed too, but you woke up on your own a bit later," Sienna continued, biting a hair strand. "So, we brought you here, as you know. Everyone was so curious, seeing you asleep."

Oh no. They must have heard her snoring. A boy from the Linguistic Sector had once described her snoring as a *troupe of men sawing away at a pile of logs.* A horrifying experience, it had been.

Grecia straightened her gaze. She had to ask Sienna about the emotion she'd feel every Regulation Day. She needed to know if all the kids here had really felt it too—if the emotion had something to do with failing the examination. Just as Grecia was about to open her mouth, Sienna waved at her to stop. "Before you ask me—and I know you were going to ask me this—I'll explain to you how *I* ended up here," she said. "It's easy. I used to be from the Kinetic Sector. You know, sports and dance and everything that has to do with body movement. I was a swimmer." Her face, body…everything froze. It was as if her body had stopped functioning, her brain being flooded by the feel of water passing through.

Sienna shook her head, and her gaze returned to Grecia. "Sorry. Got distracted. Whatever. I failed the examination. My muscle memory, and stuff…I was not fit for that Sector, I guess…I mean, I like the sport, but maybe it wasn't my real talent. And I preferred being in a super dangerous place than having to be stuck in Alcatraz. I think you get it. With my twin, I made this place right after we ran away around two to three years ago. A place for others like me, who decided the Outside was better than Alcatraz." Nostalgia filled her eyes, making them glow. "I miss my home."

Grecia's thoughts left her mind. Her pharynx cut short, making her unable to talk. The strange emotion didn't matter anymore. It didn't matter if the kids from Home felt it too.

Because they were broken. The kids from Home had taken that part of them that was broken and had made it into a beast, a beast that was willing to survive even during the most difficult of situations. Even when being in the Outside.

They missed Nepenthe. Unlike Grecia, they hadn't come here with at least a small level of desire to do so, or with a goal like freedom, but because it was the better option. That moment, she decided that she would be the bandage to their wounds, the medicine to their illness. Or at least she'd try.

More people were affected because of Nepenthe's ways. Destroyed, broken inside.

I hate Nepenthe, Grecia thought, fierceness burning in her eyes. *I'm glad I left. I'm glad I can help now.*

With the patient determination of a spider, even something as intricate as a web can be fashioned again and again. And with that same patient determination, something as powerful as change could be made over and over again.

Well, not change…change was too risky.

"Anyways," Sienna said, "I'll go gather some food and water. Stay with Brink, he's also new. He failed the recent examination too, so he's only been here for two days. Returning as soon as I can."

Grecia's stomach growled at the mention of food.

There was only a small amount of water left, and Grecia drank it all. She and Brink shared the bananas and apples.

"What do you like doing?" Brink asked, his feet dangling from the large stone he had made his seat.

Brink wasn't as social as the others. He and Grecia had taken quite some time to talk, with Grecia presenting herself first. He was a pretty average boy, with brown, average hair, and a plain, average face. He was like one of those kids one glanced at in the supermarket. He was a few inches shorter than Grecia.

She thought about Brink's question. She liked painting, but she also liked hanging out with her friends, running around in the park, talking with her mother…

Veronica's sweet voice engulfed Grecia's mind, telling her to flee, telling her to do what she felt was right. Her brain flooded with pictures of Veronica. Her mother's eyes twinkled with laughter and her teeth glistening as she smiled. A vulture gnawed at her chest as she thought of what she had lost.

It was alright. Veronica was happy now, because Grecia was happy. She had said that herself.

Brink's made-on-purpose cough, and his expectant face interrupted Grecia's deep thinking. He tapped his fingers on his lap.

"Can you answer?" Brink asked, raising his arms in exasperation. "I asked you at least a billion times. Or at least, I think so. Math is not my forte."

"What?" Grecia asked, traveling in time through her brain, trying to extract the boy's question.

"I asked you what you like to do." He pronounced each word carefully.

"I..." mumbled Grecia. She'd prefer not to say anything that had to do with her loved ones, for the sake of herself and Brink.

"I like art," she said, grinning. "Especially painting. Painting is *the best.*"

"Oh," Brink said. "Draw something for me. I'm bored. Seeing something might be interesting."

His dull expression told differently, but he probably wanted to pass time doing *something* instead of staring blankly at the ceiling.

"But there isn't any paper here." Grecia inflated her chest, as if wanting to look fierce. "I'm afraid it isn't possible for me to draw something for you." She hoped it would make the boy laugh.

Brink rolled his eyes, and Grecia's face flushed in embarrassment.

"Do what you have to do. Use what you have, like rocks," he said, picking his nose.

Grecia's face scrunched itself, and her mouth went wide in shock, horrified. But not because Brink had picked his nose.

Drawing rock against rock? What kind of substandard human being would do such a thing? Drawing was art. Not caveman stuff. However, Brink was already sharpening an especially small stone with the help of the strong wall next to him.

She didn't remember fixating her gaze on the boy, but soon Grecia was staring at him with wonder.

"Why are you looking at me like that?" Brink squeaked, blushing. He folded his arms crossly, waiting for an explanation.

Grecia's face became a bright tomato, turning her back against Brink.

Whatever.

The whole room vibrated with the echoes of the sound of rock against rock. It was as if the metallic part of Cayenne's favorite pencil were being dragged through the wood of her desk.

Grecia didn't look behind her for the next quarter of an hour, until the rock was completely edged and sharpened. Brink turned around and offered the stone to Grecia.

"Here. Use it for drawing."

"But—"

"Isn't this your hobby?" The boy savored the word *hobby*, as if it had been the first time he had used it in real-life situations. As if he had once known the word, but not used it for a long time.

Which Sector had he been from? She softened her scowl. Fine, she was going to use the rock for Brink's proper entertainment. She didn't want him to hurt any more than he already was.

Pleased with her decision, Grecia grabbed the tool as if it were a precious, ancient diamond. Or better—a new generation paintbrush, yet to be released for the public.

"Now can you draw?" Brink asked, raising his eyebrows.

Grecia gulped down a retort. "Okay."

She took the rock from his outstretched hand, turned to face the wall, and started carving. And she didn't stop.

The rock became a pencil, precisely sharpened. The wall became a gray, concrete canvas, one in which she could effortlessly carve.

It took her hours and hours. She was so immersed in the drawing that she didn't notice the other kids gathering around when they returned. Grecia hardly blinked. Her body had been transported into a new world of creativity.

Something not only stirred in her, but it overtook her mind, her body. The rest of this world had become an unimportant blur that vanished into the far recesses of her memories, and a blanket of passion and joy fueled her.

Time was meaningless. Space was nothing. Just Grecia, the pencil, and the wall.

In a blink, she was done, sadly, and her vision snapped back into reality.

She had drawn a woman. A woman with carefree, flowing hair and lovely, detailed eyes. The nose, the lips, and the eyes had been so intricately engraved that the carving didn't look like it had been made from raw stone.

The children gathered curiously, gawking in wonder.

"How did you do that?" asked Maya, pointing at the art.

"I gave her the idea," Brink stated in a timid voice, "so I—uh —get the credit." What a jealous little boy he was.

The only one who responded to him was Sienna, who kindly gave him a thumbs up and patted him on the back.

"Who's that?" Maya asked.

Grecia had been so concentrated on drawing that she had been unaware of *who* she'd been drawing.

"It's nobody," she spat.

However, *Mom* was the only thought that resonated in her mind.

Grecia's body was at Home, in the forest, surrounded by unknown children. But her soul was still in Nepenthe.

"What was the crying for?" Maya asked. "That was *very* awkward."

Grecia blushed, remembering how she had shed quite a few tears after carving the portrait.

"Maya," Washington said after a chuckle, "you cried a lot when you first got here. I mean it. We all did. This girl over here, Grace, she isn't crying much at all compared to Brink when he showed up the other day."

"My name is *Grecia*," she corrected as Maya giggled.

Washington smiled, and when Grecia glanced at Brink, he turned away with a reddened face.

The giggles in the air were oddly…heartwarming.

They rolled about the room like spinning tops. Although they weren't melodic at all, their mere existence warmed Grecia's heart.

So they do have their happy moments. That's great.

Everyone, Grecia included, held a branch over a fire. Each crackle meant a darker tone of brown for the chunks of fish at the ends of their branches. From raw to edible. From hunger to satisfaction.

"Alright, people," Washington yelled. "That was enough time for the fish to cook. Go on and eat. Hurry up."

Guess he was from the Cuisine Sector. A chef hat would have looked great on him.

Without waiting, Grecia's teeth dug into the fish's flesh, a crispy yet soft feeling clashing with her tongue, which was wet from drinking tons of water.

The fish was warm. Hot, in all honesty. But that didn't stop Grecia from putting out her fire of hunger.

She stared at the flames in front of her. Hunger wasn't the only thing that had been bothering her today. She couldn't keep herself from thinking back to her escape.

A few words prickled inside of her. Seven, to be exact.

I knew you were going to fail.

What had her mother meant? Veronica had said that Grecia's father had told her that she'd fail, but it still didn't make any sense. How had *he* known that?

As an orange flame roared upward, eating its way through the wooden pyramid at its base, Grecia could almost see her mother's face, smiling at her, saying how proud she was...

Grecia rubbed her eyes dry. No, not again. She wasn't going to embarrass herself.

She had been so focused, so terrified about running away when she'd failed the Exétasi, that she hadn't thought about why she'd failed the Exétasi in the first place. She had always been a talented artist. Even the examiner had said that the possibility of failing was nearly zero.

Yet here she was.

Whatever had happened, it didn't have to do with her neurons, or how much information her brain contained. Or how smart she was.

If only she could remember the word Veronica had mentioned. Something about activity in some part of the brain. Then she could ask someone who had been from the Scientific Sector about it. If only...

Forget about it. She was here, outside, and free. She didn't need to worry about why any longer. It wasn't like she'd be returning to Nepenthe.

Grecia curled her fingers around her sneakers' shoelaces, carefully twisting them, untying them. When her feet broke free from her shoes, Grecia bent down, grasped the sneakers, and hurled them into the fire. With a sigh of satisfaction, she then furled her socks away as well.

Grecia chomped on her fish again. It was cold now.

She was barefoot. Barefoot like the kids here, in Home. She was part of them now. And not part of Nepenthe anymore.

"Why don't I have a father?"

That had been the first question Grecia had asked her mother at the age of seven. Grecia usually asked her teachers at school for clarity, but this question, she knew, couldn't be answered by any teacher or tutor.

Veronica remained seated, her head down, and a shadow cast a dark glow onto her face. She opened her mouth to say something, but as if the words had gotten stuck in her throat, she pressed her lips together grimly.

"Why don't I have a father, Mom?" Grecia asked once more, her voice harder, sharper this time. "Why does everyone else have two parents? Why am I the only one with just a mother?"

Grecia's mother turned her head towards her daughter in slow motion, and when her eyes landed on Grecia's teary eyes, she sighed.

And then, Veronica finally explained everything.

Everything she didn't know.

"I have no idea, Grecia," she said, her head sinking in her sweaty palms. "I really don't have a single idea." She launched herself into her daughter's arms. "I'm so sorry."

Grecia stood motionless, chin trembling and lips quivering.

And she hugged Veronica back.

"It hasn't been easy for me either," her mother whispered into her ear. "But we're gonna make it together. We're gonna reach the end of this dark tunnel."

Grecia closed her eyes, tears streaming down her wet cheeks. Yes, they would cross through this dark tunnel. Not alone.

Together.

Veronica came back home with a cardboard box under her left arm the very next day. She placed it on the dining table before rubbing her sweaty hands on her navy leggings.

"What's that?" Grecia asked. She had been sitting on one of the chairs next to the table, eating an apple to conquer the grumbling hunger she had suddenly felt.

"A little something." Veronica flashed a warm smile at her.

Grecia beamed, her eyes sparkling. "Is it something for me?"

After a moment, Veronica burst out with chuckles. "Grecia, no, it isn't a gift for you."

She pouted in disappointment. "What is it then?" A frown painted her face in a darker color. In an angrier color. What could her mom have possibly brought?

"Well," Veronica said, delicately pushing a few strands of hair behind her ear, "some new customers contacted me today. They want me to make a blue cover for a notebook with the cloth I make clothes with."

"Oh. Nice I guess."

"You're probably thinking, what's in it for me?*" Veronica continued. "I've been thinking...it'd be great if you could write a little note for our customers. I left a bit of important info out, but the customers want the notebook cover for their son whose birthday is coming really soon. And I know you love birthdays."*

Grecia smiled at the floor, her posture loosening. She knew what her mother was going to say next.

"And, well, also because...who wouldn't want a birthday note from Grecia, the best daughter in existence?"

She giggled. "Thanks, Mom. Love you too."

And she meant it.

There was no one in this world who could cheer Grecia up like her mother.

She wrote the note right before Veronica started packaging the product. Grecia couldn't help but feel warm and fuzzy inside, seeing her mother beam at what she had written.

Veronica was probably reminiscing about the day Grecia had first written something by hand.

No, not probably. Surely. Completely surely. Because, well, she was Veronica.

7
FLASHES OF SILVER

Three days passed, and it finally came. Camping day. No, not *real* camping, but that was what Sienna and Juniper called it.

Eyes were trained on Maya that morning.

The only confused soul in Home was Grecia. A look of puzzlement crossed her face as she searched for an explanation, peering at Sienna, who was sitting right next to her.

"We're waiting for Maya to confirm that it's the last day of the week. You know, camping day," Sienna whispered, leaning closer. "We always forget, and since she used to be from the Mathematical Sector, it's easier for her to remember."

As a response, Maya, who had been leaning on the wall and staring at the floor, looked up with a lit-up face. "Yes! It's camping day!"

Cheers roared through the room, echoes bouncing in the tunnels, making it sound like many more people were there, urging them to continue with their celebration.

Grecia seemed to be the most thrilled. She jumped up and down with her hands raised in the air. She formed a circle with her mouth, whooping. She had always heard of camping but had never done it, not even with Veronica. In Nepenthe camping was said to be dangerous and mundane. Based on the reactions of those in home, however, the words Grecia associated with camping now were now fun, fun, and more fun.

Brink, wearing a confused expression, laughed nervously. Being a newbie as well, he was probably extremely bewildered.

"How many days will we stay there?" Grecia asked eagerly.

"One day," Juniper said without hesitation.

Grecia's body went slack. "What?" she asked, incredulous, eyes wide.

"Oh, don't worry," Sienna said. "I'm sure you'll have fun. Lots of it." Juniper received a glare from her twin afterwards. Again.

Since those words came from the nicer twin, Grecia cheered up a tiny bit.

"Also, you gotta take advantage of today," Sienna continued. "You'll be outside without having to work. Being a newbie and everything."

"Okay," Grecia said.

"Get ready, kids," Juniper hollered. "And one bowl each, except Grecia and Brink. Yes, Washington, we'll cook the fish outside today, you should know. Alright now, everyone grab one or two apples to eat on the way."

The children did as instructed, and on they went to camp.

Brink and Grecia walked in front because each one of the others carried a heavy bowl in their hands, slowing down their pace. She wondered why the bowls were heavy if there wasn't any content in them—she assumed it was because of the material itself and its original weight. They were all surrounded by trees, closing in to make a small empty path.

"Almost there, y'all," Juniper yelled. "Almost there. Keep going or else you'll miss the real fun."

That was enough for everyone to keep moving.

Soon, the narrow pathway broadened into an autumn-colored beach with rocks of every size, from boulders to grains that got stuck between Grecia's toes. Beyond that lay a flat lake, which reflected the day's cotton candy clouds. Leafless trees cast shadows onto the clear water.

Woah was the only word Grecia managed, goggling in amazement. Perhaps because nature liked stirring drama, the wind started blowing at Grecia's hair. This made the scene look emotional and dramatic, and Grecia felt it too. She pushed her hair back into its original position, behind her ears, with a scrunched-up face. "This place is really pretty."

"It is, isn't it?" Washington said with a sigh. "Welcome to the world outside of Nepenthe." There was a forced cheerfulness, what looked like regret dulling his eyes.

Cheer him up. Do something, will you?

"What do you like the most about camping?" Grecia asked, putting a hand on Washington's shoulder. "The sun? The food? The people?"

"I just like how I can relax on these days." It was an instant reply, as if he'd had it prepared.

Grecia nodded, although she didn't fully understand the meaning of his words.

She and Washington stood next to each other, staring at the wide expanse of twinkling water. She'd never seen anything so wonderful—she bet that she could stare at the lake for days without getting bored. The scenery was like a diamond ring—at first, it just looked alright, but as one kept their eyes on it, they noticed more intricate details, and once they looked at the full scenery once again, it looked delightful.

They all reached the edge of the lake and placed their belongings in dry land.

"Alright, everyone," Juniper yelled with an optimistic smirk. "Let's all jump into the lake." She took in a deep, dramatic breath before screaming, "NOW!"

Juniper jumped. A thunderous sound filled the peaceful air as water came jumping at everyone on the ground. Juniper's clothes were plastered to her skin as she emerged from the lake, and the others followed suit.

"Three, two, one—JUMP!" Maya roared before splattering into the sparkling surface. Washington and Brink followed her lead.

Before Grecia knew it, she and Sienna were the only ones on solid ground.

"Go ahead," Sienna said, patting her shoulder. "It'll be fun." She had a twinkle in her eyes, a twinkle that urged her to do so.

"What about you?" Grecia asked. "Weren't you a swimmer?"

Sienna sighed, shaking her head and turning away. "I prefer not to talk about that."

Grecia stood, motionless. *Well, guess that was a* no. *Strange.*

She buried her now-naked feet into the ground, squatting, ready to jump into the fun.

Three, two, one—JUMP!

The water ate Grecia whole, making her unable to breathe and open her eyes. If she had been another kid, they might have gotten startled, but for Grecia it was a pleasure to forget about everything. About her worries. Her struggles. To forget she was alive.

The water moved softly, embracing Grecia as closely as her own skin. Caressing coolly, eddying in its wake. She pulled her head out and watched the droplets drip from her hair—transparent, but opaque when she looked closer. In the breeze her hands trembled, yet the morning soon warmed her back.

The only thing present at that moment, that place, was complete euphoria. Glee. Elation. Ecstasy.

And one more word.

Freedom.

Grecia laughed aloud, her open mouth facing the sky. She kneeled, lowering herself more and more until the water reached her chin. It was then that she saw it. Movement in the water, a ripple. Barely a dart of silver, yet fast.

Grecia screamed. Her voice pierced the air, perforating the kids' ears like an annoying coach's whistle. She jumped, trying to distance herself from the aquatic monster, only to sink into the water once again.

She felt a force on her shoulders, increasing the volume of her yells.

"Hey," Juniper said, shaking her as she fell silent. "What's wrong with you? That's a fish, dummy."

"Get away!" Grecia screamed, pushing all the air out of her lungs. "Get. Me. Out. Of. Here." She thrashed, like a hamster squirming to get out of its owner's hands. She kicked whenever she could, punched as soon as there was something to hit.

"It's a *fish*," Juniper repeated, rolling her eyes. "It's just a darn fish. Calm down. Geez."

That moment, Grecia finally heard what the older girl had to say, but it only confused her further. "You mean fish that are alive?" she asked, eyebrows furrowed in disbelief. "Those are from ancient times. When people killed animals and ate them."

"Gosh," Juniper muttered under her breath. "How can you explain the fish that you ate yesterday, then?"

A revelation hit Grecia. "You mean…"

"Yeah, the food you ate is from *ancient times*." As Juniper said the last two words, her pitch went higher, probably to mock Grecia. Juniper was Juniper.

"But," Grecia stammered, "I was taught that animals are dangerous and things like that."

"Do you really still believe everything you learned in Nepenthe?"

Grecia freed herself from Juniper's grasp, heading toward where she'd seen the fish earlier. She widened her eyes, waiting. It wasn't long before her vision caught another one.

With scales like the most delicate of armor plating, the fish made its way through the lake, choosing to get out of her way. Grecia moved her hand in the same way as it flexed its body, wanting to feel the same motion. As she stood there, feet in the mud, her eyes wandered with the fish.

It was pretty.

Her gaze fixated on the others, who freely played in the water, ignoring the fact that to Nepenthe, they were as human as that silver fish.

"Let's race!" Maya yelled. "Race! Race! Race! Race!"

"But I'm horrible at swimming," Brink whimpered, hitting the water's surface with his hand.

"Hey, just give it a try," said Washington with a wink. He lay a hand on Brink's back. "If you beat Maya, I'll give you a piggy-back ride."

Brink's face lit up.

Grecia turned her head to Sienna, who was sitting on the soil, staring at the others with a miserable smile. What was wrong?

"Whatever," Maya yelled. "Catch me if you can!"

As Grecia watched everyone race, a splash of water rocketed from her side, hitting her square in the face.

"Heyo, loser," said Juniper, crossing her arms. This time, Juniper didn't snicker. She pulled a genuine smile. Of course, not the same one Sienna always wore, but it was filled with brightness nonetheless. That had to mean *something.*

Grecia laughed uncontrollably, inflating her surroundings

with a carefree static, as she took revenge on Juniper with another splash. And another. And another.

Two hours before sunset, Juniper was the first to leave the lake. Water dripped from her *everywhere*. Her hair, her clothes, and her fingernails. She left a trail of liquid behind her as she walked out.

"Everyone, leave now!" she shouted from dry ground. "We have to return before sunset."

Nobody complained. Not even a squeak. Grecia frowned, but then shook her head. For a split second she had felt déjà vu.

One by one, kids left the lake, all joining Juniper on the sand.

"Alright everyone," Sienna said in a gentle but stern voice. "Juniper and I will collect some fish. Washington, you collect materials for the fire."

Washington gave a thumbs up as he parted towards his work. But he left somewhat reluctantly, as he lacked any happy energy in his footfalls.

Grecia watched the twins as they worked with elated expressions. Juniper waded through the water while Sienna stayed dry, crouching by the edge of the lake. Their quick movements were enough to collect five huge fish, along with several bowls of water, in no time.

"Not working is plain fun," Maya said, extending her arms. Her voice broke the calming silence that had once been a soothing blanket for them.

"Yeah," Brink said timidly.

Grecia turned her head toward Brink, but he avoided her

gaze. What was wrong with the guy? Did he have feelings for her or something?

"Now, please be quiet," Brink added. "I wanna enjoy the silence."

What followed was only the pecking of the woodpeckers, the buzzing of insects, the chirping of birds. Nothing else, except for the occasional yell coming from Juniper. It was a pleasure to hear what nature had to give to humans. No beeping of alarm clocks, nor ringing of the bell of her school.

Nepenthe was wrong. Animals don't destroy; they give.

Before even half an hour passed, Washington emerged from the trees, bearing a few branches and rocks in his arms. He lay them softly on the sand.

Juniper and Sienna walked up to the rest, holding five buckets with fish and water filled to the brim. Grecia could tell the loads were insanely heavy, as their arms went stiff, muscles popping up. Living in the Outside had surely given them strong arms.

"Maya," Sienna called. "Did you bring the shard of glass?"

"Yup." Maya pulled it out from her dusty sweatshirt's pocket, which glinted brightly against the sunlight. She extended her arms, angling the glass to the sun's location. A ray passed through, hitting the branches and rocks like a laser.

Smoke lifted from the floor, and soon it turned into the flames of a fire.

"Let's eat some fish," Juniper said, with water dripping from her outstretched fingers.

What happened next was expected. Eating, laughter, fun, a heavenly smell in the air. Camping day had been perfect…except for one lingering question.

"Sienna?" Grecia mumbled, scratching her head. "I was wondering—"

"Why don't I enter the water?" Sienna said without meeting Grecia's eyes. That girl could read minds. "It's a long story."

Grecia focused on the older girl, her curiosity building like a cat fixated upon its prey. She sloped her head, waiting for at least a brief explanation, until Sienna finally spoke.

"Possession," she said. "It's dangerous, really. Once you possess one thing, you'll want more. And more. And more. Until you want what seemed impossible in the beginning. When you realize that you can't get what you want, everything breaks down."

Sienna didn't say a single word after that, so Grecia took another bite of her fish.

8

THE MYSTERIOUS COTTAGE

Leaves crunched under Grecia's feet as she tried to keep up with Washington's pace. Her pants matched the rhythm of her footfalls, creating a not-so-pleasant melody.

Today, her week as an escort for Washington and Maya had started.

"Wait for me!" Grecia yelled through cupped hands. They had only been walking for about twenty minutes, but she was already beyond exhausted.

Washington chuckled, a few feet ahead of her. "Gotta toughen those thighs up if you wanna survive here in the wilderness, Grecia. You too, Brink."

Grecia noticed things about the forest that she never had before. The tree trunks were much thicker than the artificial ones in Nepenthe's sole park, and upon touching them, had a rougher surface.

Although Grecia had already grown accustomed to the singing and chirping of birds, she still wasn't accustomed to how...*real* they looked. A pigeon stopped pecking the branch next to it and turned its head toward her. Its unblinking eyes tore into Grecia, as if saying, *What have you done to nature, human?*

Grecia looked away. Even birds seemed to hate Nepenthe. Or maybe Grecia's brain was playing tricks on her. Who knew? Either way, that pigeon was plain creepy.

Brink staggered behind Grecia. "I don't remember walking being this hard."

Washington laughed aloud. "Don't worry, we're almost there. We'll be working in the same place we camped." He halted and sneezed a few times before regaining his balance.

"Gosh, what a relief." Grecia wiped the sweat off her forehead with what remained of the sleeves of her already tattered tie-dye shirt. "The fish better be really good." She broke into a smile. "Dibs on the fish untouched by Brink. I've got the feeling his hands have the power to ruin good food."

He glared at her, pouting.

When they arrived, Washington splashed his cupped hands into the lake, pulling up a handful of clear water to his lips. He let the water trickle into his mouth until the liquid in his hands ran out.

"You should try it too." Washington ran a damp hand through his short, crispy hair. "Makes me relax before work."

"I'll pass," said Grecia.

Brink nodded.

"Alright then." Washington pulled the sleeves of his brown shirt above his shoulders. "Let's get to work."

"Okay, I think I'll get it this time. Can you repeat the instructions?" Grecia positioned her fists on her hips with a confident smile.

She and Brink had been waist-deep in the lake, trying to

catch fish for at least thirty minutes (with no success), while Washington had watched from the sand with his arms crossed. Well, at least that was what he was supposed to be doing, according to Juniper's instructions. He was actually in the lake alongside the two, helping them directly.

Washington sighed. "Sure, but this is the last time. Juniper told me I should tell you the instructions only once, but this is like, the fifth time or so."

"Okay, nice," Grecia replied. "Hope Juniper doesn't kill you."

Washington proceeded to stand with such stillness that it looked like he was frozen in time. He dipped a hand into the water. "Fish won't approach warm, foreign objects, so make sure you stay still for at least ten minutes so that your hand cools down."

Grecia imitated his actions, and Brink followed. "Okay, gotcha."

"Then, wiggle your finger to imitate a worm."

Grecia didn't make the same mistake she had made in the last tries—wiggling one of her fingers before the ten minutes ended. She stayed still, eyes fixated on Washington.

"Now, continue wiggling your finger until a fish approaches. When it does, snatch it by its gills, and do it fast, because these creatures are really strong." Washington motioned his arms to resemble the actions he had described.

Grecia nodded and turned her head to the lake.

I'll patiently wait for ten minutes. This time, I will *catch a fish.*

She didn't patiently wait for ten minutes.

It couldn't have been more than five minutes before Grecia opened her mouth once again, words flowing out of her mouth naturally once again. "Hey, Washington, I'm curious about something."

"Yeah?" Washington crossed his arms.

"Why are you so...chill? Like, it's not really a bad thing, but...I don't know, you're so much calmer than the others."

He ran a hand through his face before facing her with a quiet laugh. "Grecia, you've got it all wrong."

She cocked her head in confusion. "What do you mean?"

"This may sound depressing...and I swear that I'm not one of those teens who pretend to be depressed. I just think that I've worried for too long. Worried about my friends. My family. My grades. My life." He shook his head. "I don't think there's much to worry about now, as naive as that sounds. I mean, yes, there's a high chance I'll be killed by some weird animal or die of a disease outside the city, but if that counted as a reason to worry, I would have to worry twenty-four-seven. I don't want my life to be like that. And, well, I don't know if this makes sense, but worrying… it reminds me of Nepenthe." He closed his eyes at the sound of the city's name. The city he despised so much.

Or was it the city he missed so much? Grecia would never know.

"Well...what about you?" Washington asked.

"Huh?"

"What's your story?"

Grecia pressed her lips into a straight line. "I don't really have a story," she lied. But for whatever reason, those words *did* seem true.

"I do," Brink murmured after not having revealed his voice for quite some time.

Grecia smiled, encouraging him to go ahead and speak.

"My parents told me I wasn't enough for Nepenthe. That I was dumb. That hurt me, and to be honest, I kind of believe those words are true. And, well, that must have interfered with my brain. Because I failed the Exétasi." He kept his voice in the lowest volume throughout the whole revelation.

"Oh." Grecia lowered her head, and the trio fell silent.

None of them talked until Grecia finally caught a fish six minutes later. And then another, and then another. Four in total.

Brink's words haunted her.

There were so many ways to interpret them—did he hate Nepenthe? Was he insecure because of his parents' insults? Did he regret being so *dumb*, even though he really wasn't?

These questions swam around her head while she marched down the same forest trail as yesterday with Brink and Maya, who couldn't stop chattering about her first day outside Nepenthe. She kept her head low, watching her bare feet step on the dry leaves, an abundance of warm colors. If this had been her first day in the Outside, she might have been curious about or even fascinated by her surroundings—but today, Grecia could only think about the hurt everyone in Home carried.

She had wanted to be the band-aid to their inner wounds, but now she questioned her abilities to do so.

"...so, then I was like, what the heck? The woodpeckers aren't robots? Impossible! And then Juniper was like, hey, are you dumb? And for some reason, I laughed," Maya was saying. She sure loved to talk. The smile on her face was so broad that it looked like her cheeks might explode.

"Okay. Interesting," Grecia muttered under her breath, still shuffling through her thoughts. There had to be a way to help these kids…

"Oh, right, I forgot that little detail—"

"Can't you just shut up?" Grecia said unconsciously, her voice heavy with exasperation. She bit her lips, eyes drooping. "Sorry…I—"

"I agree," Brink cut in. "Like, why are you so...bright? Like, in an annoying way?

Grecia's eyes grew. He must have been truly annoyed if his thoughts were flying out of his mouth, because that was simply out of character. Well, at least out of character for the Brink she knew, but considering everything he'd told her and Washington the other day, she still hardly knew him at all.

Oh.

"Is it really that much?" Maya asked, fidgeting with her hands. "I'm just happy. Is it too much to show all my happiness in a situation like this one?"

Grecia looked away. She had never seen this side of her, and for some reason, it disturbed her. The way Maya had switched from one emotion to another in such a short time...it creeped her out.

"But what is there to be happy about in this situation of yours?" Brink asked, voice trembling. "We've lost everything! All of us! You, Grecia, Sienna, Juniper, Washington...even me!" He burst into tears, his shoulders bobbing.

It was then that Grecia heard Maya's giggles.

Her *giggles.*

"Oh, so you're in that phase," Maya chuckled, rolling her eyes. "Don't worry though. As soon as Juniper assigns you a real job, you'll be happy again." She took a deep breath before bursting into another fit of laughter.

Grecia staggered backwards, stumbling upon contact with a thick branch on the ground.

Brink glanced at Grecia, a concerned look painted onto his face. He was probably wondering what the heck had impacted her so much to send her flying backwards.

"To answer your question," Maya continued, "you know why I'm happy? I'm happy now because while I was new to this whole Home thing, I didn't really have a sense of purpose."

Grecia leaned against a tree. It felt like sandpaper under her forearm, coated with dirt.

"But Juniper gave me a sense of purpose."

Before Grecia knew, she was running.

Running away from Maya.

Running away from the questions that chased her.

Is Maya correct? Whether it's Nepenthe or Juniper, is my life nothing without someone ruling over me? Someone setting rules, giving me orders, choosing my job?

Apparently, Washington and Sienna saw her from somewhere, because their voices resonated in the air.

"Grecia! Stop! Where are you going?"

But she didn't stop. And she ran, ran, and ran.

Soon, Grecia's Kinetic Sector-level speed slowed into a trot, as she panted with her legs barely keeping up with her train of thoughts. She laid her hands on the sides of her head. Never in her life had she been so disturbed. And with that, she really did mean *never.*

How could Maya possibly mean that?

Grecia's self-made marathon continued until she could run no more. The ground slipped under her feet, and she fell on her face, dirt coating whatever clean spot was left on her face. She didn't bother standing up. She lay still on the same spot, sucking in handfuls of dust with each ragged breath.

She blinked the dust off her eyes, tears streaming down her face to help with the work. Grecia leaned on her forearms before cautiously standing up, a hand on the tree next to her. She turned her head in slow motion to dissipate the stiffness in her neck, and then she inspected her surroundings.

I better not be lost in the middle of this forest...

She was most definitely lost.

Although the elements and characteristics of the forest she

knew were still present, Grecia could tell she had never been here before. The tree trunks had an unnatural light color—white combined with brown. Well, it was probably natural considering how Grecia had only seen the artificial trees in Nepenthe and the ones close to Home, but they seemed unnatural to *her*. The tree trunks were considerably thinner than the ones by Home, like this part of the forest was weaker than the part she knew.

Grecia sighed. How the heck was she going to return to Home when she didn't even have a vague idea of her location?

For now, she'd have to seek some shelter. It was way too dangerous for her to wander around like a meek sheep in a place she barely knew.

After resting for some more time with her back leaned against a tree, Grecia set out to find whatever waited for her in the wilderness. And for some reason, she was pumped to find it.

It probably was because anything was better than thinking about what Maya had said…

Grecia closed her eyes, her teeth digging into her dry, cracked lips.

Grecia trekked along an imaginary trail as her eyes flew around. Her jaw tightened. She was already familiar with situations like these. Except the context had been completely different.

Grecia chuckled, thinking about how free of worry she had been back then, when she and Veronica would go to Nepenthe's Park to play a game. Whoever found more birds (artificial ones, at least) would win and get to choose what they'd eat for dinner. She remembered how she would play the game as if her life depended on it, her eyes wide, her mouth open, and frowning with concentration.

But what was so special about this game, at least for Grecia, was how her mother had never treated her like *just* a baby while playing the game. Veronica had always treated her like an equal—and that meant the world to Grecia.

And Veronica meant the world to Grecia.

She stopped in her tracks as soon as her eyes caught a weird flash of the color of chocolate, a few feet from her current location. Grecia continued moving her legs in a constant rhythm until she stood in front of what seemed to be an old cottage.

The dully-painted door was falling off its hinges, its still-shiny knocker dangling as if gravity had an extra effect on it. Weeds had grown between the mortar, the kind that would have overtaken the neighboring houses with ease if it were to be placed in Nepenthe. Cinnamon-colored, wooden dowels covered the surface of the cottage in a disordered manner, and the flat, timber ceiling creaked loudly against the wind.

What was something like this doing outside Nepenthe? And how did it look...relatively preserved?

Grecia cringed as soon as she stepped onto the porch. A squeaky sound (which might as well have been a screech) filled the air. If the sound had been a physical object, it would have been a thin, sharp blade, capable of piercing any ears nearby. Grecia put her index fingers inside her ears to block the noise.

When Grecia finally reached the front door, she nodded confidently before pushing it open. Another squeak filled the air.

When Grecia's eyes finally adjusted to the blackness, her lips parted open.

The first thing she saw was red. Not the aesthetically pleasing red of roses. The frightening type of red. The red that one sees when someone bleeds.

There was blood everywhere.

There was blood splattered on the broken wood floor. There was blood on the purple, wallpapered walls, and there was blood on the white ceiling.

It seemed to be only composed of one room, as there were no

doors except for the one she had just opened. The three light-bulbs hanging from the ceiling were shattered, shards of glass scattered through the floor.

Grecia gulped and stepped inside. The house had a salty, delicate smell. But it had some nightmares sprinkled into it, some fear. Whoever had lived here hadn't been happy.

Well, at least they were surely happier here than in Nepenthe.

Right?

Maya's words started ringing in her head once again, making Grecia mutter, "If only Brink hadn't asked her that darn question."

She settled on the closest corner of the wall on the left, trying to tear her mind away from Maya's voice. She closed her eyes, teeth digging into her lips. But no matter how much she tried, her thoughts always landed on those dreaded words.

Grecia peeled her eyes open, but that didn't help much at all. The bloody smudges on the walls, made her sick to the core, and her breakfast climbed up her throat.

Time went by quickly. With the blink of an eye, the sky turned dark, and the heat of the sun dissipated.

But the moment Grecia heard voices other than Maya's, time stopped.

"Grecia?"

"She must be around here…"

A shy squeak.

She recognized those voices.

A creak rippled through the air, and close thuds reached her ears. Artificial light, which Grecia supposed came from a flash-light, landed in front of her.

Sienna, Washington, and Brink walked through the door with caution, making their footsteps as light as possible.

They had found her.

9
THE NOTES

Grecia sighed with relief, rubbing her stiff back. This hadn't been as bad as she thought it would be. She had imagined she'd be stuck here for at least a week, trembling in the cold and her stomach grumbling with hunger. However, Sienna, Washington and Brink had found her in a matter of hours.

"Great to see you," Washington tapped Grecia's shoulder from behind, and leaned against the wall.

She nodded, rising to her feet.

"This place…it's just…creepy," said Brink, next to Washington. He embraced himself. "Can we go now?"

"It sure is…" Sienna slid a hand through a blotch of dried blood on the wall farthest from Grecia. "But I think we should stay here for a bit."

"Wait, what?" Washington turned his head to her sharply, bewildered. Grecia stared at this image of Washington, one she had never seen of him before. "Were you even paying attention to what Juniper said after Maya explained everything to us? That wasn't part of the plan. Juniper told us to find Grecia and come back immediately."

"Listen," Sienna said after a pause, "this place looks like it was once inhabited by a person. We should look for objects that could be helpful for us in the future."

Washington sighed. "Yeah, you're right I guess."

"We could also take advantage of this opportunity to be on a little"—she coughed, eyes directing themselves to the other three —"fun quest."

He cocked his head and arched his eyebrows but shrugged his reluctance off. "Welp. You're the senior here, so, I guess we must obey you."

Grecia couldn't get over the bloodiness of this place. Of all the red stains on the walls. She stood with an awkward pose, head down.

She still hadn't wrapped her head around what Maya said. Her thoughts toward Juniper reminded her too much of how citizens thought of Nepenthe, and it terrified her.

The only thing she knew was that she was glad Maya hadn't come as well. Grecia knew she wouldn't be able to see her in the same light anymore.

Grecia gulped. Not knowing what to do, she stood next to Washington who had been staring intently at the farthest corner of the room. "What are you looking at?"

Washington shrugged. "What do you want to look for?"

"What do you mean?"

"You know…this place is filled with objects, at least according to Sienna. Is there something you'd like to find?" His curious eyes tore into her.

Grecia blinked, her mind racing. In a stupid attempt to answer his question, she spoke the first thing that came to mind. "Uh…maybe a necklace? My mom loved necklaces, and, well, I want her to stay alive in my life." She winced, realizing he'd probably make fun of her for mentioning her mother.

However, Washington smiled. "Let's look for a necklace, then."

He set out on his search and left her.

Strange.

Sienna turned a hundred and eighty degrees, grumbling. "There's nothing here." She shined the flashlight. The light wasn't too shiny, and it barely lit up the room. But as she moved around, shining it in different parts of the cottage, a gleam caught Grecia's attention.

"Wait, stop," said Grecia, pointing at the left corner, the one closest to the door. "Can you shine it there again?"

"Uh, okay?" said Sienna, and she did as asked.

There it was. A slight glint.

Grecia ran to the mysterious gleam and squinted her eyes. She folded her fingers around the shiny object reminiscent to a handle, poking through the wall, and tried to pull it out.

"Stubborn gleamy thing," she muttered. She put more power into her pulls. One. Two. Three. Fou—

A loud click reached her ears.

And the left wall split in half, revealing a workspace.

This place didn't smell of sadness. It smelled of curiosity. Mysteries yet to be solved.

There was so much more in here than in the other room. Everything was made of wood. The desk sitting in the center, the fallen chair next to it, the empty bookshelves in the farthest right corner. Even the books on it had a dusty, brown-ish color. There wasn't much detail she could see because of the lack of light, but she was sure that if this workspace had been properly bathed in light, it would've looked incredibly aesthetic—something she wouldn't have been able to resist making a painting of.

"Now this is some adventure," said Sienna, gawking at the new environment. She trotted towards the place, arms dangling from her sides. "Who made this place? What was it used for?"

"Cool," was the only word Brink said. His face was one of a bored person, but Grecia knew his heart was beating inside. That secretly, he wanted to know everything about this mysterious workspace.

Because, really, who wouldn't want to?

"Come here y'all," said Washington, who was staring at the desk. "There is some really creepy stuff here."

"Creepy? I don't like creepy," Brink said, biting his lips. Fear danced in his pale cheeks.

Sienna grabbed Brink's arm and dragged him to where Washington was located, and Grecia followed with short steps,

And indeed, what was on the desk was creepy.

They were crumpled sheets of paper Grecia hadn't noticed before. On them lay a pen broken exactly in half, dried ink splattered below it. How had it broken in such a clean way? Nobody knew.

Words were scribbled on all the paper, and most of them weren't understandable. Grecia could read the occasional *the* or a *maybe* or a *of course,* but those words didn't help in understanding the message of the letters.

Grecia was about to head out to another corner when her eyes caught two words.

Amygdala Creature.

Amygdala. It was the word! The word her mother had mentioned! But why was it written in some creepy, old piece of paper? Who had written it? And why had that person written it?

What did *Amygdala Creature* even mean?

Grecia's vision ran through the letter at full speed. It found several other understandable words, like *project*, or *evil*, or *hypnotizing.* Grecia put all those words together in her mind, but they wouldn't fit. The puzzle had too many pieces missing for it to work.

Grecia scratched her head with frustration. One way or another, this thing had to do with herself. Her identity. She just didn't know in what way.

"Excuse me," she said, squirming through the three teenagers. As she did so, Brink and Sienna wandered off to the edges of the workspace, leaving her alone with Washington in front of the desk.

She grabbed the letter and put it only a few inches from her face, and doing so, an object slipped from the desk.

Another object they hadn't noticed.

A necklace.

"Guess you found what you wanted," Washington laughed, doing the thing that I don't remember its name.

"Yeah," Grecia said, forcing out a nervous laugh. She kneeled and picked it up, the necklace twirling as she lifted it into the air. It was the shape of a heart broken in half, but in a cartoonish way, with all those unrealistic spikes. Though she couldn't clearly see it, it seemed to be emerald green. On it was engraved the letter *L*.

Why would something so childish be among serious, eerie letters in the middle of the woods?

Her head was still encased in the cage of questions. Questions about the crumpled paper.

Questions about this place, the person who had lived here, and questions about herself.

"Hey," said Washington, at her side. "Nice necklace."

Grecia looked down. It glimmered even without light, and it swayed with every movement from her part. "Kinda weird how I found a necklace right after saying I wanted to find one, huh?" she asked.

"What do you think it was for?"

"Huh? What do you mean? It's a necklace. Necklaces don't serve a specific purpose."

Washington shook his head. "Everything serves a purpose, whether it's a shallow one, like being decorative, or a deep one, like reminding someone of a loved one."

Grecia scratched her neck. "I don't know. It was probably just decorative."

Washington shrugged. "Seems like it."

She laughed in a nervous tone, and moved to her left, where the bookshelf stood with magnificence.

Sliding her fingers through the book spines, she dusted off the surfaces with delicacy, and her eyes met with words. Words, words, and more words. Who knew dusting off spines of books could reveal so many letters and phrases?

A certain word caught her gaze. *Diary*, it said.

Curiosity is sometimes a monster that tears into your soul. It wasn't long before Grecia started reading the diary.

DAY 1

Dear Diary,

People from ancient times used to ~~right~~ write about their daily lives in notebooks, sharing their most intimate secrets and feelings. Basically, they talked to inanimate objects. Sounded kind of crazy, so I decided to give it a try.

Oh wait, the wind just made a corner of this page move a little bit. Are you asking me to tell you about my life?

Wow, this feels extremely dumb.

Never mind. This kind of does feel fun. Well, I escaped Nepenthe today. It was all planned, and I really don't regret it. Although the life conditions in the Outside are horrible compared to the city, I feel happier here. I feel like a huge burden has been lifted from my shoulders.

I walked for about three hours before finding this place. It's kinda old and seems to be pretty much dead. But fortunately, I enjoy building things, so that isn't really a problem. There's also a really cool office kind of room. There's a desk, some bookshelves, and even a pen and a notebook.

That notebook, my friend, is you.

It feels really weird to be writing so informally, to be honest. In Nepenthe, I had to write formally 24/7. Well, trying new things out is always a good thing, am I right?

I'll have some rest for the rest of the day. So, until tomorrow, farewell.

~ Louisiana

P.S. Yes, I do know how to spell "write." I studied in the Governmental Sector for a reason. It's just an inside joke.

DAY 2

Dear Diary,

Food. That's all I'm thinking of right now. To demonstrate that, I shall write a very inspiring paragraph:

Food. Food.

Holy crap, I just wrote a useless paragraph and wasted much of my energy. Genius.

As you may have noticed by now, I'm not in a good mood. At all. I'll go outside in a few minutes to collect some fruit. If there is fruit. Or perhaps some fish. I saw a lake on my way here.

Bye.

~ Louisiana

P.S. I just returned from my little walk, and wow. The fruit is amazing. The flavor itself may not be as tasty as the fruit from Nepenthe, but they have this unique, fresh feeling. I'll see if there's any fish in the lake tomorrow.

DAY 42

Dear Diary,

I'm a murderer. I'm a murderer and nothing else.

I sometimes understand why people from ancient times talked to inanimate objects. Sometimes, the information you have is a burden so heavy that you want to share it with someone. With anyone. But you can't. Because if you do, everyone will hate you.

Which is why you can head to diaries. Things that don't have a mouth.

While catching fish today, I saw an old man. He was accompanied by two girls who looked the same. I don't know what I was thinking, but as soon as I saw the man, I threw a rock at him. He just...he reminded me of Mayor Neville. It triggered so many memories. I lost control of my own body...and ...

By this entry's opening line, I think you could guess what happened.

~ Louis

DAY 102

Dear Diary,

Louis here. This will probably be my last letter to you. Besides the fact that my old pen is running out of ink, this house is breaking apart. The animals have been clawing at the walls every night, and I'm worried they might someday break through.

I should try to fix the weakening wall, but I just don't have the energy to do so anymore.

To be honest, I'm not scared of dying. The moment I crossed that border, the moment I left Nepenthe, I knew my destiny was sealed. I was just too stubborn to admit it. What are the odds of me, a simple twelve-year-old, surviving the wilderness for more than a few months? Anyone who believes that to be possible is ignorant.

I used to be ignorant, even just a few days ago. But I finally came to the realization that…I'm not really happy here.

I was skipping through this notebook's pages today. While reading through my first entry, I noticed that I had *felt* happy while writing it, that I *felt* as if a burden had been lifted from my shoulders. But I was never really happy. 102 days ago, I had unconsciously known that.

Tonight, I'll make noise, noise to attract wild animals. This cottage has not only been protected by camouflage and the extremely large number of weeds on its surfaces (their growth helped by yours only). It has also been protected by the lack of sounds coming from it. I have already accepted that I'll die soon, and I don't want my death to be a surprise.

I regret leaving Nepenthe. I regret deciding to leave so impulsively.

Though it may not be for the reason you're thinking of.

When Grecia had found the dusty notebook hiding between the bookshelves, she hadn't expected to read the whole story of a stranger called Louisiana. But she had.

There were so many so many things that troubled her about Louisiana's entries, but there were two that especially bothered her:

First, Louis had killed an old man. An old man accompanied by two girls who looked the same. Had those two been, by any chance, Sienna and Juniper? And had that old man been the guy who had helped the twins when they first left Nepenthe, the one Juniper had quickly mentioned when Grecia had first arrived?

Perhaps, thought Grecia, *the wild animals Juniper always mentioned weren't really animals at all. Perhaps, seeing the man being killed had scarred her so much that she wanted to protect everyone, in such a nasty way, from all the dangers, not just the animals, that they could face in this forest.*

Grecia gulped, running a hand through her black (and now messy from her days in the Outside) hair. Had she misunderstood Juniper all this time?

The second thing that bothered Grecia was the last two sentences of the very last entry.

I regret leaving Nepenthe. I regret deciding to leave so impulsively.

Though it may not be for the reason you're thinking of.

Why had Louis regretted leaving Nepenthe? What if in the future, Grecia regretted her past decisions too?

Had she made a terrible mistake?

Grecia bit her lips, closing the notebook shut. Dust emerged from the pages, which caused her to sneeze.

"What you got there?" Sienna scurried towards her with an eager smile. "Any cool secrets?"

"What? No." Grecia shoved the notebook back into place. "The words aren't legible. Nothing cool over here."

10

THE CLIMB AND THE WOLF

They soon left the cottage, the night's darkness enveloping them, and set out to return to Home.

According to Sienna, they had to climb trees to get back to Home, because night was when predators were most active. Walking on the ground among bears and wolves didn't seem like a good idea.

Grecia gulped, remembering how Sienna had said the trees were approximately sixty-five meters tall, according to Maya. Sweat trickled down her neck.

She held her hand against the rough trunk, searching for an opening that could serve as a grip. She'd seen Brink do it. She'd seen Washington do it. Now it was her turn.

When her fingers touched an oversized bump on the trunk, they wrapped themselves around it, and Grecia pushed herself off the ground. Instead of being left dangling as she had expected, her feet lifted and ended up only a few inches above the ground. Grecia lifted her left arm and wrapped her fingers around a branch, lifting herself upwards. She repeated the process over and over. Grabbing a branch, pushing herself upwards. Grabbing, pushing. Soon, her shoulders were burning.

Grecia lifted her chin and grimaced. She still had a long way to go. Her next goal was to get to the part of the tree where branches were spread further apart, which would make climbing much easier. According to Sienna, climbing was the ideal way to get to their destination. Through the branches, they could jump from tree to tree, moving forward. When Grecia had asked Sienna why they couldn't use the ground, she hadn't received a response.

"Use your legs!" Sienna yelled from below. "You're putting too much pressure on your arms!"

Grecia did as she'd been told, swinging her leg to the ledge she had used last time. As she did, her toes pressed against the short bump, leaving her foot in an uncomfortable position.

"Ow," she whispered to herself. As she reached out to grab another ledge, her foot slipped, leaving her dangling fifteen feet from the ground. Her arms burned so much it felt as though they were turning to ash. Her heart beat viciously against her chest.

"Grecia!" Sienna yelled once again. "Put your foot back!"

Grecia inhaled a lungful of air and swished her foot back into position onto the bump

Though her heart didn't stop insisting on being let free from her chest, the rest of the climb grew easier. She eventually entered a world of thin branches that could be confused with giant spider webs. She carefully set her foot on one of them and sighed.

"That was pretty fast," Washington said from the tree next to hers. Grecia couldn't get a clear image of him through the branches between them, but she could infer through his ragged breaths that his chest was going up and down.

"I did it faster," Brink said from behind. "She almost slipped, and I didn't."

"Yeah, sure," Washington said. Grecia rolled her eyes.

"Good job!" Sienna screeched. Her voice was pretty loud, as she was more than thirty feet below them. "I'm coming!"

"Okay," Grecia said through frayed breaths. She shut her eyes, trying to catch her breath. And as she did, it was suddenly dawn, and she saw something...something that, in her opinion, could only be described through a detailed drawing.

The white heaven-bound birds were as brilliant rays from wind-dappled seawater; their brightness amid otherwise infinite blue, gliding as free souls. In each wing-given arc were the tips of a conductor's wand, a music for both eyes and soul, bringing a wave of sweet earthly joy. The birds flew through that ever-developing canvas of the dawn, as if their wings were fine quills, drawing such buoyant hues.

One of the tiniest birds lifted its head and screeched. All sounds had different tones that could indicate the emotion of the individual making it. Although screeching mostly showed craziness and anger, that one made Grecia's heart heat up. It sounded so happy. It sounded so...free.

The bird glided through the sky, twisting in its pathway. It was now heading towards the water. Grecia knew it wanted the freedom to do whatever it pleased. It wanted the thrill of breaking the rules. Soon, it reached the surface and chirped, dancing around and ruffling its feathers.

The bigger birds started screeching from above. This time, they were startled screeches, screeches that sounded like alarms. The surface of water below the little bird started bubbling, and a navy-colored being broke from the surface, swallowing the creature whole.

A whale.

Startled, Grecia peeled her eyes open, and once again it was night. Had that been a vision? A dream? Had it been a simple, random one? Or had she seen it for a reason?

"Hey," Brink said. "W-why are you so silent? Are you daydreaming?"

Grecia gulped and pushed herself forward with the help of a few branches.

"Brink. Grecia. Follow me," Sienna said. Because the blanket of darkness had covered Grecia's eyes, she hadn't noticed Sienna was right in front of her. "Washington also knows the way, so don't worry about him. Did you hear me?"

Grecia nodded, and then realized Sienna couldn't see her. "Yeah." Her smile dissipated when she thought back to the vision. And then Maya. And then Louisiana. "When will we arrive?"

"In a few—"

A raspy howl came from below, freezing the two girls right in their tracks. And then a scream.

Oh, Grecia thought. *So the wild animals are real. No wonder we're in the trees. Walking on land through the night would have been a death sentence.*

"Brink!" Washington yelled. "Brink, hold on!"

Grecia gasped, and rushed through the branches, each one crunching beneath her feet. She didn't wince. She rushed past Sienna, past Washington, eager to make sure he was okay.

Brink had slipped.

Now, his fingers barely there, Brink was dangling with only one arm with a strong grip. Tears streaked his cheeks, and his chin was shaking. More than seventy feet below him, a wolf was barking the sanity out of him, growling every five seconds. Grecia couldn't see through the branches and the darkness, but she had seen pictures of wolves in books. She was sure they were creatures she didn't want to meet.

"Help me," Brink whimpered.

"Hang in there," Grecia said, inspecting the branches around her. Helping the boy up would be way too hard. If she wanted to reach his hand, she'd have to lay down. That might cause the branch to snap into pieces, which wouldn't end well. But there was no other way to help him. Standing up wouldn't work. Sitting would make her fall. So, she did the most impulsive thing one could have done.

She lay down on the branches.

"Grecia…" Brink took a shaky breath. "That's too dangerous."

"I don't care." With a stretch, she grabbed his fingers. "Come on, pull yourself up."

Crack. Crack. Creak.

She gulped. If Brink did not act quickly, they would both fall to their deaths.

"*Come on.*"

Brink, closing his eyes, hoisted himself upwards. With the added weight, the sound of cracking branches filled the air. "Grecia, if we die, I wanted to tell you that—"

"Oh my gosh, shut up! Let's get out of here!"

Brink closed his eyes, and with one final push, set his feet on the branches. Grecia released his hand and grabbed the boughs above. "Hurry up!" Long cracks drew themselves on the branches below them.

Brink, with wide eyes, scrambled among the dry leaves like crazy, following Grecia. They both gripped the branches and swung themselves forward with such force that finally, the branches behind them collapsed.

Grecia bit her lips, panting. "You were bragging about not having slipped, like, three minutes ago."

Brink lifted his shoulders, as if he wanted to shrug but couldn't, because he was holding onto two branches. "Nobody's perfect."

Grecia frowned. "You're weird."

"Oh my gosh, are you okay?" asked Sienna once she reached the two of them. "Grecia, what were you thinking? You could have died! Why didn't you wait for me?"

Grecia's frown deepened. "I just saved Brink's life, and that's how you thank me?"

"Grecia…"

"Thanks for saving me." Brink cut through the conversation with a nod of acknowledgement. "And sorry, for my, uh, melodramatic sentence back there."

Grecia gripped the branch above her harder, and gave a short, awkward nod.

"Can we rest for a bit?" Washington said from behind Grecia. His eyes were still shaking from the incident. He directed his head towards a group of thicker branches to the left. "We could sit there."

"I think we all need some rest," Sienna said, head down. "Let's go."

They all adjusted themselves on the thicker branches, Grecia sitting next to Sienna farther away from the two boys. They hugged their knees, staring at the sky.

The night was oddly peaceful. Stars lit the sky like snowflakes in the night, yet appeared still, like an old photograph. Grecia smiled, feeling the wind blow her hair into a tousled mane. Were she out in space, riding the limits of the known universe, the stars would move, the galaxies tumble and dart. But for now, with her arms around the branch of a windswept tree and her head leaning gently on the bark, the starlight kept its familiar pattern. The constellations, who'd witnessed centuries and millennia just the same, watched over this moment.

Grecia whispered to Sienna, "I'm sorry for getting angry back there."

"I should be the one apologizing," Sienna replied, scratching her neck. "I just kind of worry too much." Silence lay over them, but it didn't last.

"I wish everyone could understand Juniper," Sienna said soon after.

Grecia cocked her head. "What do you mean?"

"Just…everyone but Maya thinks she's mean. That she's just a sarcastic jerk. But it's not like that." Sienna's eyes reflected against the twinkle of the stars. "She's stressed, you know? I'm also pretty stressed. But it's much worse for her. Even though she's hard to comprehend sometimes, she always has good intentions."

"Huh." Grecia crossed her arms. "As soon as I woke up in that cave, she was a jerk. What do you mean she isn't?" She knew her words sounded quite rude, but she couldn't help it.

Sienna ran a hand through her bushy hair. "She feels really responsible for all of us. She cares about us and wants to keep us safe, because the Outside truly is dangerous. She believes the only way to keep everyone safe is to be strict and, as you say, a jerk. Remember how I told you about the guy who helped us out when we first left Nepenthe? Juniper feels like she needs to help you in the same way he helped us. It's hard to explain."

Grecia rubbed her arms. "And why are you telling me this?"

"Because you need to understand that the Outside isn't the heaven you think it is. Have you ever wondered why it's just us outside Nepenthe? Grecia, there used to be more people in our little group. More people at Home. Like, more than twenty." She lowered her head. "They all died. Most kids don't survive the brutality of the Outside for more than five years after their escape from Nepenthe. That was what the man who helped us said. He was the only one to become an adult before dying here. They all…they all died before becoming adults. And that's what will likely happen to us too."

Chills ran up her spine, and Grecia shuddered. She clasped her fingers together. That was a lot to take in.

"Oh. I'm sorry." Greica's voice barely escaped her throat.

She may have not seen the wolf itself, but even its growls and howls were enough to make her tremble. If being so strict was the only way for Juniper to protect everyone, did that mean the Outside was *that* dangerous?

"Sienna," Grecia said, "I have a question."

"Yeah?"

"You seemed to enjoy the thrill of doing something you shouldn't be doing today, at the workspace. But if you want that thrill so much, why didn't you swim today?"

She winced and looked away. "I already told you. Possession is dangerous."

"But how is swimming possession?" Grecia flailed her arms with frustration. "Don't you want to be happy?"

"For me, swimming *is* possession, Grecia." Her voice hardened. "Imagine losing all your passion. You should know. Drawing on rocks isn't the same as drawing on paper, right?"

Grecia hesitated, and then nodded.

"Swimming in a lake, it just isn't the same as swimming in a pool, with lanes, with a tech suit on. I miss the control days when we had to break our personal records. Just…touching the wall, turning around, and looking at the board, seeing you lowered your time…I miss all of it. I'm suffering, Grecia. Passion is something that makes people live on. Dreams come from passions. Without a passion, all your will to live withers away. If I swim in that lake, the nostalgia will be too much to handle." She hugged her knees. "I don't want myself to get that bit of fresh air, and want more, knowing I can't have it. Temptation is dangerous, you know?"

Grecia didn't know what to say, because in part, Sienna *was* right. Grecia pursed her lips, staring at Sienna's side-profile.

The least she could do was lie.

"Sienna, you should swim. When I carved on the stone, it felt pretty good. Don't let your thoughts stop yourself from doing what you really love."

Grecia caught her gaze. They sat staring into each other's eyes until Sienna announced, "We're resting for too much time. Let's get going."

Grecia spent the next several days playing, having conversations, carving, and occasionally observing her drawing of Veronica on the cave wall, guilt welling up in her chest.

After the day of her first masterpiece, Grecia chiseled other things, like dogs, cats, and her friends' faces.

Besides the occasional memory of leaving Veronica, or when she thought too much about what Maya had said or what she'd read in Louisiana's journal, Grecia's life was perfect. She had friends, food, drawing tools, protectors (Sienna was a good one, Juniper… not so much) and a decent place to sleep.

A place where she was *free*. Where everyone was treated as a human, no matter their intelligence.

A place filled with people whom Nepenthe had broken, including Grecia. Though she didn't know if they had also felt the strange emotion, their company was enough for her to feel as though she weren't alone anymore.

Even being an escort for Maya and Washington was enjoyable. She was getting better at catching fish, though with Maya it was quite hard for her to do so. But at least it was something.

Little did she know that all the thoughts about Louisiana and Maya were more than ready to attack her. That the emotion was waiting for the right moment to strike again.

Disaster was on the way.

11

REAL WORK, REAL LIFE

Grecia passed her first day of real work in hunger.

She had expected a better day, one in which she could actually help the kids from Home. One in which she would get to hear more of their giggles. She had hoped for a day that would be as easy as she'd first thought, where all she'd have to do was follow Juniper's easy instructions.

She fell to the rocks with empty hands. The ache was dull, as if some lazy torturer was standing right behind her, only applying enough pressure to be an annoyance. It sat there, to the side of the right shoulder blade toward the spine.

But standing up, actually moving, and doing the work Juniper had told her to do was another story entirely.

She had to work. It was her job to help them, even if it hurt. She had to do it.

As Grecia tried to stand, using her knees as a reinforcement, needles prickled at her stomach and thighs, and every time she tried again, another needle was added to the multitude. When she was finally able to force through the stings, she wrapped her fingers around the bucket's edges.

She groaned as she thought back on Juniper's instructions.

"Fill this bowl up with water. As much as you can. And catch five fish. Return as quickly as possible. If you return empty-handed, there will be consequences. Serious ones. You already know the way, so I won't need to take you there."

It was heavy. There were no other words good enough to describe its weight.

How did the others manage to carry these buckets? Bringing it here had been hard enough. How did Juniper expect her to carry it back, filled up with water?

The worst thing was, she still needed to catch at least five fish. *Five.*

No, that wasn't the worst thing. The worst thing was that she'd done a good job as an escort for Washington. She'd done decently with Maya.

But now, with no eyes watching her, it was impossible for her to feel enough pressure to do what she had to do. Especially with the constant thought of Louisiana's journal and Maya's story poking her brain. They made concentrating an impossible job- something only doable through a miracle from heaven.

C'mon Grecia, this isn't too bad. You need to help the people who fed you for two weeks straight. Two weeks is a whole lot. Besides, you already know how to do this. You gotta concentrate. That's it. Concentrate, ignore all your unnecessary thoughts and just work.

Ignoring the obnoxious prickling in her limbs and in her mind, Grecia rose from her position and splashed into the water.

Cold water seeped into her now-dusty shirt, stealing the heat from her back as fast as the wind stole from her face. The drops came together to run into Grecia's eyes and drip from her chin.

Though helpful, that didn't quite dissipate the ache.

"Let's grab some fish," she muttered, placing her left hand inside the lake. She waited and waited and waited, hoping the fish would come sooner than later.

A flash of motion passed right through Grecia's legs. She tried snatching it by its gills as Washington had taught her to.

Had Louisiana had to worry about catching fish when she had first escaped Nepenthe?

The thought left Grecia unsettled, and in the blow of distraction, her fingers barely grazed the fish. It flashed away, leaving Grecia with the added pain of failure.

"I'm not giving up," she said in between breaths. "I swear I'll return with what Juniper asked for."

She continued until sunset, failure after failure, thought after thought.

Grecia returned to Home empty-handed.

Well, almost empty-handed. The handles of the heavy bucket of cold water dug into her skin, leaving ugly, red marks. The burden in the bucket was so great that Grecia thought of nothing but the growing pain in her shoulders as she stumbled down the path surrounded by trees, towards Home.

Grecia stumbled through the door, the bucket almost falling from her grip. She leaned on the wall nearest to her, panting, and set it down. Sweat trickled down her neck, rolling down and seeping into her already-wet shirt. She glanced at the others, who were gathered in a circle on the center of the room.

"Looks like day one didn't go so well," Juniper said with a smirk after catching Grecia's gaze. "I can see you got the water. Where's the fish though?"

"Juniper..." Sienna started, but her twin waved her off.

"You didn't catch any fish, did you?"

Grecia looked around, searching for help. "I-I didn't..." she trailed off. Lying wasn't an option anymore, as everyone could clearly see that she had failed. "It was too hard, and there were some…inconveniences. But I have the water." Eyes rained on Grecia, and she waited for Juniper's response.

"Can you explain how *he* did well?" Juniper asked, pointing at the frightened Brink. "He brought five fish, as I asked. And came here much earlier than you. Much earlier."

"I— "

"Explain."

She wanted to explain because she *knew* how. Brink hadn't been disturbed by Maya's story. He hadn't read Louisiana's journal. He hadn't questioned his search for freedom, if he even had one.

Grecia lowered her head in fake shame. What would the consequences be? "Sorry. It was too hard for me. But—"

"No buts. For you, today's dinner will be water, because that's the only way you helped."

"What?" Grecia stared at the older girl, incredulous. "But—"

"I said, *no buts*. You only helped with that. Your newbie days are gone, Grecia. You have to understand that. You get more if you work more. That's the rule."

Grecia's teary eyes locked with Sienna's, and the air grew colder.

"She's right. I'm sorry. Work harder tomorrow. That's the rule." Sienna's voice was tight.

"Okay," Grecia mumbled.

This was her fault. Juniper was right; she should have worked harder. She shouldn't have let these crazy thoughts about freedom thrive in her mind.

But was that even possible?

Grecia sat by the bonfire with everyone else. The heavenly smell of burning fish filled the air, making her nostrils flare in temptation.

She shouldn't have let Maya's story overtake her. She shouldn't have read Louisiana's journal.

Her stomach snarled and howled and from it came the not-so-subtle undertone of pain. She clutched at her stomach, pulling this way and that in an attempt to silence her hunger, but to no avail. It cried out even louder, earning her a few curious stares.

In Nepenthe she didn't have to work to be fed…

Maybe this wasn't the freedom she'd been looking for.

It was a slow pain that ate at her, one that left her drained and empty.

People say that the first day is the hardest one. They say that it's the first day when we start learning, and that the work on the second day comes with surprising ease, along with some kind of strange optimism.

Wrong. Wrong. All wrong.

Grecia stepped into the freezing water. Her stomach gurgled and screamed, *Please feed me!* Her second day was the same as the first. It came with the same needles from yesterday. The same thoughts from yesterday. Perhaps even worse ones.

Grecia gulped, holding back tears. Here she went again.

The hunger numbed Grecia, and the exhaustion didn't help at all.

Darn fish. Darn fast fish. Can't you just move around slowly?

Grecia groaned and splashed at the water with fury, creating a miniature wave that soaked what remained of her dryness. She couldn't help but let go of the tears.

The next day, fruit was added to her list of things-to-collect. She failed. Then again. And then again.

Every night, tears seeped into the leaves that had once been magical. Every night, hunger slowly bit into her stomach, her consciousness, water being her only source to tame it. Every day, she tried her best to get what she was asked. A bowl of water. Two fish. Fruit.

Every day, she tried to discipline any thought related to the journal or Maya's words-to keep them away from her mind, to stop them from distracting her from her tasks.

Occasionally, she grabbed one apple, or one fish. But it wasn't enough to calm the beast of pain inside of herself. What if Home wasn't the correct place for her to be in? What if she needed to go somewhere else?

Somewhere beyond Home. Somewhere farther away.

Grecia couldn't help but think about what Louis had written in the last entry of her diary. *I regret leaving Nepenthe. I regret deciding to leave so impulsively. Though it may not be for the reason you're thinking of.* Was that reason, perhaps, that Louis hadn't been able to find freedom in the Outside, just like Grecia? Those two sentences prodded at her brain every night.

Well, not really. It wasn't just two sentences that bothered her.

It was *definitely* more than two sentences.

12

NOTHING BUT DOUBT

After four days of fasting, a surprise arrived for Grecia.

Her heart thumped in accordance with slow, shallow breaths. Serenity was plastered across her face as she slept. At peace, her consciousness swirled in the land of dreams, oblivious to the physical world. The only time she could be at peace. The leaves rustled against her breath. There were a few grunts, but nothing more.

"Grecia."

I'm dreaming. Nobody is calling me.

"Grecia, wake up."

It was better here than in the real world.

"Grecia, wake up before Juniper finds out."

It was when a heavenly, familiar, yet distant smell hit her nostrils, that Grecia opened her eyes, one by one. Sienna was sitting next to her, cross-legged, odd objects sitting on the floor in front of her.

Fish. Actual food. Three of them.

Grecia sat up, all the sleepiness that once resided vanishing.

"Sorry, they're cold," Sienna whispered, putting her index finger on Grecia's lips. "I had to hide them for some time."

Grecia tried to sob in gratitude. She tried to hug Sienna, to whisper words of thanks. And she tried to refuse, to tell her that she deserved this hunger for not working the way she had needed to.

But nothing came out.

Instead, Grecia clasped her gift with all her might, as if her grasp were an admission letter to the world's greatest university. Her grip tightened on the fish, the surface squeezing through the gaps between her fingers.

She didn't even gaze at Sienna, didn't even say a word before she gobbled up what she'd been given, devouring everything within a few seconds. Calming the monster inside, even if only a little, was enough for her.

By the time Grecia looked up, Sienna was gone.

She never got to say thank you.

During their everyday breakfast, as Juniper shared her instructions for the day, all the children, Grecia included, had been seated in a circle with their legs crossed. The twins, sitting in the center of their circle, handed one apple to every child.

Every child except Grecia.

"So, little *Grace,* how do you feel?" Juniper had said mockingly.

"No offense, but your rules don't make sense. If I don't eat, I'll be less able to work and even more tired."

The others stared at Grecia with disbelief. As if she'd broken the most important law in the world or a promise that had been kept for centuries.

Juniper's eyebrows furrowed, mouth twisting into a frown. "Oh?"

"You should give me food instead of making me starve," Grecia said, this time with more determination.

Even Sienna, of all people, was shocked.

The emotion, after so much time, had made her heart beat a hundred miles per hour. It filled her lungs, made her clench her hands into fists, dig her teeth into her lips.

"What's wrong with you?" Juniper's voice radiated with warmth, but it was piercing at the same time. "All these kids, *all* of them, bring exactly what they have to every day. More than they have to, even." She pointed at the others. "And you're telling me that what I do doesn't make sense?" She shook her head, incredulous.

Grecia dragged herself farther away from the circle.

"I..." Grecia didn't know what to say.

"This is for your own good," Sienna muttered from where she was seated. Grecia switched her gears, this time glancing at the older girl. "Please, trust us. You need to."

Juniper shot a scowl at her twin. A scowl that read, *Please, shut up.*

"This is for saying that our rules don't make sense," Juniper added. "If you return without the fruit, the bowl of water and the five fish, you won't even be able to drink water."

"What?" Grecia shouted. Who did this girl think she was? A dictator?

It was then when it dawned on her. Children obeying instantly.

"This is for your own good."

Grecia's eyes widened, and she shut them with all the power she had left.

The world outside the walls wasn't any different from Nepenthe.

How quickly it had changed. At first, Home had been heaven, a place where she thought she'd found real freedom.

Now, it was a storming hell. Only a place for starving and suffering.

With its own good elements, of course, like Sienna.

Just another version of Nepenthe. Perhaps worse.

Grecia wanted to see Veronica again. She *needed* to see her. She wanted to eat with Cayenne and Liam in the McDouglas Burger Shop. She wanted to walk in the park. She wanted to complete assignments from the Artistic Sector. She wanted to live in a place without creepy diary entries, without people telling her that she was nothing without someone ruling over her. She wanted Nepenthe back.

But she couldn't go back. Because if she did, she'd go straight to Alcatraz.

Grecia's stomach roared like never before, the beast of hunger gnawing at her again. Wet wool crowded her brain, muffling her thoughts.

There's a certain level of exhaustion that equates to insanity. At what point you consider yourself insane depends on the person. For Grecia, it was when she wanted to dislocate her soul from her body. When she wanted to sleep for days and weeks and even years.

Grecia's fatigue was insane.

She paced back and forth across the sand. Should she try once more to catch fish in the lake, or should she save energy for later?

She wasn't only exhausted physically, but mentally. All these thoughts, all these worries, days with nothing but water, everything but rest…

Grecia froze. Her skin was washed with white paint—even her lips were barely there as they shifted to an ugly, light shade of purple. She took a few steps backward, and with a final grunt, she fell as though her puppeteer had let go of her strings.

Grecia woke up to never-ending darkness. Wherever she looked, there wasn't even a spark of light to smile at. She turned her head upwards, and she saw it.

The moon.

It looked beautiful—its edges glowing, light spots on the surface here and there. In the monochrome sky, it looked like a silver ballerina, her aura shining gracefully and doing pirouettes with ease.

Wait. The moon had come out.

Which meant the sun had already set.

Despite her situation, Grecia was quick to react. "Oh no," she mumbled. "Oh no. Oh no. Oh no. No!"

Wolves. Bears. Whatever wild animal hiding behind the bushes.

They were coming.

13
THE CHASE

No. She couldn't have been out for so long. It was impossible. Surely Sienna would have found her like she had last time, when Grecia had stumbled into the old cottage.

But no matter how many times Grecia blinked or pinched her arm, the moon stayed in its spot.

The worst thing was the monster of hunger still gnawed at her throat. At her stomach. And it was almost done with its treat.

She knew the monster of thoughts was soon to come.

No. That couldn't be. She hadn't worked at all, and…Her thoughts trailed off, leaving only an echo in her head.

"Hello? Is someone out there?" Grecia stood up, dull aches nipping at her limbs. "Anyone?"

The only response to her calls was the chilling breeze.

She needed to do something. If she returned like this, she wouldn't even be able to drink water.

Fortunately, and unfortunately, someone else decided for her. Or perhaps something.

Grecia's ears caught a growl, deep and terrifying, and she turned around to face a few bushes. An animal emerged from the shadows, saliva hanging from its mouth, and rabid barks slipped from its tongue.

A wolf.

Its brindled fur didn't move an inch, even with the strong wind. It had a fair snout of a beautiful black shade that twitched every time Grecia took a step backwards.

She had a few seconds to contemplate the beauty of the animal before it howled once and charged toward her.

Grecia ran. Her feet slipped outwards on the wet autumn leaves as she rounded the corner, the crisp air shocking her throat and lungs as she inhaled deeper, faster. With each footfall, a jarring pain shot from her ankles to her knees.

Grecia fully understood why Louis had regretted leaving Nepenthe. The honorable city was a place far better than the Outside, and Louis had left without thinking it through.

Just like Grecia.

The monster of hunger vanished. The dryness in her throat wasn't relevant anymore. She could only think of her life. Getting caught meant getting *eaten.*

She screamed, yelling for help, piercing the air with despair until her throat went raw.

The wolf growled with ferocity and barked. Running on a treadmill at full speed would never compare to the feeling of running from a real threat.

She didn't know where she was going. Home? The place was too dark for her to even know if the way was familiar or not. Grecia searched for trees to climb, eyes wild.

The branches were too high.

I need to run.

This time, it wasn't freedom that spoke to her.

Run. Run. Run.

Seconds felt like minutes. Minutes felt like hours. Because a rabid, killing beast was chasing her, ready to shed blood from its soon-to-be victim.

Where did she have to go?

Grecia thought back at what Louis had written in her journal. That she regretted leaving Nepenthe. Was returning to her home city the right choice? Was Maya right? Did she have to be under someone's rule to feel fulfilled? Given the choice between Nepenthe or Juniper, whose rule would she choose?

Her shoes caught a broken branch, and she lost her balance. She fell slowly, suspended in the air.

How did everything crash down so quickly? So easily?

She crashed into the ground, her skin striking a pile of rocks. Her bones jangled in a way they shouldn't have. Without even looking, Grecia knew there was blood seeping into the dry leaves. The leaves she had once considered beautiful.

With torn and dirty skin, she wept.

Nepenthe had been right. Nature only brought suffering and pain.

The wolf barked, stronger, closer. It rattled Grecia's head, forcing her to move on, to drag herself away from death. She gripped the dirt with fury, and with one more push, stumbled back onto her feet.

That's when she saw it.

Nepenthe. The invisible walls. How she'd ended up there, she had no idea. Perhaps her inner instinct had directed her to her place of origin, to the place where she belonged.

Perhaps the words in Louis's journal had resonated in her head so many times that her body had simply trusted them.

Oh, but who cared? She could either let the wolf devour her or return to Nepenthe and end up in Alcatraz.

Veronica's sweet, gleaming smile flashed through Grecia's mind. Eyes made from coffee beans, hair flowing like ink on paper. "Mom," Grecia mumbled with her chafed throat. "Mom!"

Aroooo. The howl sounded like it was only a few feet away, possibly less. The wolf was closing in on her, and if Grecia didn't move, she'd never get to see her mother again.

"I'm sorry," Grecia croaked. "You were right. I was wrong. I'm sorry for running away. I won't question Nepenthe anymore. Please, let me live."

She wasn't speaking to anyone in particular. But saying what she had learned—it refreshed her heart.

"Please, let me see Mom one last time."

A few more barks. Shorter distance from pain. Twenty feet. Fifteen feet. Ten feet.

Grecia finally made her choice, sprinting with all that she had left, which was close to zero, toward the walls of Nepenthe. Her limbs went numb. There was nothing to feel, nothing to hear, except for the barks.

Her heartbeats thundered against her head, giving her a perhaps final sense of life. *Bump. Bump. Bump.*

When she crossed those borders, she'd be safe. No animals could get inside.

Five feet.

With her final strength, Grecia propelled herself through what separated freedom from suffering. Order from disorder. Perfection from imperfection. Nepenthe from the Outside.

Before Grecia knew it, the chilly wind vanished.

She was in Nepenthe. Her home. She didn't care about the fact that she had failed the Exétasi, that Alcatraz was waiting for her.

All that Grecia cared about were her breaths. Her life. She was alive.

Grecia stared at her trembling hands. Blood.

Pain.

Everything went black.

PART TWO
WHEN THE GLASS SHATTERS

14
THE BRIGHTEST YELLOW

Was she dead? Had all of this been a dream?

Grecia floated. Nothing hovered around her, neither light, nor darkness.

What had she done? She was going to end up in Alcatraz. She was going to get her memories and knowledge of all things erased. She'd die in that detestable prison, either out of hunger or cold, with nothing to eat except for some scrapes of trash, and with surroundings as filthy as a rat in a sewer.

Well, there wasn't much she could have done. She could either starve or get killed by that darn wolf.

Grecia had gotten her punishment. For doubting the government. For doubting the people who really knew what was right for her. For her future.

Sorry. Sorry. Sorry.

She repeated those words over and over, with the hope that they'd change the course of her future.

Certainty pulsed through her brain. Certainty that all along, the citizens of Nepenthe had it best. In Nepenthe, Grecia had never been hungry, had never been on the verge of death. She had never had to work to fill her stomach.

What did the Outside lack that Nepenthe had? Rules. Laws.

And Grecia was certain that it had been the lack of those laws that had made the Outside such a horrible place.

And it had been the presence of them that had made Nepenthe such a grandiose place.

She had already seen the brutality of the Outside. She knew how brutal a place without a structure like Nepenthe was. Grecia wouldn't doubt Nepenthe anymore.

Never again.

There was a tug near Grecia's shoulders. Then another. And another. They were already taking her. Grecia gulped, bracing herself for what was to come.

The tugging halted after a few more, continued by a voice.

"Wake up. You're okay now, I promise. I can tell you're about to wake up."

No. Not again. She was not getting tricked this time, and definitely not by seemingly kind voices.

Grecia's eyes rebelled against their owner. Her eyelids peeled back against her desire, and when her eyes fully opened, a powerful ray of light blinded her.

No. No! She was in the cave again. She was being stared at by Sienna and Juniper again, ready to take her to Home and starve her.

It was the kind of brightness that seared into your retinas, making you close them for fear of going blind. A brightness that would make dull snow look like it came from summer. It could even rival the Sirius Star itself.

Where was she? What was this place?

Curiosity upon Grecia's mind, she kept her eyes open, shedding tears from the horrible yet fascinating brightness.

It was when her pupils adjusted to the light that Grecia saw the girl, sitting next to her on a couch.

A teen, to be precise, maybe about seventeen years old. She

had pale skin and freckles spread about her face like confetti. Her thick, frizzy hair was spilled in front of her shoulders, covering part of her cheeks.

Oh, and her eyes...Her tiny night-black irises were surrounded by sapphire blue strings, and thick ones for sure.

"Oh," she said with a jump. "You've…woken up." Her lips parted in surprise.

Only two weeks and four days, and Grecia had almost forgotten the feel of couches. The softness of the couch she lay on startled her, as she had grown used to sleeping on rocks and leaves. Her wounds had vanished, along with her ripped clothing, replaced by a brand new, shining outfit.

It was a simple one. A light green t-shirt, along with loose, black pants. Not fancy, but just as comfortable as Veronica's hugs.

The teen looked around with uncertainty, which showed that she didn't know what to do with Grecia. "Greetings," she continued, collecting her brown hair strands to make a ponytail. She wore a light green collared shirt with a circular, silver badge that said *Nepenthe Governmental Center.* Her pants were the same as Grecia's, but tighter. "My name is Amber." She stole gazes at the door, waiting for someone to storm in and save the day.

Grecia couldn't have been more puzzled.

"What is this place?" She scooted away from Amber. "Where am I? I'm supposed to be in Alcatraz! How do I even remember who I am?" She wheezed like an exhausted cheetah.

"Calm down," Amber said, and instantly, Grecia's muscles relaxed. How could an average voice be so soothing? It was like a marshmallow melting in hot chocolate.

She found herself sitting on a couch in a stranger's room. Had been sleeping in it, actually. Grecia shuddered at the thought.

The room belonged on a magazine cover. A crystal chandelier hung from the ceiling, giving out a regal mood. Paintings of

Nepenthe's school, framed with gold, dangled on the vivid walls. A bookshelf made out of marble, which had intricate carvings of flowers, sat next to the window with countless books stacked on its thick shelves. Couches the color of mint were spread throughout the room.

But what stood out the most to Grecia was the bright, sunny color of the walls.

Amber ran a hand through her exhausted face. "Grecia Rivera, am I right?"

She nodded after hesitating, uncertainty crawling up her mind. How did Amber know her name?

"Sit up. Let me tell you some things."

"First tell me where I am." Something about Grecia's voice was unstable, as if her brain couldn't process the events clearly. "Am I…in another city or something?"

"I promise that by the end of the day, everything will be clear." Amber sighed, staring at the empty walls. "My name is Amber Walsh. I'm eighteen, and as you should've already guessed, I am, or at least *was,* from the Governmental Sector."

Grecia cocked her head, waiting for more.

"Right now, we're on the third floor of the Nepenthe Governmental Center, the building where creatures are held until they are sent to Alcatraz. You're not in the same situation as them, though. You're being given a second chance.

"On rare occasions, the Nepenthe Governmental Child Control gives second chances to special children, and you're one of them."

"But…" Grecia said, frowning. "What do you even *mean,* a second chance?"

"It means you'll return to your parents when you do things in the right way."

A forgotten memory popped into Grecia's head. One time, when Grecia had been sitting on a thick tree branch, waiting motionless for a soccer game to finish, she dozed off and plummeted ten feet toward the ground, slamming onto her back. The impact had knocked every wisp of air from her lungs, and she lay there struggling to inhale, to exhale, to do anything.

It means you'll return to your parents when you do things right.

That's how Grecia felt now—trying to remember how to breathe, unable to speak, totally stunned as the phrase bounced around inside her skull.

But this time, it wasn't because of pain. It was because of a fusion of amazement and disbelief.

"But it doesn't make sense!" Grecia exclaimed. "How? Why? Why am I being given a second chance? There must be something about me that's making you do this. I mean, of course I want to return to Mom, but—"

"You'll understand when it all ends," Amber said. "I promise."

Promises. How many broken promises had Grecia experienced?

But staring at Amber's kind eyes that burned like gas fire and carried the warmth of a sunlit surface, Grecia couldn't help but trust her.

She now knew how it was to be in an imperfect place. She knew that Nepenthe always made the correct decisions. Trusting the government would be the...best decision.

Grecia didn't know what it was that made that room look like it was inviting her to believe that. Perhaps it was Amber's presence, or the lack of fancy objects.

Or perhaps it was the color of light in the air. Yellow. The banana tone, to be precise.

Grecia had finally given in to Nepenthe's embrace.

"Let me take you to your room. If you do things right, you'll return to your family in about five weeks, on September first." Amber's face beamed.

Five weeks.

Grecia now had the chance to return to Veronica and live in her cozy embrace. She could have a normal life again.

Maybe Nepenthe *had* listened to her prayers.

Grecia grasped at her neck, and her fingers connected with a cold, smooth surface of the necklace she'd found in the bloody cabin. Holding on to its pendant, she inhaled a breath of sweet air. She had to give this to Veronica. Her mother loved necklaces, and this was a beautiful one.

Grecia's mind wrapped itself around the thought. She'd use the necklace as a motivation to do her best for the next five weeks.

As Grecia turned to face Amber, she saw that her lips were quaking.

"What's wrong?" Grecia asked.

Amber stood from the couch, and the fog cleared from her eyes. "It's nothing. Follow me to your room."

15
ANOTHER SCHOOL AND FANCY WORDS

The color yellow brightened the entire third floor of the Nepenthe Governmental Center.

The lobby was a giant space, to say the least. A great mahogany table sat at the center of the room, and its marshmallow-white tablecloth made it look like a smooth cloud. A digital clock with touches of Victorian Era-style hung from the farthest side of the room. The deep yellow, marble walls glinted against the light from a chandelier that hung from the ceiling. Crystal strings shot from the lightbulb encased in a sphere of glass, forming the shape of a diamond.

The chandelier wasn't the only source of light, however. Artificial sunlight streamed from the windows that faced the beautiful city of Nepenthe.

"Woah." Grecia gaped at the scenery out the window as she walked, following Amber to her room.

There were also several wooden doors—eight in total. Five on the left wall, the one they had just come from, and three on the right wall, the one they were heading towards.

"Are there more people here?" Grecia asked.

"Oh," Amber said. "There are two more people. Viktor is a

boy who got a second chance too. Twelve years old, like you. Stanton is my friend. He works here with me."

But Grecia was barely paying attention, as she looked back and her eyes drifted to the smaller and narrower door, the one right next to the one she had come from. She noticed something about it she hadn't noticed before.

It wasn't wooden, but metallic.

"What's that door?" she asked, pointing at it.

Amber pursed her lips before saying, "Employees only."

Something about the way Amber said that bothered Grecia. The volume of her voice had been higher than usual, and Grecia didn't get why she had pursed her lips…as if hesitating. The two continued walking towards Grecia's room, awkward silence laying between them.

To interrupt the quietness, Grecia said, "Where is everyone? You know, the workers."

"Only my friend Stanton and I work on this floor." Amber said, head straight. "The thing is, our goal here is to make the second-chance kids feel comfortable. At home. Too many workers might be overwhelming."

Why are they giving me a second chance, though? Grecia couldn't help but wonder. *Why me, exactly? It can't be random…*

Grecia gazed at Amber, the question about why she'd been selected for a second chance almost slipping from her tongue, but she stopped herself. Why she'd been chosen didn't matter. All that mattered was doing her best to return to Veronica.

"What do I need to do to go back home?"

Amber halted, face gleaming with apprehension. "You'll find out soon."

Grecia nodded with disappointment, and they continued walking.

Soon after, Amber stopped in front of a brown, wooden door.

"Go in," Amber said. "Make yourself at home."

When Grecia didn't do anything, staying in stillness, she twisted the doorknob and opened the door.

The bedroom contained a bed, a table, a chair, and a tiny bookshelf. Once again, what stood out the most was the color. The room had blue walls with beautiful murals on them, hand painted by an artist who knew what they were doing. One mural displayed a laughing child with books tucked under her arms. The colors were like nothing else—vibrant, strong.

"There's a schedule on your bed. I also left a milkshake and some cookies for you on the desk," Amber said to Grecia's back, still standing in the lobby. "Read it carefully. I'll come check in on you soon."

The bedroom door creaked shut, and as Amber's footsteps echoed through the lobby, Grecia stood alone in what would be her home for the next five weeks.

Do things the right way. Grecia stared at the paper on her bed, curious about what her schedule might entail. *What does that even mean?*

Apparently, Grecia was going back to school. Kind of.

Grecia read her schedule once again, to have it all in her mind.

RIVERA, GRECIA. AGE 12, CITIZEN 18945, ARTISTIC SECTOR

SCHEDULE

7:00 a.m. Wake up (Brush your teeth and clean up)
7:30 a.m. Breakfast
8:00 a.m. Corresponding class

12:00 p.m. Lunch

1:00 p.m. Corresponding class

3:00 p.m. Free time

7:00 p.m. Dinner (Brush your teeth)

9:00 p.m. Sleep time

Clothes to be changed every week

Teacher: Stanton Carmichael

Room: A2

Type: Amygdala

Amygdala. That word again.

Grecia shook her head, then stared at the world through the bedroom window as a distraction from her deeper, more worrying thoughts.

The tranquility of the dark sky married with stars calmed her.

"Grecia," she said aloud. "What matters is the present. Don't let the past affect what you do now. Just move on."

She had to move on.

"How do I do things right?" Grecia said unconsciously.

Of course, there were many more questions running through her head, but she restrained them.

Don't worry. They know what they're doing.

Don't worry, she repeated, as though she were trying to convince herself. *Don't worry. Don't worry.*

Grecia sighed, sipping at the milkshake Amber had mentioned. That instantly made her racing thoughts slow down.

What's more, it was cookies and cream flavor, her favorite.

"So," Grecia said as the sound of straw against drink filled the air, "I'm back." She dropped her cup as its contents drained out. "Crazy, huh?"

She grabbed a cookie, playing with it with her fingers. It was dotted with delicious chocolate chips.

Cookie crumbs crunched under her teeth. She felt like she was eating food from heaven after having eaten fish and fish and fish and nothing more, except for the occasional fruit.

Giggling, Grecia missed her footing, falling upon the bed. This time, the fuzziness wasn't startling, but relaxing in all forms. She toppled into it, relieved to rest her weary feet.

She had a lot to be thankful for.

Grecia squished the silken mattress. She pressed her cheek to the fresh, velvety pillows. They were irresistibly soft and cloud-like.

Crunch.

Something crackled under Grecia's back. To confirm the noise, she rolled around on the bed again, and that same sound rippled through the air.

Crunch. Crunch. Crunch.

Alarmed, Grecia carefully slipped off the bed. Was it a monster? A hidden animal?

She cautiously tip-toed to the place where the crunching sound was coming from. One has to be careful when a possible monster is hiding under their bed. She removed the bed sheet, revealing a tiny envelope.

It had a soft, yellow tone, but a softer one than the room she had woken up to. There were decorations printed on it, intricately designed to look like it had come from ancient times. Curly decorations, minute drawings of birds.

An envelope? thought Grecia. *An envelope made the sound?*

For some reason, chills spiked her back.

The envelope was pristine, as she hadn't been rolled around over it.

Grecia's hand slid through the opening of the envelope.

As the sound of paper against paper reached her ears, a letter emerged, slipping from its original home and into Grecia's hands.

The page's tone was the same as the envelope and smooth to the touch. The scribbled words were bumpy, which implied that the words had been erased and rewritten on top of each other.

"What is this?" Grecia asked, scanning the room.

But the smoothness of the paper, the bumpiness of the words…it all demanded to be seen, to be read.

Grecia gulped and forced her eyes to direct themselves toward the dreaded letter.

Greetings,

Though I do not know whom you are, or whether I'll be there when you read this, I am certain you've been through events of a great extent of difficulty.

I have been through many happenings as well, those which I still cannot comprehend, and those which I could have avoided if not for the outright ignorance of my past self.

This is why I am requesting that you do not engage in conversation with me, as I, like you, cannot afford any distractions from doing this right. I shall do what I am asked to do; what Nepenthe asks me to do. This way, I'll be able to go back to my family, and if you focus, perhaps you may too.

I hope this letter made it clear that I'm not here for a social life, but to make use of the second chance Nepenthe has gifted me.

Best regards,
Viktor Collins

Grecia's eyes danced between the letters and commas, her brain eating up every word. By the time Grecia lifted her head from the paper, she groaned, knowing she could have read it without hesitation had her pathetic fear not slowed her down.

The letter was from Viktor, the other second-chance kid living on the third floor of the NGC.

"Well," she said aloud. "That's one strange kid. His way of writing is plain weird."

When Grecia stared at her empty cookie plate and mug, something clicked. Everything became as coherent and logical as the fact that gravity prevents us from floating into space.

What did Nepenthe love most? Multi-talented children. Those were the students who would become government workers. If Grecia wanted to claim her second chance, she would need to impress Amber and the other NGC workers.

Viktor was clearly from the Linguistic Sector. His writing was fancy, and he wrote weird words that Grecia didn't understand. If Victor could teach her how to write and think like him, she could impress the NGC workers and claim her second chance. Nepenthe surely wouldn't send a multi-talented child to Alcatraz.

Grecia grinned as the last piece of the thousand-piece puzzle finally clicked in.

Viktor was wrong. *Doing things right* wasn't only about following orders but becoming multi-talented. Throughout the next five weeks, Grecia would need to prove that she was exceptional, that she was worthy of being a citizen of Nepenthe.

Tomorrow, I'll tell Viktor what I discovered. I'll tell him how we can help each other earn our freedom and return to our families. We can both have our happily ever afters.

Even if talking to Viktor was the exact opposite of what he'd told her to do in his letter, she'd do it.

Grecia scratched her neck (there had been quite some mosquitos in the forest) before collapsing onto her bed for the second time that night.

How nice it was, to be back home. At least partially.

But her journey to freedom wasn't over yet. Her destination had simply, once again, shifted out of reach. Now, freedom was her mother's embrace. Her childhood home. Her friends from school, Cayenne and Liam.

Grecia didn't think about the possibility of failing. She didn't think about Alcatraz. Oh, but who cared? Everything she longed for was only five weeks away.

16

THE BLONDE BOY

Grecia spread the avocado over the toast and placed the sliced tomatoes on top. There was an odd joy in her subtle smile and loving gaze.

A good breakfast toast was enough to brighten anyone's day.

An alarm in the lobby had woken Grecia up, blasting so loud that it spread through the walls of every room on the third floor. The obnoxious blaring had jerked her out of her peaceful, celestial sleep, and the worst thing was that she hadn't been capable of hitting the snooze button.

But again, she had important things to do. A mission to complete.

7:01 a.m.

Amber had been outside of Grecia's door, waiting for her. The older girl led Grecia to the communal bathroom to get cleaned and brush her teeth before leading her to the breakfast table in the middle of the lobby.

7:29 a.m.

Grecia had taken a seat at the table, dishes of all kinds spread out in front of her.

"Enjoy your meal, you two," Amber said as she made her way toward one of the many doors. "I'll be back to bring you to class."

Viktor was the only other person at the table, which, as there were five chairs, made the table look empty. He was sitting right across from her. He wore the exact same outfit as her—a lime greens shirt and black pants.

Instead of immediately telling Viktor the plan, as she'd originally intended to do, Grecia stared at the boy's hair.

It was so blonde. The strands resembled the countless hued stems of a golden wheat field, swaying in the summer sunlight. But, oh gosh…his paleness…

Is he sick or something?

Grecia took a bite of her avocado and tomato toast before speaking.

"Hey."

Viktor ignored her as he chewed, staring at the half-eaten toast in his hands with dreadful eyes.

Maybe he didn't hear me, she thought. *Let's try again.*

"Hey."

The boy sunk into his chair, avoiding eye contact with her. He didn't talk. Didn't look. Didn't stare.

"Hey," Grecia said, stronger than before, tapping her feet on the floor as she bit her lip. "Hi. I'm Grecia. I need to talk to you about something."

Viktor took another bite of his toast. His dull, brown eyes—an uncommon color for a blonde boy—stared at whatever possible that wasn't Grecia's face.

Grecia gave up on conversation and dug her teeth into her own toast.

Sheesh. What is wrong with this guy?

Grecia realized that telling Viktor about her plan wasn't going to be easy. At all.

When she glanced at him again, her eyes widened. She was confident that she'd seen him somewhere before, but she couldn't remember where.

17
MEETING STANTON

After the bell had rung to mark the start of her and Victor's classes, both Stanton and Amber had strolled out of their respective rooms. Amber had emerged from the room Grecia had originally woken up in, and the door to Stanton's room mirrored Amber's from the other side of the lobby.

But Grecia's eyes drifted to the prohibited door, curiosity energizing her body. *No. Don't do it.*

"Viktor, let's go," Amber said with what seemed like a forced smile. "Oh, and Grecia? This is Stanton." She pointed at the young man by her side.

Stanton was a few inches taller than Amber, and he appeared to be about two years older than her. His long, curly hair—black as charred wood—was held in tight braids. The occasional loose strand of hair fell across the dark skin of his face. His outfit consisted of a green collared shirt with a pin—just like Amber's—and black jeans.

"Hey," Stanton said with a nod. "Let's go."

Grecia jumped from her seat, her shoulders painfully stiff. Unlike Amber, Stanton glowed with authority, and Grecia worried that one wrong move in his presence would send her straight to Alcatraz.

Why does Viktor get the nice teacher?

"Okay," Grecia croaked. She glanced over her shoulder, watching Viktor as Amber led him toward one of the classroom doors. She hadn't had the chance to tell him about her discovery and how they could work together to impress the NGC workers.

"I'll try today in the afternoon," she whispered as she reached Stanton, stopping in front of him.

"What?" He halted, staring at Grecia. "What did you just say?"

Grecia peeled her eyes away from Viktor, facing Stanton. "Um…nothing."

"Tell me." Stanton narrowed his eyes, which burned with obligation.

"Alright! Alright. I said I was going to try today in the afternoon."

"And what does that mean, exactly?" Stanton leaned closer, scrunching his eyebrows.

"I-I'll try being kinder to Viktor," Grecia rapidly said, eager to move on. "Yeah. That."

Stanton's brows loosened. He turned around and walked toward one of the classroom doors, closely followed by the shaken Grecia.

Sheesh. What was that all about?

Hoping to improve his first impression of her, Grecia splashed some brightness into her mood. "I'm excited for class. Why didn't I see you yesterday?"

"I wasn't in this part of the building. I work in my room before your morning class, and I work on a different floor afterward. The same goes for Amber. She was with you that evening because it was…" He trailed off, trying to fetch the right word. "A special occurrence."

Stanton opened the door.

The classroom was the same size as Grecia's bedroom, but it was almost completely empty. The only item in sight was a blank, white canvas on an easel with a sage green armchair in front of it.

Grecia's lips parted into an opened-mouth grin. Every fiber of Grecia's being vibrated with anticipation. Adrenaline coursed through her veins, and her hands trembled like an earthquake.

A room without distractions, without loud people, and without other artists to compete against. Just Grecia, the chair, and the canvas. And of course, her new teacher, Stanton. After weeks of carving on rocks, painting felt like something reserved only for people of high class. A luxury.

"W-why?" Grecia could barely say the words. "Why is this here?"

"We arranged everything when we heard that you would be given a…uh…second chance, after you reentered Nepenthe," Stanton said, shutting the door behind them.

Grecia shuddered at the fact that she'd once been living on the Outside, hunting and collecting fruit with a group of misfit children when a beautiful room like this existed in the world.

"Thank you. It's very cool. I like it a lot." Grecia beamed at Stanton as he leaned against the wall.

Surprisingly, Stanton smiled back. His ear-to-ear grin brightened his dull face like the moon at night.

"Right. Let's get started. We're three minutes and twenty-four seconds late."

Grecia painted what some would call a masterpiece.

The scene depicted an animal—a wolf, to be specific, crouched in fear in front of the view of a city with narrow, tall, and rectangular buildings, splashed with neon colors. Its ears were folded, and its eyes' usual sharpness had dissipated, replaced with the roundness of a full moon.

But it was no masterpiece to Stanton.

He hummed from behind the chair, studying the canvas.

"Well, it's not bad," Stanton said in a bland tone. "With some work, you have potential, kid."

"Thanks," Grecia said with a quick nod, trying to look professional. "My dream has always been to have a painting of mine displayed on Nepenthe's school ceiling."

Strange. I nearly forgot about that dream.

"That's good." Stanton contemplated the painting, a layer of what used to be a blank, white space. "We'll analyze and correct some mistakes after lunch."

The alarm trumpeted, marking the end of class.

"Go eat some food, Rivera. I'll be in my room."

"Your room?" Grecia asked. "Is that the room you came from this morning? The one across from Amber's?"

And across from the prohibited door?

"Yeah. My room. Now, go eat."

"What do you do in your room?" Grecia asked.

"Go eat."

Grecia bit her lip, recognizing her mistake of questioning him. She scurried out of her art classroom, legs and arms more energized than before, rather than tired from the movements needed to complete her showpiece.

As Grecia emerged into the lobby, she almost stepped back when she saw the plates on the table.

Chicken noodle soup, bitter greens with tomatoes the size of peas, barbecue slices as thin as paper, noodles in a red sauce, cheeses served with sweet blue grapes. The sight left her mouth watering.

Grecia took a seat at the table and dug in. An explosion of all kinds of flavors and textures sprinkled her tongue. One second the juicy barbecue got crushed by her teeth, the other her throat was getting warmed by the salty soup. Next, Grecia slurped the noodles, their soft texture enough to make her smile from pleasure.

That is, until Viktor emerged from his classroom and sat at the furthest seat away from Grecia.

Sheesh, Grecia thought. *That guy. He never answered me, and now he's avoiding me. Not cool.*

Although she tried to stay calm, she couldn't help but feel the claws of desperation and worry tightening around her throat.

Grecia took a deep breath. Viktor obviously didn't plan on speaking to her during meals, but it wouldn't be smart for them to discuss such an important matter in the lobby anyway. There was always a chance that Amber or Stanton might overhear them.

Grecia stared at the door next to her room. The door next to *that* one led to the bathroom, and the other five rooms were the employee-only room, Amber's room, Stanton's room, and the two classrooms.

That must be Viktor's room.

18
THE (SOMEHOW) SUCCESSFUL SPEECH

After a second class with Stanton, Grecia spent her free time before dinner practicing her speech.

Well, not exactly a speech—more like a ridiculous attempt to persuade Viktor to collaborate with her.

"Look. We need to do our best to return to our parents. Well, for me, my mother. But whatever. What does the Nepenthe government love the most? Exactly. We need to teach each other what we know to become sort of multi-talented children, making us favorable for, you know, freedom."

Grecia sighed as she said the word *freedom.*

Only a few days ago your destination was somewhere that wasn't even inside Nepenthe.

No. Grecia shook her head, unable to think straight.

I didn't. The past is the past. Now, focus.

Grecia inhaled as if she wanted to suck all the oxygen of Nepenthe. Then she exhaled, the stress and worry leaving along-side the carbon dioxide.

"Let's start once again."

Practicing was a flash. Dinner was a flash, even with Viktor close by. Brushing her teeth was a flash.

Sticking to the plan wasn't.

Grecia stood in front of the door she dreaded the most. Viktor's room.

The two second-chance children were currently alone on the third floor of the NGC. As Stanton had explained, he and Amber worked in a different part of the building during the evening, but Grecia had no clue what time they would return. She would have to be quick.

Keeping her plan a secret from Amber and Stanton was crucial. In order to truly impress them, she and Viktor would need to pretend that they hadn't helped each other at all—that they were multi-talented by nature. This would both shock and impress the NGC workers into sending them home. Amber and Stanton might even release them from the second-chance program early.

As Grecia stared at the doorknob in front of her, she lost control of her rapid breathing, and her legs began to tremble.

All Grecia had to do was storm into Viktor's room and tell him the plan, but she couldn't bring herself to open the door.

He'll probably say no.

How horrifying it felt to think of the event that hadn't even happened. Not going back to Veronica all because of an egocentric and shy boy would be a nightmare.

What if I'm wrong about my plan? What if this isn't *doing the right thing?*

Quit being afraid of what could go wrong, stupid, another part of herself countered. *Think of what could go right and smile. Now, do you want to go back to Mom or not?*

It was now or never.

Grecia took a final step and touched the doorknob.

Here we go.

Closing her eyes, now with only black in her vision, Grecia gave the knob a twist and swung the door open.

Plain, white walls with scribbled numbers and words in black ink greeted her. She arched her eyebrows. Viktor's room's walls were way too plain and boring compared to hers.

A wooden desk sat on the furthest side of the room, a bed identical to her lying on the opposite side. In other words, Viktor's room was no different from Grecia's, the walls being an exception.

"I see that you have finally decided to enter." A calm Viktor sat at his desk, eyes fixed on Grecia. Apparently, he had been scribbling words on what seemed to be his journal. There were a few blank pages in front of him, and his right hand held a pen. His muscles and face were relaxed, as if he had been expecting this all along. "Do you take me for a fool? I expected you to enter my private space to tell me things I don't care about. Now, I kindly ask you to retreat."

Grecia stared at the boy, dumbfounded. He hadn't spoken a word at the table today, but he had made a whole speech as she'd entered his room.

Viktor looked thinner than Grecia had thought he was, cheekbones visible. She had been so fixated on his blonde hair and on his pale skin that she hadn't noticed how unhealthily skinny he looked. Even though she could tell he was nervous, thanks to the sweat trickling down his forehead and trembling chin, his eyes burned with passion.

What surprised her the most was his voice. It had a heavy, elegant accent. She had heard that kids from the Linguistic Sector had a special way of speaking, but listening to it directly was enough to take her aback.

When his quivering eyes met with hers, she realized why he had looked so familiar.

He was the tall boy with ruffled blond hair that she had bumped into on Regulation Day, just a few weeks ago.

"You should be more careful," Viktor had said. *"You have probably ruined the whole crowd's pace."*

"Well, pardon me, Your Majesty," Grecia had replied, trying to imitate his Linguistic Sector accent. She had nearly walked away, but his eyes had stopped her. They had glinted with misery—the same misery that lingered in his eyes now.

Not a word formed inside Grecia's skull. All the practice vanished, leaving her with nothing but confusion.

"I…" Grecia bit into her bottom lip, staring at the now silent, blonde boy. "I…"

Viktor's lips parted, like there was something in mind he wanted to say, but the command wasn't working.

The embarrassment left her cheeks flushed. *Maybe I should just go back to my…* But her mouth started working before the thought was completed.

"I don't know why you're so weird," Grecia said, stepping toward Viktor, "but I have stuff to tell you."

He cringed, as if terrified and disgusted by her vocabulary.

"I think I know what doing things in the right ways means," Grecia continued, ignoring the boy's rude expression. "You know that what Nepenthe loves the most is multi-talented children."

Grecia gathered her confidence, and her voice became louder with every other word. She took another step.

"I know that you won't like it, but I have a plan. You teach me words, and I'll teach you art. Then we'll be semi-multi-talented and…yeah. We'll impress Amber and Stanton, and then they surely won't send us to Alcatraz." She shrugged with a nervous grin. "I think we should teach each other things at night, after dinner, so we can learn from each other."

Phew. I finally said it.

Grecia had made her declaration of hope, the grand speech

she had been rehearsing for hours, and now the silence lay on her skin like a venom. It seeped into her veins and immobilized her brain, leaving her pupils dilated and her hands quaking.

Viktor pressed his lips into a thin line, eyebrows lifted. He didn't even hurry to save her feelings, fill the void with a non-committal statement of appreciation. With a final movement, he turned his back to Grecia.

"Okay," Grecia whimpered as her heart fell into the black chasm. "Guess that's a no."

But before she could exit the room, disappointment hanging in the air, her ears caught one sentence.

"You're smarter than you look," Viktor said. "I agree to your terms."

Grecia's face cracked into a huge grin before tears rippled out of their home. She had done it. She was doing things the right way. She was going to return to Veronica.

"Oh. Good," she said, trying her best to hide the bumpiness in her voice. "To-tomorrow night, okay? We'll start tomorrow night."

Grecia slammed the door into its rightful place, and as she tumbled into her bed, tears of joy seeping into the blankets.

Her goal, freedom, wasn't far away. Her destination, Veronica, wasn't far either.

Learning a few hard words was going to be worth it.

VIKTOR

19
AN OLDER BROTHER

First it was his brother.

When Viktor had finally grown comfortable in the NGC, the girl came. And that was nearly *three weeks* after she should have come. Another bad thing? Viktor recognized her as the girl who had stopped in the middle of the school hallway on Regulation Day, and their first impression of each other hadn't been the best.

What alarmed him the most, however, was that she wanted to drag him along with her plan to return to their parents. That one thing Viktor didn't want.

On the other hand, there was an inevitable spark of hope in him. Not because he wanted to return to his parents, of course, but because the opportunity to learn about art was the greatest gift he had received.

Viktor lay on his bed, nothing in mind but one phrase.

Embrace your bad memories so they never happen again. It was his motto. It was what described his whole life, ever since his older brother had left.

No, he didn't leave. They took him.

Who were '*they*? Viktor didn't know. Didn't care. Didn't want to know.

Embrace your bad memories so they never happen again.

Viktor chanted those words in his head. It was the phrase with the most simplistic language Viktor had made, yet it was the most meaningful.

Don't become her friend, he thought. *You'll get hurt again.*

He was only doing this for the lessons. To become multi-talented so that he could someday enter the Governmental Sector.

Viktor slowly closed his eyes, drowsiness washed over him like a stormy wave. His anxiousness clutched to the bad memories that pulled him into his dreams…

"So, how was your first Regulation Day?" Mr. Collins asked, arms crossed. "Are you happy with your choice?"

"I suppose I'm quite content." Viktor scratched his head. "Entering the Linguistic Sector was my second choice. So, that is pleasant."

Only a few hours ago, an event he had been waiting for since the age of five had finally occurred. The Settling. *Like the other kids turning eight this year, Viktor had chosen which Sector to study in. But unlike the others, who had chosen theirs with joy, he had chosen his bitterly.*

The boy stared at his hands. They were the same hands that lacked enough talent to earn a spot in the exclusive Governmental Sector. His application had been rejected, forcing him to choose one of the normal five Sectors just like everyone else.

Viktor had failed to achieve his greatest goal.

"What's wrong?" Mrs. Collins asked. The family of four sat together at the table except for Elliot, who was working on a musical project in his room. "Are you okay?"

"Positive." Viktor forced a smile. "I am absolutely fine."

"Alright, then, Viks." Mr. Collins stood and wrapped his arms around him. "You did an amazing job. Now, go rest. Tomorrow will be an amazing day, I can assure you that."

Everything happens for a reason. *With that final thought, Viktor scurried into his room, and crumbled onto his bed. What a chaotic day it had been.*

The boy stared at one of the many stacks of books spread across the floor. This stack contained those that made him feel nostalgic, the pages that had fueled his imagination throughout his early childhood. Among them were books like The Nightmare Thief *and* The Secret Life of My Neighbor. *Of course, the characters' decisions were nonsense, even for a boy as young as Viktor. But at least they had a certain ability to entertain.*

His eyes caught the cover of When the North Wind Stops. *A hardcover with a minimalistic design, only containing the drawing of a cloud, the title, and the author's name.*

It's been six years since I've read through that one, *Viktor thought.* Was that when I was two? I do remember I only saw the pictures though.

Maybe I should go through it now.

He grunted while rising to pick up the book from the stack. One of the quirks of owning too many books—messy piles of them everywhere. It was always a challenge for Viktor to find the book he was looking for.

There it is.

Viktor grabbed When the North Wind Stops *and sat on his bed, eager to flip through the pages.*

"Hey."

A voice came from the door, and Viktor raised his head to spot his older brother standing in the doorway.

"Huh? Elliot? Were you not working on an important project?"

"Well, yeah," Elliot said. He had somehow gotten into his room without making a sound. He smirked mischievously at his younger brother. "But I think that Viktor Collins being part of a Sector is more important. Don't you?"

"But—"

"Too late. I'm coming in."

"But—"

"What you got there?" Elliot asked, eyes wide as he took a seat next to Viktor on the bed. "That book? Oh, gosh. It's been a while."

"How do you know about it?" Viktor replied, holding the book closely with a light grin.

Elliot chuckled, ruffling Viktor's hair. "I remember seeing you read it, like, every single day. You'd laugh like a maniac."

"Huh. Interesting."

"It just…it brings back memories." Elliot rubbed his eyes and yawned. "Whatever. I'm sleepy. And I need to finish that music project. Good night."

"Good night, Elliot," Viktor said, waving.

"Congrats, by the way." Elliot halted right in front of the stack of books and faced Viktor. "Now that you're in a Sector, you'll be around like-minded people all the time. It won't be long until you make a friend."

"Well, can you describe what making a friend is like?"

"You'll find out someday." Elliot smiled.

"Elliot, it will be fine."

Four years had passed, and Viktor sat on his older brother's bed with Elliot's hands clasped in his. It looked like the brothers were engaged in a handshake, but instead of greeting each other, they were saying farewell.

With their hands in each other's grasps, they were saying goodbye.

"Viktor, what if…" Elliot's eyes locked with Viktor's. His skin turned a tone lighter, making his face look unhealthily pale. "I don't feel so well."

Elliot was two years older than Viktor, yet between the two of them, it was the younger brother who was the most comforting. Elliot tended to sob too often for a citizen of Nepenthe, about once every two months.

Tears streamed down Elliot's jaw, and his chin trembled like flames blown by the wind.

But it was Elliot's shaking hands that showed his vulnerability.

"Viktor…" he sobbed, gulping down a yell every now and then. Elliot's hair, between the color orange and red like fire, would have been neatly combed if not for the hours he'd spent under the bed covers, pulling at them with dread.

Viktor lowered his head, swallowing his own cries. "You will not fail the Exétasi; do you hear me? You will stay with me. Alcatraz…" Viktor trailed off. Saying that one word was enough to throw him off track. "You will never end up there."

"I'll sure miss the Musical Sector. The coffee shop. Our house. Our family. I'll miss all of it." Elliot sniffed bitterly. "But especially, I'll miss you."

"Elliot!" Viktor yelled. "You are staying here. You are simply anxious since tomorrow is Regulation Day. That is all." He patted the older boy's back softly, and gave a hopeful and cheerful, yet heart-broken smile.

It wasn't the same for Elliot.

"But you don't understand," he coughed out the words, banging his fists into the pillows. "You've always been the smart one. And if you had performed just a little better in art, you'd be in the Governmental Sector. But look at me. I'm a complete failure, understand?

These last months I've been having much more trouble than the others. I'm going to fail the Exétasi tomorrow, and then I won't be a human."

Elliot's words stabbed Viktor in the heart. "But..."

There was no but. *Elliot was right, and Viktor was smart enough to know that.*

"You are not a failure to me." Viktor looked up at his older brother. That same older brother he had always looked up to. The brother with whom he shared countless, beautiful memories with.

It was Elliot who had given him hope for the future. For his future. With Elliot's jokes and optimism in his life, Viktor had started to believe that there was nothing out there to fear, that sunshine and beautiful books was all there was.

No, you will not fail the Exétasi tomorrow.

Viktor had reassured Elliot in his head, but for some reason, he couldn't make himself tell Elliot aloud.

It didn't matter anyway. Viktor's warm grin said it all.

"I believe in what Nepenthe believes," Viktor muttered. "I am certain they will not fail a person as amazing as you."

They sat in silence for a while.

"Viktor?" Elliot whispered. His cries had halted. "You're the best friend I could ever ask for. Remember that."

And, cuddled in each other's arms, Viktor and Elliot drifted into what they hoped to be an eternal sleep.

Oh, no. Not death.

Rather, a never-ending comfort.

Calmness. Warmth. All in each other's embrace.

It was two days after that. Viktor sat on the floor of his closet, and this time it was his turn to grip at his hair.

He would have been in Elliott's room if not for his mother's commands. Her words still resonated in his head, a voice that hammered against his sanity.

"You won't get even a little bit close to Elliot, understand? He isn't even your brother anymore. He's just a creature. He doesn't have enough information in his head, and that's that. He'll be locked up in his room until people come to get him to banish him. Now, go prepare for school, okay? See you in a few minutes. I'll take you to school today."

Brick by brick, his walls came tumbling down. As Viktor punched the closest walls, creating a storm of thuds, the tears in his eyes turned the colorful strips of his clothes into a blur of grays and browns. He didn't care who heard; he broke down. The sobs punched through, ripping through his bones and veins. He pressed his forehead against the closet's wood and began to let his heart yank in and out of his chest. It pulled back in like a yoyo. Over and over. In and out.

All his life, all of it, crumbled in his fingertips.

He could still see his brother's face. The brother who would never complain, who never said no. He wanted to scream, to yell his thoughts from the rooftops.

This was all his family's fault. His parents. If not for them, Elliott would be cracking jokes to him. They'd be happy. He would be happy.

But deep inside, Viktor knew it was Nepenthe's system that took his brother away. He knew it. But he couldn't accept that fact. He still trusted Nepenthe.

Even with his eyes shut, the tears' gateway to the outside world wasn't fully closed. Tears streamed down his cheeks.

He wouldn't make any friends. He wouldn't even talk to other children. He wouldn't become this close to anyone ever again. Not when every six months, the Exétasi would be waiting to steal them away.

Because in the end, he'd get hurt.

The worst memories weren't from when Viktor failed the examination. The worst memories weren't from when he got knocked out by guards that had come to escort him to Alcatraz, only for him to wake up on the third floor of the NGC. The worst memories weren't when he was told he had gotten a second chance without any explanation. The worst memories weren't when Viktor started having constant flashbacks, all of them triggered by the smallest of things.

The worst memories weren't when a strange, mysterious emotion would arise every time his parents ordered Viktor to do something. The same strange emotion that he'd felt ever since his brother left for Alcatraz. The worst memories weren't even from when he saw his brother on the hologram during the next Regulation Day.

They were when his dear brother was taken.

Now, living on the tightrope between freedom and Alcatraz, an annoying, talkative girl was offering Viktor the chance to return to Nepenthe as a multi-talented child. There was even a chance the government officials would offer him a second chance to join the Governmental Sector. He could become a teacher, just like he'd always dreamed of becoming.

But still, a permanent scar itched in his heart.

When the officials had arrived to take his brother away, Viktor hadn't left his room to say goodbye. He had known that it would result in agony.

That it would result in his heart shattering a little more.

20
THE BLUE JOURNAL

Sunday, January 26th.

With a pencil, the boy wrote the date on the wall, where he took track of every day he spent in the NGC building. The same building in which the mayor worked.

The boy stared at the first date, in the lower part of the wall. Thursday, January 2nd, and the last one. Sunday, January 26th.

It was quite funny for Viktor, how in ancient times, Sunday was a day for rest. How lazy it seemed for him, to have a full day dedicated to idling.

Anyway, what time is it?

Viktor usually never woke up later than about 6:00 in the morning, as his memories kept him awake late into the night, but it didn't bother him much. He had been waking up extremely early since four years ago, so that he could study subjects other than linguistics.

Oh, how much trouble he had with art. Luckily, that day at night, he'd learn some of it.

Viktor stared out the window, empty of curtains. To the boy's ears came no noise, as if everything that made sound had been destroyed overnight. The same was for light, as the sun had only then started peeking into the world. Viktor flicked the light switch on, and an electric glow bathed the room.

Viktor headed to the desk and sat down, where his most valuable possession lay. A journal sat heavy in the palm of his hand. It wasn't particularly large or thick, but inside were written so many life lessons he'd learned over the past few years.

The smooth, black edges, which were made of cloth, weren't as pleasant to touch as the blue that dominated the cover. Its roughness represented the many years of use the notebook had endured. Blue was Viktor's favorite color, not because it was what people called the *color for boys*, but because it represented honesty and reliability—the qualities Viktor valued most.

What Viktor loved the most about his journal was the content—what some people would call *quotes*. The boy flipped through the pages, contemplating the phrases he scribbled down over the years.

He stopped at page twenty, one of his personal favorites.

Being a teacher isn't just about teaching, it's about building the foundation of civilization. After all, how could children take advantage of their talent without someone to learn from?

By now, the pencil marks were slightly faded. When had Viktor written this quote? Two years ago? Three?

Viktor slid his hand through the paper, memories flooding in. He remembered the day his teacher had assigned an essay about his dream job. Of course, he had chosen to write about teaching.

Viktor balanced a fountain pen on his fingertips. It was what he did whenever boredom came upon him. Balancing *was* his specialty, at least when it came to kinetic proficiency. Whether it was a pen or his body, Viktor was good at precision and control. Those weren't his only abilities, however. The violin and algebra were other things he enjoyed, as well as modern history and genetics.

But of course, nothing could beat writing for him.

Viktor held his journal as if his life depended on it, which it kind of did. Ever since the officers had taken his brother away, the journal had been his bridge to relaxation, to some decent amount of peace from the raucous outside of his head. It was the object that Viktor had chosen to bring with him after failing the Exétasi, when the authorities had told him he could only bring one thing to the NGC.

It had been then that his suspicions sparked. Suspicions that his reason for failing wasn't an ordinary one.

Now, Viktor Collins, aged twelve, slept and ate somewhere that wasn't his home, the result of a second chance in his hands.

Then the girl came. Grecia Rivera. Someone whose name he heard from murmurs between Amber and Stanton soon after she was detected crossing the walls, someone who completely ignored his letter.

"I wonder if she feels the emotion as well," Viktor said. It was a normal thing for him to speak to himself, because he was the only person he could count on. "It is strange. Being from the Linguistic Sector, it is unusual, really, for me to encounter an event or object that is not possible for me to describe."

Viktor's eyes widened when he looked out the window. It was already morning.

Beyond the invisible borders stood the definition of a forest during autumn. A carnival of gold and orange everywhere. Viktor couldn't help but wonder what it was like Outside. What kinds of unspeakable mysteries lay beyond.

21

RAIN OF TEARS

For the first time that he could remember, Viktor did something during class other than studying, writing, or talking.

He cried.

It had all started during breakfast.

Like always, Viktor didn't care about the food. Maybe that was why he was so thin, why he became ill so often—though with Nepenthe's medications, he would always heal in a matter of minutes.

His legs resembled twigs, wrapped in nothing more than pale skin. He had a chest so frail that the bump of each rib was almost visible through his green shirt. His face looked as if he hadn't eaten well in months.

Viktor frowned at his plate. A sandwich, along with a cup of milk. Why did the food look so dull when the smell was angelic?

"Hi," Grecia said. She was right next to him.

Viktor almost jumped but refrained from doing so. His personal image was an important thing.

"Hey, relax," she continued, patting the boy's back. Was his tenseness really so noticeable? "You don't have to be shy or anything. We're going…through similar things, I guess."

She keeps chattering on and on…what is wrong *with this girl?*

Grecia leaned closer to him and whispered, "So, how are we going to study today? At night?" Her eyes shined with excitement. She seemed to be even more hyperactive than she normally was.

Viktor hated it.

"Hello?" Grecia said, trying to imitate the boy's accent. "Mister Viktor? Or whatever." She chuckled, snapping her fingers in front of Viktor's face.

He grunted, and she pulled her hands away from his face.

Is it possible for you to stop speaking to me as if we were friends? It is utterly annoying, yet you continue. But he couldn't make himself say it. Couldn't make himself tell Grecia.

He chomped his sandwich away, piece by piece. The milk helped the bread slide down his throat.

Viktor didn't care. He didn't care about anyone. He only cared about what Grecia had called him.

Mister Viktor.

He turned his back towards Grecia to hide his bloodshot eyes from her.

His fury boiled the moisture in his face. But he couldn't show his true self. His emotions. What he felt. Viktor couldn't be himself.

Why show your real self to other people? It's useless—it only makes people pity you.

The boy gulped down his sobs until he couldn't anymore. Viktor stood up, without even taking a second look at Grecia or the way his chair was now out of its place.

He wanted to shout, to cry out. But he simply walked away in silence towards the bathroom before Grecia could say another word.

The boy splashed water on his face. The water poured down, dripping from the edges of his hair, as his everything turned into a foggy illusion.

The water was colder than his heart.

"Elliot!" Viktor squealed with delight as his older brother approached him from across Nepenthe Grand Park. Elliot had been talking to his friends while the nine-year-old Viktor had been observing the green, spiky grass rooted in the ground.

"Hey, Viks," Elliot shouted, raising his hand as he ran toward his little brother. His crispy, orange hair bounced on his head. Although he had long limbs, his pace wasn't the fastest, not even in the Musical Sector. "What're you doing?"

Viktor turned to the grass. It was rough and shaggy like uncombed hair that hadn't been washed with decent shampoo for days, yet its smell told otherwise. The lovely aroma, a combination of honey and pinecones, made his skin prickle with excitement. The grass under his palms were almost like his favorite blanket back at home.

"I was just observing the grass," Viktor said before shutting his mouth. "Oh, pardon. Just *isn't necessary in that sentence."*

"Seems like your Linguistic Sector way of speaking isn't complete yet," Elliot said, ruffling his brother's hair. Viktor giggled as Elliot's fingers slipped into his armpit, and the tickles rippled through his body.

"Stop," Viktor hollered through a fit of giggles. "Stop! I don't want to laugh but– Shoot!" He rolled on the ground, and the prickly grass only tickled him even more.

"Oh, so the smartest boy in the family can't resist some tickles?" Elliot said tauntingly.

Instead of becoming a furious little squirrel, *as his parents would call Viktor whenever he'd get angry, the boy giggled even more.*

The edges of Elliot's lips spread further apart.

"But you aren't brave enough to tell Tiana that you have a crush on her," Viktor continued the word duel. "Even if she's your best friend." He prepared for the final blast of tickles, the strongest enemy until that moment.

But that final blast never arrived, as Elliot's hands halted mid-air. Elliot tilted his head and sat beside his little brother.

"You know what?" Elliot said. "Tiana isn't my best friend." He looked to his left, where Tiana drank from a juice box along with his other friends.

"Is that so?" Viktor asked, curiosity brightening his eyes. "Is it William?"

"No."

"Elijah?"

"No."

"Logan?"

"Nope."

"Angelica?"

"Incorrect answer."

Viktor groaned, pulling at his hair. "Who is it then?"

"Well," Elliot said with a grand smile. "My best friend is a boy named Mister Viktor."

"Greetings Amber," Viktor said glumly.

"Greetings," Amber said back. "How's it been going, with the new girl?" She hesitated before saying the last three words. "It might be good to talk to her, be her friend. I can imagine you miss your friends a lot."

"I might try out your suggestions," he said through gritted teeth and a pained smile. He was smart enough to know that those words were a good way to end a conversation about this specific topic.

"Good." Amber said with a smile. "Now, let's get started with class."

The room's walls were draped in paint, the color of pale smoke. A paper-thin screen was stuck to the farthest wall from the door, and a digitizer pen with a thread tied to it hung from a hook next to the screen—tech that replaced what was used to be known as a blackboard and chalk.

On the opposite wall stood Viktor's desk, a miniature version of the table in the lobby. He sat at the desk with an elegant notebook and pencil in front of him.

"Well then," Amber said. "Have you memorized the words from yesterday?"

"By all means." Viktor nodded with confidence.

"What does inchoate mean?"

"To be only partly formed." He halted, and a sigh left his mouth. "Pardon. The word *only* wasn't necessary in that sentence."

"Your mouth speaks the truth," Amber said with her typical smile. "You're very smart."

"*Very* isn't necessary in that sentence," Viktor said with a smirk.

A sudden sense of *déjà vu* washed over him. He shook his head, blinked, and looked forward to continuing with class.

But the person he saw in front of him wasn't Amber, but his mother.

... *What?* Viktor frowned.

It was then that it hit him. He had had this exact same conversation with his mother before his life came crumbling down.

Am I... hallucinating?

Surprised, the boy shut his mouth and his eyes fluttered. Amber, once again, came back to his vision.

Snap out of it! You have gotten over this such a long time ago.

Stanton and Amber had reminded him of his parents for some time.

At first, Viktor had hated it. Two people, both older than him, and of opposite sexes. Seemingly caring.

However, not much after, he had gotten used to it. He'd started to consider them as just teachers. Not parental figures.

It was Amber with whom he felt the most comfortable, after Stanton. Of course, it wasn't as if there were many others, but the way they treated him was special. After seeing his mother and father dump Elliot in such a way, he had mistrusted them terribly, enough to make the strange emotion be present whenever they ordered him to do something.

But they weren't people to whom he'd tell secrets, or hug whenever feeling down. He didn't even want to smirk in front of them. He didn't do that to *anyone*, anymore. But, well, it was necessary for him to talk to them. They were his teachers, after all.

The three weeks before Grecia came, it wasn't bad. Stanton and Amber would take turns for each day. One would stay with him, teaching him and simply being present. The other would be working wherever they had to in the NGC building. A different teacher each day, a different way of learning each day. And there was no inconvenience whatsoever as to learning, both teachers, Stanton and Amber, having studied in the Governmental Sector and having been taught all subjects.

But then, that girl came…

"Viktor?"

The boy snapped back to the class when Amber called him.

"Yeah?" he said and shook his head.

"I asked you a question," Amber said. "Which word means *wasting time*?"

He got immersed back into his world of words and letters. His world of vocabulary.

"Is it," he started, "dilatory?"

"Correct," Amber said.

They continued with the other ninety-eight words of vocabulary studies. Viktor got them all right, though he struggled with the word *martinet*.

Next was writing each word fifty times. Normal schoolwork from Nepenthe.

Writing an essay in exactly five minutes is expected of a student in the Linguistic Sector.

Viktor tried to crack his knuckles. After a failed attempt, he sunk in his chair in embarrassment. Fortunately, Amber hadn't seen him.

"The question for this essay is…" she cleared her throat in an exaggerated manner, obviously to tease him, but he refused to give in. Eventually, Amber gave up and continued. "When you were brought to the NGC, you were told that you could bring one object with you."

Viktor nodded, a shiver making his head spin.

"Why is this object so important to you?" Amber asked. "Write more than five hundred words regarding this question in three minutes or less."

She pulled her *Nuntius*—a gadget that looked exactly like a small tablet—from a bag beside her, lying on the floor. Amber took it everywhere, at least according to what Viktor had seen. She pressed the Nuntius' screen a few times, until a clock appeared on the screen.

"Three minutes starting in five," Amber hollered, "four…"

The boy grabbed his pen with so much force that he worried it might break. His muscles turned rigid as he stared at the blank pages on his desk. Words and sentences in his head either flew away or got caught, which meant only a few of them would be written on paper.

Not that it mattered.

"Three. Two. One. Go!"

Viktor scribbled in his notebook, the ink flowing naturally, as if it were born to form those words. In only a minute, a whole page was filled up, inky words engraved into it.

It was a wonder how the boy could write so swiftly yet maintain great calligraphy.

Five minutes passed in a blink.

"Stop," Amber said. She approached the boy, tapping at the Nuntius's screen. When she reached the desk, she let go of her Nuntius, and it hovered over Viktor's notebook.

The Nuntius made a deep buzzing sound.

"Next page," Amber said when the buzzing stopped. However, Viktor knew what he had to do before he was instructed. The boy flipped to the next page, and the buzzing continued.

The gadget stopped floating, and Amber caught it before it fell wherever it had been intending to. She gazed at the screen and cleared her throat.

"According to my Nuntius, you wrote five hundred and eighty-one words." She smiled, clearly satisfied with her part-time student. "Good job."

But Viktor wasn't happy for his success, nor was he proud of himself for the few hundred words he had written.

Don't do it in front of her. Not in front of someone, he thought.

Yet it was inevitable. Writing about his journal, why it was so important for him, and why he had brought it to the NGC had been too much to bear.

His eyes became glazed over with a glassy coating of tears. When he blinked, they dripped from his eyelids and slid down his jaw. Viktor bit the insides of his mouth in an attempt to hide the sounds that threatened to escape from his mouth.

"I need to go," Viktor said, rubbing a few tears away. "I'll return when I can."

He left the classroom and stepped into the lobby. After taking a shaky breath, he ran towards his room, heart racing. Bumping with a few chairs in front of the mahogany table, but quite rapidly for someone who had never been in the Kinetic Sector. As soon as Viktor entered his room, he sank into the corner, hugging his knees as hard as possible.

Viktor woke to the soft singing of his parents from the hallway, just outside his room. Instead of laughing with excitement and running to his family, the boy turned his head to the opposite side and stared out the window. Viktor guessed it was about four in the morning. It was the best time of the day, when people weren't laughing, or talking, eating together.

The sky seemed brighter today, happier. Perhaps because it was Viktor's tenth birthday.

"Happy birthday to you," his parents sang. His bedroom door squeaked as they opened it. "Happy birthday, little Viktor..."

Such a funny fact, how that song survived for so many centuries. Oh, and not only the song, but the whole tradition of birthdays. A cake, a few candles sticking out of it to indicate the person's age, and gifts.

Perhaps some things had been perfect since the beginning of their existence.

"Happy birthday, Vik!" Elliot screeched from behind their father's back.

"Shush," their father said back. "It's four in the morning. We don't want to wake our neighbors."

In their mother's hands sat a plate, with a cake on top.

A creamy, pink icing coated the cake, and a large strawberry stood at the top.

Viktor couldn't even imagine living in a world without genetically modified strawberries. Strawberries that weren't nearly as sweet, not nearly as red nor juicy nor big.

The boy scurried off his bed and almost ran into his family. Taking advantage of how close he was to them, Viktor embraced every one of the people he loved the most. His mother. His father. And especially Elliot, his brother.

"My sincere thanks," Viktor said. By then, the advanced vocabulary had been sinking into his daily conversations. "I have an immense love for you. All of you."

"We do too." Mr. Collins squatted, his height shrinking enough for him to not have a significant difference in height between his son. Being from the Kinetic Sector, and having practiced basketball, the man was too tall for his arms to reach Viktor. "Happy birthday."

A warm hug makes any person's day. At least if they have a heart.

"Viktor?" Mrs. Collins said with a huge grin. "We prepared a gift for you."

She gestured at Elliot, who shyly approached Viktor. "I hope you like it." The hands that had been hidden behind his back that were now in front of Viktor, held a flat object.

Even before his brother could say another word, Viktor snatched it from him, wonder sparkling in his eyes. His lips quivered from excitement. But as soon as he realized what this gift was, the brightness in his face dissipated. "Really?" he asked. "I already have two notebooks. And I'm happy with those."

Elliot sighed, his gaze drifting to Mrs. Collins. She nodded.

"Well," he started. "I guess I can tell you where it came from. We bought it in the bookstore. It was one of those cheap ones." He smiled nervously as if begging for mercy. But apparently, he wasn't done yet. "You know that clothing company, Veronica & Co? That famous one? Well, they're all famous, but you know which one I'm talking about. And the owner of the company helped us make the cover more special. Since your favorite color is blue, we asked her to stitch something blue into it. And it ended up like this. I personally think it's really pretty." His nervous smile widened.

Viktor could only stare at this simple gift. He didn't want to make his family feel bad.

"You paid for a notebook and decorations as well?" he said. "Then, I adore it." He grinned from ear to ear, making his eyes look so small. "I'll only use it for special things."

His parents chuckled, and Elliot sighed, probably in relief.

"Oh, right. Forgot to mention something" Mrs. Collins said. "The lady who works there has a kid, and she wrote a note, since this is a birthday order. I was told she's very enthusiastic about people's birthdays."

"Is that so?" Viktor asked, slowly opening the notebook. A light, pleasant smell, similar to vanilla, made his nostrils quiver. The lined, yellow-ish pages were smooth and thin betwixt his fingertips.

As said, a little note was tucked in between the very first two pages.

Happy birthday!!!!!!!! Even though I don't know you, I hope you like my mommy's work.

Clearly someone who wasn't from the Linguistic Sector. Oh, but who cared? The journal was growing on him. Besides, if Mr. and

Mrs. Collins had bought it, it should have been for a reason. The elders were always right.

Viktor turned around with a smile and blew at the candles with such force that in a second, his surroundings were inky.

Now, the journal was the only thing that could connect Viktor to his brother. His thoughts. The world.

Creak.

"Viktor. Are you okay?" Amber said from the doorway. Her close footsteps elucidated that she was walking towards him.

"Viktor. Look at me."

Miraculously, he did.

Amber's face showed the kind of gentle concern that reminded him of his favorite teachers. She lightly touched Viktor's shoulder, and instead of tensing like he usually did, he slumped forward. It felt as if he had drunk a soothing cup of tea.

"That question I asked must've triggered some bad memories, didn't it?" Amber asked.

The boy nodded, and his eyes twitched.

"I'm sorry." Amber stroked Viktor's hair. "But I believe that was for the better. It must've reminded you how good Nepenthe is, deep inside. If the government was evil, they wouldn't have let you bring the object. We actually care about our people and their relationships with others."

Nepenthe being evil? Why was she saying this? He didn't even think about the city in such a way.

"I know," Viktor sighed. "I'm lucky to have lived here for all my life."

"Viktor, you need to understand how good Nepenthe is.

That'll motivate you to want to do things the right way. To go back home."

The boy nodded throughout Amber's talk.

"What's more," Amber continued, "we actually give second chances. You're receiving a second chance."

"You are certainly right." Viktor smiled at her.

"Hope that made you feel better. Now, I have to work upstairs," Amber said, standing.

"Please wait," Viktor grabbed her arm as she stepped towards the door. "I have a question."

"Yes?"

"Why did you not stop me from running away? Class…class is too important for me to act in such a way. I apologize, by the way."

He would have received a terrible punishment if it had been a normal class in school. Leaving class without permission was something only animals would do.

Oh well. He *was* a creature. He had failed the Exétasi.

How strange it was, to think that now he was the same as the people he'd seen in the holograms of Regulation Day. The only difference was that he had received an unusual second chance.

Why had he received it? Why Grecia? Why not any of the others? What was so special about him?

"No need to apologize," Amber said. "Like I said, Nepenthe cares. We care." She walked out of the room and gently closed the door.

Viktor's gaze drifted to his journal. The object he had chosen over a photo with Elliot. Over his limited-edition pen. Over every single possession of his.

Nepenthe cares.

22

THE ORIGAMI CRANE

Slowly and with great care, Viktor ripped a page out of his journal.

And then another.

And then another.

Thirty seconds later, ten pages lay on the ground. Sweat trickled down his neck as if he had run a mile at full speed. He knew that he and Grecia would need resources to teach each other, and lined paper was definitely going to be one of them.

Even though Viktor had planned to do this, it was painful to actually rip these pages out. Pages that could have been filled with his deep, sincere thoughts. But he knew it was necessary. Besides, he wasn't letting Grecia touch his journal. Not even for a second.

Viktor wrapped a hand over it, walked to his bed, and slid the journal under the bed sheets.

For safety.

The more he thought about Grecia's statement, the more flawed it was. *We'll start tomorrow night.* What was that supposed to mean? What place? What time?

However, Viktor was smart enough to know at what time she

was going to come. Or the fact that she *was* going to come to his room in the first place. Grecia probably thought he wasn't going to go to her room (which was true), and she was the type of person whose excitement was hard to contain. That's why she'd eaten so quickly at dinner, and that's why Viktor had tried to follow up with her. So he could get prepared.

He stared at the pen lying on his notebook.

Guess they'd have to share that one. It wasn't like it could get ripped and separated from its other pieces.

Viktor rubbed his arms anxiously. But at the same time, there was a thrilling tingle in his heart. He was actually going to try out teaching. His dream job. A rare opportunity was within his grasp.

Only concentrate on the learning and the teaching. Ignore Grecia. If her idea is right, I will return to Nepenthe, and most probably even enter the Governmental Sector.

His mentality wasn't that he was going to return to his parents. Or his friends. He was returning to *Nepenthe*, and that was that.

But what if he gave up on being happy, and gave in like Elliot did? What if he didn't follow Grecia's plan? That wouldn't be too hard.

His slender fingers pressed into his knees. His whole body shook, bones rattling in fear of all the possible outcomes. His heart pummeled against his ribcage.

Calm down, Viktor thought. *If you said yes in the first place, you surely are going in the correct direction.*

Grecia came to his room a few minutes later.

After he didn't give a response to the knocking in his door, the door creaked open, revealing Grecia's face. She smiled and stepped in, lowering herself next to Viktor.

"Hi," she said, waving her hands. "Let's start. Who goes first?"

She was truly exceedingly obnoxious.

The two sat on the floor, cross-legged. With only paper and a pen distancing them, Viktor's hands rattled in anxiety.

"I'll start," she offered, when, once again, Viktor didn't respond. "Wait, aren't classes supposed to start with the students presenting themselves?" Grecia stared at him. No response. She shrugged. "I'm Grecia. I *was* from the Artistic Sector. I like cookies and cream milkshakes, and I absolutely *love* painting. Also, there's this emotion…uh, never mind. Yeah." She grinned nervously at Viktor.

Memories of his brother's smile flashed through Viktor's eyes.

No.

"I know you aren't going to present yourself in exchange," Grecia continued with a cough, a hint of annoyance in her voice. He found that amusing. "Whatever. Let's start with origami."

Viktor couldn't help but let his curiosity spark. New vocabulary was what every student from the Linguistic Sector desired. "Origami?"

"Yeah." Grecia slid a paper sheet towards her, making him tense. "You're going to do what I did four years ago. When I was *eight.*" It was quite obvious she was fighting a snicker. "Anyway. This *is* art. It isn't advanced, but it's necessary to learn how to use your hand."

I do *know how to put my hand into use. I have written more than a few dozen words today*, Viktor thought, rolling his eyes.

"This one is my personal favorite." Grecia folded a part of the sheet, as Viktor's eyes went wide in horror. And then again. And then again.

What was she doing? How could she fold paper? Paper that could be used for writing? Paper from *his journal*? Just as Viktor was about to yell *are you crazy?*, Grecia set her work on the floor.

It was beautiful.

It looked like…

A crane.

Grecia had formed a crane out of paper.

Viktor's sciencey side glowed with fascination. However, the exterior of him stayed gray, dull. "How did you make an object resembling an animal out of paper?" he asked calmly.

Grecia chuckled. "I'll show you again." She grabbed one more sheet, and this time, Viktor paid attention to her careful movements, the movements that formed such a beautiful form.

Viktor gawked at the result once again.

"This is origami," Grecia said. "Your turn."

What did she mean? She had only shown him the process two times! However, Viktor wasn't going to display his feelings in front of that girl. He'd displayed enough already.

He nodded and started making his own crane.

And oh, gosh. How strenuous it was. Arduous. Burdensome. Onerous. And those were only four words of the dozens Viktor could use to express his utter pain. His fingers twisted awkwardly at an attempt to fold the paper as naturally as Grecia had. He folded and unfolded it multiple times, teeth digging into his lips.

"That's one good crane," she said as he lifted his work.

She couldn't have been more wrong.

On Viktor's palms lay a deformed kind of creature, several parts ripped because of the boy's unnecessary force. There was no beak, and one wing was half the size of the other. In other words, on his palms lay a failure. A completely, utterly embarrassing failure. Viktor frowned. He hated being bad at something.

"Try again," Grecia gestured at his deformed crane. "Continue until it's…not bad."

The *not bad* was not reassuring at all.

"Can you not show me the process step by step?" Viktor asked with irritation, crossing his arms.

"Memory is an important thing in the Artistic Sector." Grecia said, and after that, kept her mouth shut.

Viktor huffed in irritation and went to work once more.

And so, he spent the next half hour trying to form a charming inanimate object.

He folded and twisted, crossed his arms in annoyance and scratched his head, trying to remember the order of the steps.

But by the end of that time, Viktor held a beautiful paper crane in front of him. Compared to his first try, at least. He still had the problem with the wing size, but it wasn't too bad. Even Grecia admitted it.

"That's enough for today," she said. "Tomorrow you gotta try again." She paused, eyes sparkling with excitement. "Now, teach me some stuff."

Unconsciously, Viktor cringed as he heard the word *stuff.* Such a terrible, simple word. No sophistication at all. Horrifying. But that was off topic.

It was the moment Viktor had been waiting for. Trying out the career of teaching.

This is the plan. Only talk about topics related to the subject. Do not answer Grecia's off-topic questions. Easy.

"Today we'll be teaching you a few words," he paused soon after staring to speak, cheeks warming up. "I meant I. I'll be teaching you words." It could be guessed with only a few sentences that Viktor was much more than anxious.

He gulped one last time, and gently grabbed his pen with a plan in mind. The pen's tip touched the paper's surface, and it slid through the page with each movement of his hand.

Soon, he handed the paper to Grecia, words scribbled on it. Not the messy, unorganized type of handwriting though. The type that looked like printed out text.

"Here," Viktor said. He couldn't believe he had actually spoken to her. A few times now. What was wrong with him?

Grecia's brows furrowed, the frown on her face more pronounced than a 4D movie.

"What the cookies does *acclimate* mean?" Grecia exclaimed, hands on her head.

What did *what the cookies* even mean?

"Seriously? *Acclimate* means *to get used to a certain environment*?" She scratched her head in confusion. "Why not use that phrase instead? Linguistic folks are weird."

Viktor wasn't amused. What's more, he was deeply offended. But why should Grecia care, the same way he didn't care about her feelings?

"Right. Memorize each word's meaning. And write them down twenty times with the papers that remain," he said, his face staring back at her coldly.

"What? Twenty words, twenty times?" Grecia scrunched up her face.

"I wrote one hundred words fifty times today." Viktor's expression remained the same.

Grecia couldn't do anything but oblige. She crouched until the tip of the pen touched the paper. The scribbling started.

Funny.

After this, Viktor would tell her to write a long essay in a short time. The same class structure Amber had used earlier that day.

The question for the essay was: *Why did you choose the Artistic Sector?*

Oh, it wasn't because Viktor wanted to know. He'd just pulled a random question out of the big pile of random, basic questions teachers usually had for the essays.

Viktor took a look at Grecia's face. Her forehead was all scrunched up as she wrote, and she was biting her lips, apparently stressed.

The time he gave her was ten minutes. Ten minutes for five hundred words was a whole lot, but he didn't mind. More time for Grecia to write meant more time for Viktor to be silent.

Since he didn't have any clock or digital countdown as Amber did, the only way he could count was in his head.

Five hundred and ninety-five. Five hundred and ninety-six. Five hundred and ninety-seven. Five hundred and ninety-eight. Five hundred and ninety-nine... Six hundred.

Viktor clapped as soon as he hit ten minutes.

"Time is up," he announced.

"Sheesh," Grecia said, biting the pen. Viktor winced. "This should be called handwriting racing."

He rolled his eyes. "You can go now," he said, ignoring her words. "I will examine your work and make you practice on the points you are bad at."

"Okay?" Grecia said as if it were a question. "Well. Bye! Hope you learned something. All future lessons will be in your room at this same time, alright?"

Viktor nodded.

And out she went.

That was... excruciating.

After staring at the door for a moment, he glanced at the essay Grecia had written, or at least, had started writing. And for some strange reason, her handwriting seemed...familiar.

Something bugged Viktor.

Grecia had mentioned something about an emotion when

she had been presenting herself, and as time passed, something kept tickling his head. Could it be the same emotion he felt?

He faintly smiled before mentally slapping himself.

23
DREAMS DON'T COME TRUE. THEY ARE TRUE.

Viktor had an odd opinion about dreams.

According to modern psychologists, dreams could give an answer to some inner questions, though not directly. They could also give advice on life. The harder part was figuring out what the visions meant.

Viktor hated dreaming. It was as if a person with no knowledge about him were giving him tips on how to write or speak. He knew what he was doing. He wanted to be happy. Happiness equaled success, and to be successful, he had to enter the Governmental Sector and then become a teacher.

Viktor was the person who conducted his life. Not a random, crazy vision he saw while asleep.

His opinion changed that night, however. But rather than a dream, he would have called it a nightmare.

A blinding light made Viktor close his eyes. The next second, he was standing on a bridge. His eyes raced through his new surroundings, and Viktor's vision lay on where he stood—the bridge.

Viktor pondered how many blocks of clay went into constructing such a structure. He pranced on the yellow surface. The variations in the hue, how parts of the clay were a more earthen brown was fascinating, which was odd, since he wasn't from the Artistic Sector. He shouldn't have been fascinated by that. Pausing on the center of the bridge, he peeked at the water rushing beneath him.

There were no bridges in Nepenthe, as there was no water to be crossed. Except for Alcatraz. There were boats, anyway. However, Viktor could recognize these from history books. The definition of the word 'bridge' also fit what he was seeing.

It should have made Viktor jump, to actually be walking on a bridge. Instead, he skipped around as if he had lived there all his life.

Another blinding light, and at the other side of the flyover stood the person he loved the most.

His brother. Elliot Collins.

"Elliot?" Viktor asked. He blinked and then rubbed his eyes. "Elliot!" he screamed, dashing towards his brother. "Come back to me. Come back!"

But as he reached the three fourths mark of the bridge, Viktor halted.

There was no air.

Viktor gasped, desperately trying to suck in oxygen. He clawed at his throat with no success. He hacked several times, staring at his brother.

He was not giving up.

He crawled, scratches forming in his knees and ankles. It shouldn't have been this painful. It shouldn't have been this agonizing. But it was. A knife poked his lungs, and shards of glass cut his limbs. And the worst part—he was sure *that there was no way he was reaching Elliot before completely running out of oxygen.*

Please.

Right then, something clicked in his mind.

He gritted his teeth, knuckles white. His back burned. It was to the point that Viktor seriously thought someone was pouring poison on his skin.

This is what happens when one collects beautiful moments with friends and family. These memories destroy them. They make their life miserable.

Viktor hated himself for loving Elliot.

Viktor woke up faster than a cat submersed in icy water. He looked around, searching for his brother. The bridge.

I can breathe. Calm down. Just a bad dream.

He threw himself back to his bed. Viktor placed his arms on top of his face and closed his eyes to block out whatever light came from the window, yet an uneasiness poked at his ribs every time he started drifting into sleep.

Sleep. It was a dream.

When he couldn't take it any longer, Viktor sat and ruffled his hair in frustration.

"I need help," he muttered. That dream…it had been different. It had been too different to ignore.

He could ask either Amber or Stanton for help, because there was no way he was asking Grecia.

I'll ask Amber, Viktor thought, glancing at the door. *She can help. She's more concerned about me, so she'll help immediately.*

However, Viktor kept gravitating towards asking Stanton. It was probably because of the seriousness he had whenever it was needed. Amber would try to cheer him up, but Stanton would be spilling the facts without hesitation.

No. I'll go with Stanton.

"Stanton?" Viktor squeaked in front of the man's room. "Greetings?" He fiddled with his fingers.

The door opened in an instant. Taken aback, Viktor stood still.

"Hey, Collins," Stanton grunted. He stood in the doorway. "What brings you here?"

He still had his braids in, and there was no change in his state. He was the same, flawless Stanton Carmichael. The fingers of his left finger were wrapped around a glowing Nuntius.

His room was definitely minimalist—it only consisted of a bed on the left wall, a white desk and chair on the right wall, and a small, black, suitcase on the wall furthest from the door. the lights coming from the ceiling were dim, barely lighting up anything.

Maybe I should leave.

"Did you have a dream? One of those bad ones? Nightmares, I think they're called," Stanton said, scratching his back.

Viktor stood there, mouth wide. "How did you know?"

"I didn't know. I guessed. There is a huge difference between the two. Knowing happens when you read those books and eat up the information, answer questions like a robot. Guessing is trying to say things you don't know, based on your own experiences."

"I must agree with that," Viktor said.

"You know, during ancient times, kids would wake up after a bad dream, mostly after midnight. Then, they'd crawl up to their parents' bed, and hug them."

Viktor nodded, running a hand through his ruffled hair. "I find that interesting."

"Anyway, tell me everything."

Viktor explained every detail, although the dream was starting to get fuzzy. He had forgotten about the bridge's color, for example. And when the oxygen vanished.

He didn't add his brother to the story. Sharing his love for Elliot with others wasn't in his list of priorities, so instead, he said there was a sign that said 'happiness.'

Stanton sighed, stroking his chin and probably deep in thought. After ten seconds or so, he said "I'm pretty sure this means there's something missing in your life."

Something missing in his life? Well, he needed to learn about art to get admitted to the Governmental Sector, but he was already learning.

"This is preventing you from reaching a goal you have, which is happiness," he continued. "I'm not an expert regarding dreams, but I'm pretty sure about this one. It's quite obvious. The symbolism and the mentioned elements."

Viktor shook his head, as if that would make matters better. "What is missing in my life?" he asked in a whisper.

How Stanton heard the boy, it was a mystery, but a reply came right after. "Look, kid," he said. "I don't know about that. I'm not your psychologist or anything of those sorts. I don't understand what's going on in that little head of yours. That's up to you. But I can tell you one thing. *Never* take a dream this symbolic for granted."

"I don't understand what's going on in that little head of yours."

If Stanton had said that on purpose, as a hint, or if it was just a coincidence, Viktor didn't know. But he did know what was missing in his life now. Or at least, he was pretty convinced about his theory.

Nobody knew about Viktor's emotions, about what he'd been through.

Who was someone who could understand all that?

For some reason, Grecia was the first person to come to mind. She was being given a second chance, after all. There had to be something they had in common. At least one thing.

Viktor imagined a thousand scenarios in his head. One in

which Grecia would cock her head in confusion. Another in which she wouldn't tell him the truth, because she didn't trust him enough. But the one that stood out was in which she nodded along with his explanation, and said, "I understand you."

Meeting people who understood and related to him was surely the key to happiness. After all, why would he have smiled, although faintly, at the thought of Grecia feeling the same emotion as him last night?

Viktor knew what he needed to do next.

"Thank you, Stanton," he said with a slight bow, "I appreciate your help. I will tell you my progress once in a while."

"That works." Stanton smiled softly at the boy and ruffled his hair. "One more reminder: do things in the right way."

24
FROM AWKWARD KIDS TO (SORT OF?) FRIENDS

Their friendship started at breakfast.

Viktor was sitting in front of the table, on the third chair from the left. His head dropped, as his thoughts hadn't let him have a good night's sleep for what remained of the night. His vision lay on the pancakes in front of him.

Thud.

There was movement next to him.

"Hey," Grecia said as she sat next to Viktor.

He glanced at her, eyes meeting those of the girl. Her face held that obnoxious smile she always wore.

"How are you?"

No. Don't do it. Don't talk to her.

But he thought back to what Stanton had said about his nightmare, and the plan that he had in mind.

You can do this, Viktor Collins.

"Greetings," he said. "G-Good morning."

Grecia stared at him, mouth agape. Then she glued her lips together and chuckled.

Had he done something weird or wrong? Viktor gulped.

"Well, hey," she said, tilting her head. She raised her eyebrows expectantly, maybe wondering whether the boy was going to miraculously respond like just now.

Viktor gulped once again, staring at his plate of pancakes. "I look forward to learning more about art." There was silence.

This was what he could call progress.

"Do you like blueberry pancakes?" Grecia asked.

"In fact, I do."

"Same." Grecia grinned.

For once, Viktor smiled back.

That night, Viktor made his first successful origami crane.

The wings were still off, but the difference between the two was close to nothing. The beak should have been bigger, but except for that, the crane was flawless.

"I'm surprised," Grecia said with a smirk. "Good job."

Viktor's cheeks ached as he forced a smile to ripple through his face. "Thanks."

"Now, draw it." Grecia said. She leaned backwards, using elbows as a support, and stretched her arms. "Use the pen and a sheet of paper."

What? I have almost never drawn in my life! How am I going to draw the origami crane?

But I must stay silent.

Just as Viktor was about to hold back a retort, a thought shot through his head. The more he talked, the closer he would get to Grecia. The closer he got to her, the easier it would be to talk to her about the emotion.

With the strange emotion blowing up in his chest, he forced his complaint out.

"I cannot accept the fact that you are making me draw something I'm not familiar with," he said. To add some dramatic effect, he crossed his arms and pouted, cringing mentally.

He was terrible at this.

At first, Grecia was dumbfounded. Her eyes went wide, and the frown she made was so hilariously serious, he wanted to burst in laughter. Viktor could imagine her thoughts. 'He acts really weird. Maybe I should have never made him socialize with me.'

"Sorry," Grecia said after a moment. Viktor sighed in relief. "Just a little surprised."

"Whatever," Viktor said, cringing at his spoken word. "I will draw the crane."

Grecia shot him a confused look before handing him his pen and a sheet of paper.

"What does *burlesque* mean?"

"I don't know. I forgot."

Viktor raised an eyebrow, fighting back the urge to say, *try harder, will you?* But he knew he could speak words not only with his tongue, but with his eyes as well.

"Fine." Grecia rolled her eyes.

By then, Viktor had become a tiny little bit more comfortable talking to Grecia. Well, *comfortable* may not have been the right word, given his situation, but rather *almost calm.* He didn't gulp before speaking to her anymore, though he occasionally became tense when answering her questions.

But slow progress was still progress.

Teaching was starting to become an activity to enjoy for Viktor. It was fun to try out his teachers' positions.

"Something that has to do with fun things," Grecia said. She puckered her lips, tapping her head. After about three seconds, her face lit up, as if she had found the reason cookies and cream milkshakes were so good. "It's like, an artistic work made to be comical. Which means to make people laugh. Yeah." She beamed at Viktor, making him look away.

"Yes," he replied with a nervous laugh.

"I only forgot eleven words," Grecia said, punching the air in celebration. "What's next?"

Viktor sighed.

It's time. He looked back at the beaming girl. *It's now or never. Act natural.*

"Today we are having, um, an oral conversation practice." Viktor forced a grin. "The question is…"

He halted, his breathing quickening. What if he was wrong? What if the emotion had nothing to do with the reason he had been given a second chance?

But of course, there was nothing to lose if he asked. Viktor took a deep breath and spoke.

"Do you feel a strange emotion?"

Grecia blinked, furrowed her eyebrows, and made a face. It could have been either confusion or anger.

I will take that as a no.

However, her expression slowly morphed into a somewhat confused kind of happiness. "The emotion," she said slowly. "What do you mean?"

"Just…the emotion," Viktor repeated. "One that you simply cannot describe. It is, to put it simply, different."

"The emotion,"

"The emotion."

"*The* emotion."

"Yes, *the* emotion."

And when their eyes locked, it was impossible to let go. Their eyes sparkled as if saying, *there's someone who also knows.*

"Does it feel weird? Like, it makes you feel adrenaline. But adrenaline that kind of makes you scared or angry," Grecia said.

Viktor nodded.

Grecia started laughing. A care-free, childish laugh. Her laughing was like ripples spreading in a pond. Soon, the ripples of laughter turned into waves of levity.

"What the heck. I just…I just can't believe it!" Grecia exclaimed.

Viktor couldn't help but smile. A dimple crinkled on his left cheek.

Funny, how the simplest things could make people become friends.

Viktor shook his head, fiddling with his fingers. No, she wasn't his friend. Just a person he could talk to about the emotion.

Someone who understood him.

"Ugh," Elliot groaned.

It was more than a month before Regulation Day, and Elliot was already banging his head into the wall repetitively.

Another groan.

Even if Viktor and Elliot studied in different rooms, the older brother's groans disrupted every second of Viktor's night.

"Honey, can you lower your voice, please?" His mother's voice echoed through the hallways, making Viktor's head vibrate. It was Elliot's loud sigh that soothed him.

Viktor cocked his head in concern. What was wrong with his brother? He had never acted in this way.

Whatever. Concentrate.

Viktor's gaze fixated on the algebra worksheet in front of him. Even if he wanted to go see Elliot, his mind forced him to keep steady in his chair, in front of his desk.

$x^2 + y^2 + 4x - 2y = -1$

The equation of a circle in a xy-plane is shown above. What's the radius of the circle?

It was a repetitive cycle. Find the answer, realize it's wrong, repeat. It had been like that for this specific question since thirty minutes ago, when he'd challenged himself to solve it at just twelve years old. Impressive, considering he wasn't even part of the Mathematical Sector.

However, he now regretted his foolish and rather courageous decision.

Concentrate. *Viktor frowned as his ballpoint pen slid through the numbers. Crossing out. Adding. Diving. Mixing variables.*

A pound came from Elliot's room.

For once, instead of trying to keep his focus on the painful question, Viktor turned his head around to face the door.

What might have happened, if it were the ancient times?

A: Shut up. I'm trying to do my homework.

B: You shut up. I'm super stressed right now.

A: Do I look like I care?

But getting this stressed over homework was no ordinary event. Everyone enjoyed their schoolwork.

Viktor looked back and forth. Worksheet or brother?

"I'll go," he muttered as he twisted the doorknob. He was in between worried and annoyed, preoccupied and disturbed.

Viktor stepped through the hallways, one foot at a time.

When he arrived at Elliot's room, the pounding had disappeared, replaced by quiet wheezing. The air filled with the creaking of an opening door as Viktor's eyes peeked into his brother's room.

"Come in," Elliot muttered.

"Greetings," Viktor squeezed himself in. "How have you been so stressed as to make sound that disturb my studies?"

Elliot's faint chuckles made Viktor tilt his head quizzically.

"Have you been stressed with your musical studies lately?" The younger of the two asked.

"None of your business," Elliot said. Strangely, he didn't say it sharply, but rather in a soft way. "I've just been having some thoughts. It's alright. Don't worry."

Viktor's eyes met his brother's. But something was different. Elliot didn't have the usual energetic glow, the sparkle that gave life to his face. Eye bags surrounded his eyes, and they had a rather glum glow.

He wanted to know what was happening. He wanted to enter Elliot's brain, see his thoughts. But of course, he had to oblige. He knew all things the elders instructed happened for a reason.

"You are stressed because of homework, am I right?" Viktor asked. He scrambled towards Elliot and gave him a hug. "I also have some difficulty with my tasks," he said. "I understand you." His embrace tightened.

Elliot's forced grin dissolved into a natural one, one filled with sincerity. Nevertheless, the sad glow didn't leave.

"It's cool to have someone understand me," he said. "It's really cool. Thanks."

At the time, Viktor hadn't understood what his older brother meant, either because he didn't know what cool *meant, or because he didn't know what truly being understood felt like.*

"Has the emotion ever made you act weirdly towards people? Like, lose control?" Grecia asked with one finger up. "Once, I kind of exploded in front of my friends. You?"

"I acted strangely towards my parents, I suppose," Viktor said. *Only them, because I didn't interact with anyone else after they took Elliot. And it was after that that the emotion started to take over me.*

He stretched his legs, as they had started to get numb from being in the same position throughout the entire conversation.

"Parents?" A perplexed look appeared on Grecia's face, but it dissipated soon after. "Oh. Right. Sorry. Yeah, parents." Her teeth dug into her lips.

Viktor winced. *That must hurt.*

But she didn't even flinch. Her lips *did* have more cuts than any other average pair, though. She must've been used to the pain by now.

Grecia pulled back her usual smile. "I can't believe I'm telling you this," she muttered before sighing. "My dad died before I was born."

Her father…passed away before she was born?

It was one of those rare situations, dying for a reason other than old age. Why had he died? How? In what situation?

Luckily, Viktor was good at refraining himself from asking things he didn't need to know.

"Anyway," Grecia said quickly, maybe to refrain the conversation from becoming awkward, "do you miss your family?"

It seemed like she wasn't as good at refraining from asking questions as him.

Words left Viktor. And having studied the Linguistic Sector, it happened to be much more ironic than it should have been. His heart and mind fell silent, as if his soul had floated away.

"I miss my family," Viktor said through gritted teeth. "Yes, I do."

Because for him, his family wasn't his parents and Elliot anymore.

It was just Elliot.

"Yeah," Grecia said. "Who wouldn't miss their family?"

Viktor's family was in Alcatraz. Elliot was gone. When Grecia returned to Nepenthe, she'd see her mom. But his family was gone forever.

The burning anger inside Viktor was extinguished when he saw Grecia's eyes. They looked so…heavy. Heavy with sadness.

Suddenly, he was reminded of the fact that Grecia had come

three weeks after him. What had happened to her? What happened for her to come so late? Had the occurrences that had happened during that time frame hurt her? Viktor decided not to ask.

"What do you think this emotion is?" Grecia asked. He was grateful for the change in subject.

"I have no idea."

"Yeah," Grecia said. She bit into her thumbnail. "Me neither."

Viktor nodded, but there was a tugging in his heart. It urged him to do something. Believe in something. But he didn't know what it was.

Instead of diving deeper into his mind, Viktor grinned at Grecia. "You are not as annoying as I reckoned."

It was pleasurable to have someone who understood him. They weren't becoming friends, obviously. And Viktor didn't plan that to happen. Grecia was just a person with whom he could discuss a topic.

But it was pleasurable, nonetheless.

For the first time since meeting Grecia, Viktor thought of no bad memories.

However, he still felt somewhat hollow.

I don't feel as full as I thought I would be, Viktor thought later that night. *What's missing? What have I done wrong?*

25
GRATEFUL

"Stanton?" Viktor called, gazing at the digital clock on the living room's wall.

6:00 a.m.

"Stanton?" He whispered one more time. "Are you awake?"

"Come in." A grunt came from inside the man's room. Without hesitation, Viktor opened the door and stepped into the room.

The scent of newly roasted coffee merged with the brittle air. Viktor's nose tingled with the familiar smell. He watched the masterful hand of the coffee maker on Stanton's desk pour the exact amounts of the ingredients into a mug in just five seconds.

Wisps of misty white rose from the brown beverage. Stanton, who was leaning on his desk, wrapped his fingers around the warm mug, his tense limbs relaxing as he slowly sipped his coffee.

"I did not know you owned a coffee machine," Viktor said.

"I use it for things other than making coffee sometimes," Stanton said, bringing the mug to his lips. "Brought it yesterday. While you were asleep."

No. While he was learning art. While he was teaching words. While he was talking about the emotion with Grecia.

After Stanton emptied the mug, he patted the spot next to him. "Thought you'd come, kid," he said. His braids were loose, now long, and wavy hair hovered over his shoulders. "Did you have another dream?"

"Just came to say thank you," Viktor said, leaning beside Stanton. "I have immense gratitude in my heart at this moment. Maybe it sounds unseemly, but I do not have any other way to say it."

"See?" Stanton said, shrugging with a smug smile. "Told you. I'm glad you asked someone about it." He ruffled Viktor's hair.

Viktor chuckled. It felt like a privilege to get to see Stanton's playful side.

"You need to take one more step, though," Stanton said with a sigh. He looked into Viktor's eyes, and added, "I think you should prepare for class."

A look of puzzlement crossed Viktor's face. Before he could ask anything, Stanton gestured to the door, signaling it was time to leave.

You need to take one more step.

What step, though?

26

AN INVISIBLE WINTER

Viktor poked at the waffles in front of him, resting his head on his left palm.

"Hey." Grecia took a seat next to him, rubbing her hands at the sight of her breakfast.

Strangely, Viktor didn't shift uncomfortably at her close presence, and neither did he try to get as far away as possible from her. Instead, he responded.

"Good morning."

Viktor gazed at the girl, who was taking a bite of a waffle. She didn't look all that annoying anymore.

"So," she said after gulping down the food, "have you gotten a bite of these waffles? They're *so good.*"

"No." Viktor looked down at his plate.

"Well, you should."

He shrugged, lifting his fork. However, before he could start eating, he noticed a bright piece of a strawberry appeared at the bottom of his plate. Cold needles pierced his skin, and his heart went wild as a memory flashed through his head.

That day. That terrible day.

"What's wrong?" Grecia asked.

But Viktor was already gone, splashing water on his face in the bathroom.

Again.

"Hey sweetie," Mrs. Collins said. "How's the studying going?"

"I'm fine," Viktor snapped.

His heart pounded. His skull vibrated. And all because his mother stood outside his room's door.

He was currently inside his room and sitting at his desk, trying to write on his journal. His trembling fingers didn't allow that, however.

"May I come in?" Mrs. Collins asked loudly, with a hint of annoyance in her voice. "My hands are getting tired."

Viktor's hands turned into fists. Let her come in and get this over with, *he thought.*

He slipped toward the door on his swivel chair, grabbed the door-knob, and twisted it.

The door opened, and in came the boy's mother. She held a tray with her favorite design. Black background with white spots. There must have been a dozen of those in the kitchen's drawers. On it were two things: a mug of hot chocolate, and a bowl of strawberries.

"I brought you some food. Thought you'd be tired." Mrs. Collins extended her arms.

Viktor closed his eyes, trying to contain the anger within. An impossible task.

"You," Viktor whispered. He didn't yell. He didn't scream or throw his journal at his mother. He could only manage whispers.

Sometimes, silence achieves more than loudness.

"You are giving me this food. Because you're worried about me or something."

Like hot lava, something flooded into Viktor's lungs. He didn't know what it was. He didn't know how to describe it. It was a kind of emotion, a feeling...what was it?

But at that moment, Viktor didn't care.

"You care about me and all that," he continued, "but you didn't care when they TOOK ELLIOT?"

He yelled at the last two words, screamed with all the strength he could muster. With only two words, his throat felt raw.

"Viktor. Sweetie." Mrs. Collins placed her hands on Viktor's cheeks, but he swatted them away. "You need to understand. Elliot isn't your brother anymore. He is a disturbance to the society of Nepenthe."

"I. Don't. Care!" Viktor yelled.

Mrs. Collins couldn't have been more shocked. Her muscles went rigid, and her skin paled. Her lips parted and didn't move.

And Viktor didn't care.

That was the first time he felt the strange emotion.

Why was Viktor so anxious about everything? The emotion? His problems? He already knew someone who understood him. What was missing?

Maybe it was because not enough people understood him. After all, numbers had power.

The class was almost invisible to Viktor. Amber's voice, her footsteps, the tapping of her fingers against his desk.

It was all invisible. Imperceptible. Inconspicuous.

And that was only the *I*'s.

It was only Viktor and his mind. Viktor and his thoughts. His worries.

He closed his eyes shut, as if it was going to help.

"Viktor?"

His eyes snapped back open as Amber's concerned face emerged from the haze.

"What's wrong? You've been kind of distant today."

The panic sparked in his abdomen, as edginess grew in his face and limbs.

He clenched his hands into fists. Numbers had power. He could ask Amber about the emotion. It was surely going to be worth the try. Asking Grecia had resulted with a positive outcome. Why not this time as well?

"Amber?"

"Yeah?" she said as her eyes quivered.

Viktor gulped before the question jumped out of his tongue. "Do you also feel an emotion?"

He expected a lightened face, a mouth speaking words only he could understand. He expected more of that joy he had felt when he realized Grecia understood him and the strange emotion.

But Amber just tilted her head. "What do you mean? Of course, I feel *an* emotion. Which one are you referring to, exactly?"

The last bits of hope dissipated from Viktor's heart. He swallowed down a second try, an explanation to his question.

He knew it wouldn't work.

"Forget the nonsense I just said. Continue the lesson. I think that it will be easier for me to focus now." The silence that followed was like poison to Viktor.

What was it that was missing in his life?

Viktor was an orb of tangled yarn. The interior of his mind was a mess, and it was forever going to be unless the strings were untied sometime soon.

That mess felt endless.

27
A BLANKET IN WINTER

Every *tick* brought a new thought. Every *tock* led to a new worry.

Every second was torture for Viktor.

He didn't hear the alarm that indicated it was time for dinner. He didn't detect anything. Viktor was inside a tornado, a tornado that sucked him into his mind and his thoughts. And he knew that once he was inside, there was no going back.

Hours passed. There was still no progress.

What's missing?

How will I be happy?

Why did this have to happen to me?

The world spun with incoherence. His head throbbed, as if he had consumed too much alcohol in a night.

"Hey," Grecia said from the other side of the door. She pounded on it several times. "You there?"

Still, Viktor didn't move. He lay on his bed, his mind a freezing winter night.

The door creaked open, and footsteps sounded from a short distance away.

"Bro, I looked for you all over the place when you didn't answer me and didn't even think about the possibility of you just being inside your room. I'm so dumb." Grecia's voice reached Viktor's ears, and then his mind.

He didn't budge.

"Let's make a better origami crane today," she said with a nervous laugh, probably having noticed something was off. "Yeah? I know it's hard. When I first made a crane, I thought it could fly, so I threw it out of my window. I never found it again."

Viktor could almost see Grecia staring at him with hopeful eyes, waiting for him to cheer up. Waiting for him to react. To say at least one word.

Waiting for him to act as if he wasn't lost in an ongoing hurricane.

And it was then that he could take it no longer.

The tears erupted forth like water from a dam. Viktor's chin shook, and the floor swayed. There was static in his head, the side effect of the ceaseless fear and pressure he lived with during these past months.

Viktor hated living inside his tight box of thoughts. He hated himself for getting attached so easily to his brother. He hated Elliot for leaving him, for making him the person he was now.

He hated it all.

Viktor found himself on a winter night. A freezing, painful winter night.

The gnawing cold cooled his fingers into numbness. It saturated his toes and spread through his feet as though it were his exposed toes on the frosty whiteness instead of his shoes. His lips turned a pale blue tone and his teeth rattled like a drill. The cold breeze folded over him, as if it were a cloak woven from the snow.

"I miss my brother," he cried. "I want him back. I don't know if I want to return to Nepenthe. I hate my parents. They let them take Elliot. They said he deserved it. He was my best friend."

The slicing wind ran past him, ears turning numb.

It was then that the blanket came.

A relatively thin one, though thicker than Viktor's arms. From deep inside his chest, the warmth welcomed him like an old friend. It kind of scared him. It was odd, feeling the cold slowly leave his heart.

It soothed Viktor. His mind relaxed, and every worry evaporated. Because he had the blanket. The blanket that would warm the coldest of his days.

Viktor slowly opened his eyes to see Grecia Rivera the Annoying, the irritating girl who always spoke, the girl he dreaded, hugging him. It was a light hug, not strong enough to squeeze him, but Viktor preferred it that way anyways.

"Hey. Stop. The snot is annoying. Calm down. I know it's hard," Grecia said, patting his back. "Just think about what waits for you once it's all finished."

Elliot, he thought. *Elliot…*

All the sweet, amazing memories he made with Elliot flashed through his vision, like a movie. He wanted to live them again.

Miraculously, Viktor hugged Grecia back.

Right at that place, that moment, Viktor Collins felt complete. Happy. He knew what had been missing during the last months. The person he cared about the most.

Viktor needed a shoulder he could lean on, an ear he could recount his struggles to.

Viktor needed a friend.

Embrace your best memories, so they happen again.

28

WHAT MADE GRECIA HUG VIKTOR

Grecia had thought there was nothing beneath the boy's grumpiness. His silence. She had thought he was simply an introvert with no social skills.

But when she saw those tears of his, dropping one by one, a realization plopped into her head.

There's always a reason behind each action.

What had happened to Viktor for him to hide his feelings all this time? Why hadn't he talked to her about his problems? Was he perhaps scared of friendship? Of course, it might be awkward to tell a stranger the deepest of one's feelings, but why had he refused to talk to her so much?

And then Viktor talked. He spilled it all out. All that weight, he released it.

Grecia didn't know any of the details. But from what she had heard, Viktor had lost his brother. That one person he could count on.

Of course, she couldn't talk about the emotion to anyone, which was stressful and hard. But at least she could count on other people to make her smile. Veronica was her everyday medicine for when she felt lonely. Cayenne and Liam were the best mood brighteners.

Even when she left Nepenthe, although the comfort was small, Grecia had Sienna. But Viktor…he didn't have anyone. He even hated his parents. Though Grecia still didn't know why exactly he had refused to count on others, the fact that he didn't have anyone was heartbreaking.

Grecia didn't want anyone to suffer the way she did. She didn't want anyone to suffer *even more* than she did. Grecia wanted to be the Veronica, the Liam, the Cayenne, the Sienna to at least one person in her life.

And at that moment, she knew what to do.

AMBER

29
THE RIGHT THING

Amber saw all of it.

From when Grecia and Viktor first met, to when they got caught in each other's embrace. From when Viktor wrote the letter, to when Grecia read it.

She saw everything. And not only her, but Stanton as well.

But why was that such a big deal? It was necessary. They were *Amygdala Creatures.* The most dangerous organisms for the government and city as a whole. How could the governmental workers not watch out?

"Amber," Stanton called from the other side of the room. "I think Viktor is asleep now."

"Alright then." Amber rose from her chair with a yawn. "What time is it?"

"One in the morning."

"Good." She gazed at Stanton with playful eyes. "Now, shall we?"

"My pleasure," he said with a light smile. He exaggeratedly bowed while opening the door that led to their next destination —the balcony.

It was a tradition they had, staring at their lovely city each

Sunday after work. Observing two creatures for hours always made fatigue seep into their brains. Relaxing, staring at the sky with a mug of coffee...it was the loveliest of medicines.

And of course, being stuck in a single room, Observatory #31, staring at a screen until Grecia and Viktor fell asleep was exhausting. Happily, the screens that they had to stare at for hours were made to be easy on the eyes. They were the color of robin eggs, feeds showing everything the two kids did after Amber and Stanton left the third floor of the NGC and were situated on the left and right walls. They were in charge of the Handlers #31—that is, Amber and Stanton.

"Heyo! My favorite ship, Stamber. What took so long?" A girl with golden hair hugged her knees, waving at them while they sat beside her.

Amber and Stanton weren't the only workers. Haneul observed Grecia and Viktor during the morning and part of the afternoon, when Amber and Stanton were still on the third floor. She was also in charge of sending the food through teletransportation.

Truth was, Stanton and Amber weren't the only Handlers either. Although their lack of contact with those outside the Observatory #31 and the third floor made it seem like it, there were actually many more creatures given a second chance on different floors, and more Handlers in charge of them. This year, countless Amygdala Creatures had been spotted during the Exétasi, for which the second chance program took up sixty floors of the NGC, with a varying amount of creatures on each one. There were also many more observatories on the tenth floor, each one in charge of a different set of Handlers.

"I don't think we're late. You just always arrive earlier than everyone." Stanton crossed his arms, raising an eyebrow. Then came an awfully long moment of silence.

"Well, did Mayor Neville cut out your tongues or something?" Haneul said, shattering the hush.

Amber chuckled. "Well, do you have anything to say? Because I don't." She stared at the expansive sky. "Except that I love the night sky."

It was, indeed, quite a beauty. The tranquil darkness of the night, fused with the bright stars was something anyone would have loved looking at.

"I do too." Stanton fell silent as he brushed a few hair strands from Amber's forehead. "Can't believe our first time as Handlers is *this* crazy. An Amygdala Creature coming from the Outside, of all places."

Amber smirked. "Which word? Write, right as in the direction, or right?" She pressed her lips into a thin line after a pause. "Sorry. An old inside joke. Crazy indeed."

"My shipping heart is screaming." Haneul said.

Amber elbowed her, laughing. Haneul wrapped an arm around both of her friends. "Just kidding, no ship here. More like the best trio ever."

They all smiled. Haneul always spoke like she wasn't a grown-up eighteen-year-old, but none of them cared. They knew that immaturity was sometimes the best pill when undergoing extreme stress.

The three of them had gone through so much together, from studying in the Governmental Sector, to training for the Amygdala Project, side to side. Haneul and Stanton meant the world to Amber. Nobody could replace those two.

They sat there saying nothing, staring at what they could see of Nepenthe. The school would be crowded in the morning, and soon, there would be a few cars passing by. But at that moment, there was nothing but silence.

Amber's gaze fixated on Stanton. She had only ever seen his hair in braids, but she liked it that way, because when they first met, his hair had been the same. Those braids were reminders of their everlasting friendship. Or, well, perhaps more than a friendship.

Truth was, Amber liked Stanton. Her feelings for him had started to develop soon after they had met a few years ago and had started to grow gradually until where she was now.

"Do you think all this training was worth it?" Stanton asked after a cough. Her concentration broke, and she had to blink several times to process the question.

"Obviously," Amber huffed. "This is one of the most important jobs for society, and you know it. We should be honored."

"I know," Stanton said. "I'm just kind of getting fond of them. It's hard to see them as…creatures. I mean, the training was necessary. I know it. There's a reason the mayor trained us. I just think I wouldn't have done bad without it." Silence.

Haneul put on the rare, solemn expression she had. "I don't really know, to be honest. I'm part of the project, but not the central part, like you guys are. I don't really have a say in this."

Amber didn't know how she would have done without the training. Maybe better? Or worse? But as Stanton had said, everything happened for a reason, especially if Mayor Neville was behind it all.

The mayor's speech still resonated in her head. It had been a lasting one, but thanks to the content, Amber couldn't help but remember it.

"There are countless mysteries about the Amygdala Creatures. But one thing we know about them is that they feel an emotion. This emotion is much more than dangerous. We call it the *Defiance*, and it appears when a person starts questioning facts. Though it may not be questioning the government itself, any person who feels *defiance* eventually will. The citizens of Nepenthe never question the government, because they know everything is being done for the better. Instead of accepting these facts, Amygdala Creatures develop *opinions* about them. This is why they are much more dangerous than normal creatures, who fail the Exétasi because of their horrifying lack of talent.

"This is why the Handlers are one of the most important workers for not only the government, but the whole city of Nepenthe. You see, the Amygdala Creatures have a quality that makes them strongly believe in what they think is right. This means that if they start trusting and putting their faith into Nepenthe, they may potentially become the most loyal citizens out there, and thus, contribute to Nepenthe's development through their talents.

"There's a question many people have been asking me. Why now? Amygdala Creatures have existed for centuries, and during that whole time, we have been getting rid of them so easily, by directly transporting them to Alcatraz. Why make a project to 'save them' now? You see, the number of Amygdala Creatures being discovered has increased by ten percent. Yes, you heard that right. *Ten percent.* This is an incredibly huge problem. We cannot afford to lose such a big amount of our population. Though we still get rid of the Amygdala Creatures whose Defiance is way too rooted into them because of the dangers they bring with them, we give second chances to those who we have hope in. Those who have a chance of changing, of becoming loyal to Nepenthe. Those whose Defiance is still developing.

"How do we change them? By making them experience how good we are. How flawless. Because experiences are what build beliefs.

"Don't get me wrong. All of us strongly believe it would be much easier to insert information into their brains. We've tried to do that two hundred and fifty-three times, but it has never worked. This is because our scientists and psychologists have come to the conclusion that we cannot forcefully put information into someone's brain, no matter how advanced humanity may become.

"This is the sole reason we train you to be Handlers. So that you can turn the most dangerous people to the most loyal and stop Nepenthe from losing a great amount of their population.

"We collect Amygdala Creatures to turn them into the best of citizens."

Defiance.

Whenever Amber thought of that word, she shivered. How could anyone question the obvious?

Such a mystery, it was. And Amber was here to make it disappear.

"Guys," she said, "just let me ask you one thing."

"Yeah?" Stanton asked.

"What are you scared of?"

Stanton shrugged, as if the answer to the question were obvious. "In a place like Nepenthe, there is nothing to fear. Why do you ask?"

Amber's eyes connected with the blurry autumn trees outside the walls. The Outside. Where imperfection lived among nature in its purest form. The red and orange covered the ground like blood, while the trees stuck out of it like the handles of knives. It looked so deadly.

How had Grecia even survived her days out there? No wonder she had decided to return to Nepenthe. This also meant her trust in Nepenthe had grown immensely. The exact reason she had been given a second chance. If she wouldn't have left Nepenthe, she would have definitely gone straight to Alcatraz, as the amount of Defiance in that little head of hers had been shocking. Luckily, her stubbornness had led her to leave and return, trusting her home city much more than before, and having little to no Defiance. An Amygdala Creature who was worth putting into the Amygdala Project.

An Amygdala Creature who came with the friendship neckla—

No. Don't think about it. There are thousands of those in this world.

"I'm scared of living in an imperfect world," Amber said. "Every time I think about it, I'm terrified."

Stanton gave a nod of approval.

Haneul sighed. "Yeah, I understand. I guess my biggest fear is Stamber not becoming real."

Amber giggled, slapping the other girl's back softly.

"Anyway," Stanton said, pecking Amber's forehead and elbowing Haneul. "Let's sleep now. We need to rest for tomorrow."

"Alright." Amber had no idea whether she had blushed, but she was sure that warmth had spread through her. Even though Stanton showed signs of affection often, treating her like a younger sister, her heart couldn't help but accelerate. "Room A7."

A tingle formed in her body, and she found herself in her room.

Teletransportation. Even though scientists had been able to make this possible, it was only to be given for special occasions, as it was extremely expensive to make and use.

Since the third floor didn't have any exits to other places in the NGC, to ensure no creatures escaped, teletransportation was necessary.

Amber grunted, slumping into her bed.

"Amber Walsh," she whispered to herself. "Whatever you do,

just stand up for the right thing. Then you'll forever live in a perfect world."

She fell asleep faster than usual. And while doing so, Amber made the terrible mistake of thinking about the necklace Grecia had around her neck. The green, cartoonish broken heart that contained the letter *L*.

The necklace that had once belonged to her friend Louisiana.

30
LOUISIANA

Amber was five when she met Louisiana.

At first it was a normal friendship, with occasional sleepovers and sharing tables in the cafeteria at school. Soon, however, the flower of their friendship started to grow, getting rooted to the soil. Not long after, it bloomed, and seemingly, the petals marked their seemingly everlasting friendship.

But all flowers wither. And this one wasn't going to be an exception.

Amber lost her friendship necklace at the age of seven.

"I'm so sorry," Louisiana said when she heard the news at school. She halted, setting her books on the hallway's floor. "Do you wanna go out to buy another pair of necklaces after school?"

"No," Amber said, shaking her head. "That necklace was different. Nothing can replace it." When she caught Louisiana's sad gaze, she added, "But it's okay. A necklace can't define our friendship, right?" She smiled.

Louisiana smiled back, but there was a gloominess sprinkled on what seemed to be her forced joy.

"You literally won't believe what I found out," Louisiana said, bursting through the door of Amber's room. It was five years later, and now they were both twelve. Louisiana had been invited to Amber's house and had just arrived. "This is the best day of my life!"

"What?" Amber stood from her desk, eyes glowing with excitement. "Is it the application?"

Louisiana took a deep breath, closed her eyes, and said, "I got into the Governmental Sector."

Amber froze in place in disbelief upon hearing those words.

Oh. My. Gosh. She got into the Governmental Sector?

Her eyes then lit up and she squealed. The two girls ran into each other, encased in a hug that would last minutes.

Amber loved it when her best friend showed such happiness, which wasn't often. When she did, her cinnamon brown hair, which was usually tied in a braid, would look brighter, and the usual tiredness in her black eyes would evaporate, leaving only enthusiasm behind.

"Congrats! Oh my gosh, I can't believe it. You're one of those genius people. That's... ah, it's hard to process. I'm so freaking happy for you." Amber gripped her friend's back even harder.

"You'll get into it next time. I'm sure of it."

Amber had also applied to the Governmental Sector, but yesterday, she received a letter that said she hadn't gotten the cut score. She had been downhearted at first, disappointed in herself. But hearing the news about Louisiana now overpowered the disconsolation.

Two years later, Amber got into the Governmental Sector with the highest score among the applicants. Now, they were both fourteen, young ladies with a bright future ahead.

"Hey," Louisiana said, sitting on a bench with Amber. The Nepenthe Grand Park was full of people today, so looking for a free bench had been tough. "Have you ever thought about Nepenthe? You know, have you ever thought deeply about how it's organized and all that?"

"Don't start talking about your nonsense." Amber laughed.

Louisiana frowned. "I'm not joking."

"Oh."

A pause. "It's just...everything seems so unfair nowadays. Have you ever thought about the lives of the kids who are banished? Y'know, to Alcatraz. I almost feel bad for them."

"Interesting," said Amber, laughing nervously. "But I mean, they're creatures, right?"

"Right." Louisiana let out a sigh.

"Which word? Write, right as in the direction, or right?" Amber smirked.

This was an inside joke these two shared. It was nothing humorous that would make someone burst in laughter, but they occasionally used it nonetheless. As ten-year-olds, they had tried making a good inside joke and had come up with that, thinking it was so funny everyone who heard would cry out in laughter. They tested the joke on some of their friends, and like that, they discovered it wasn't comical at all. But they didn't care and continued using it.

"Just right." Louisiana's face showed a drooping grin. And it was then that Amber realized how long it had been since her best friend had lifted the edges of her lips with genuinity. How long it had been since she had smiled because she was truly happy.

The day she had gotten into the Governmental Sector had been Louisiana's last genuine smile.

One week later, Amber would come to hate her best friend.

"Louisiana?" Amber called out as she observed the road, just outside her house. Dry obsidian-black pavement covered the ground, shooting towards the center of the city.

Louisiana was nowhere to be seen.

Where is she?

She usually came extra early to pick up Amber for school, and if not, she came exactly at the appointed time. But never did she arrive late.

"She must have forgotten," Amber said to herself, shrugging. "I'll just walk."

But Amber knew.

Louisiana never forgot.

Louisiana didn't show up in school either.

Amber turned her head towards her friend's empty desk, eyebrows furrowed. She shook her head.

Something had definitely happened to Louisiana.

"Do any of you know what has happened to your fellow student?" asked the teacher. He glanced at Amber, as if somehow, she would know why Louisiana was missing. She shook her head ever so slightly.

"Well, that's an unjustified absence. This will seriously affect her grade. What a pity, really. She's an amazing student." He stole the opportunity to check his Nuntius for messages or emails. None had come, considering how his eyes sped through the screen with dullness. "Well kids, we shall commence this lesson without her."

Amber got a note in the afternoon. Reading through a textbook at her desk, she turned to page 423. There lay a white, nicely folded piece of paper.

By the way it had squares on it instead of lines, Amber knew this was from Louisiana's notebook. She knew no one else who used a squared one.

When did she have the time to put a note in my textbook?

Amber cupped her hands over her mouth. What was the meaning of all this? Where was Louisiana? Today, they had promised to watch a movie at the theater, and to buy some butter popcorn.

Don't worry. This isn't a big deal.

She exhaled and unfolded the note.

Sorry. I just can't trust Nepenthe anymore. Everything about this city is wrong. I'm leaving. And I won't return.

But you will always be my best friend. My sister.

Remember when you lost your friendship necklace when we were seven? We were literally fetuses. I had tried to leave Nepenthe the day before and had taken your necklace with me. I just wanted to keep a part of you alive on the Outside as well. I wanted to stay with you.

It's in your favorite jacket's pocket.

Farewell.

Amber's hands started trembling. She dropped the note and ran to her closet, bursting it open.

She reached out to the purple jacket in the center of the rack and unzipped the left pocket. There was no necklace.

Amber's lips quivered.

After letting her heart slow down, she pulled the jacket out and checked the right pocket.

There it was.

The long-lost friendship necklace.

But it wasn't a sign of friendship anymore. It didn't represent the flower of their everlasting friendship. It was a sign of treason. A sign that, once, a traitor of Nepenthe had been her best friend.

Amber, back against the closet doors, wept in silence.

Amber couldn't concentrate in class the next day. Her hands trembled whenever she saw the empty desk in which once, Louisiana had sat at, scribbling notes on her math notebook. She had only taken notes on that one. It didn't matter if the notes were about science or literature, her math notebook was the go-to.

During music class, Mayor Neville burst through the door and coughed. "Excuse me?"

The teacher stared at him, dumbfounded. It was as if she didn't know whether to cry of happiness and kiss his hand or to act composed.

She chose the latter. "Good morning, Mayor. What makes you come here this beautiful morning?"

"I'd like to talk to Miss Amber Walsh."

Mayor Neville, only a few feet away from Amber, sat at his desk and stared at the papers next to him.

The environment wasn't a nice one. The walls were as gray as a cloudy day, with no light except for the one spilling from the window, on the wooden floor. There were countless bookshelves on the walls at either side, but they merely served as decoration. The books on the shelves look more plastic than a water bottle at the supermarket, and the blank spines revealed the fakeness of these objects. They did, however, radiate a glow of antiqueness. The mahogany desk was at least fifteen feet long, with drawers spread about the edges. This room would have looked antique and full of wisdom if not for the light-bulb on the ceiling, which showed off its artificialness with a blue glow.

Amber looked down, not daring to meet the mayor's eyes.

So much had happened yesterday. And now this?

"Miss Walsh," Mayor Neville said after a short cough. "Good morning."

"Good morning," she muttered, clenching her fingers together. "Why did you call me?" This time, she gathered her courage to meet his gaze. "Does this have to do with Louisiana?"

Mayor Neville sighed and leaned forward, laying a hand on her shoulder. "You sure are a smart girl. Indeed, I called you to discuss the creature who used to be your friend."

Creature. *Louisiana was now a creature. That hit Amber harder than a bullet.*

"Hurry up, then," she grumbled, and immediately regretted it. The mayor squeezed her shoulder even harder, the pressure making her feel like her veins were going to burst. She looked away.

"Miss Walsh, have you ever heard of the Amygdala Project?" His eyebrows arched, and his lips lifted into a sly smile.

Amber eyed the mayor with suspicion. "What's that?"

"It's a project where only the brightest students of the Governmental Sector can participate. Basically, we make Amygdala Creatures return to normal. We stop them from becoming rebels. What is an Amygdala Creature, you may ask? To put it in a straightforward way, Louisiana, that creature, is a perfect example of what an Amygdala Creature is."

The bullet buried itself deeper into Amber's skin. "I don't feel very well."

"I'm not done yet," Mayor Neville cooed. His voice was smooth, elegant, with a pitch that calmed Amber down. "Don't you want to get rid of the Amygdala Creatures? Imagine how many children and teenagers lost their best friends because of their existence. Imagine how many people suffer because of these creatures, just the way you are suffering at the moment. You aren't at fault for your pain, Miss Walsh. It's Louisiana's fault you're suffering." His voice sent a wave of warmness and comfort, a wave that indicated whatever he said was right.

It was Louisiana's fault she was suffering.

The Amygdala Creatures were evil.

Amber had to get rid of them, even if it meant inflicting pain on others. Because it would be for the greater good.

She faced the mayor once more, this time with confidence. "How do I sign up for this project?"

Three weeks later, Amber walked through the hallways of the NGC building, her shoes sliding against the slippery, white floor. Apparently, someone had forgotten to dry it up after cleaning.

Amber's foot took a bad step, and she fell to the ground with a thud. Her books, which had been tucked behind her arms, tumbled as well, skidding through the ground.

She sighed.

What a great start to being a candidate for the Amygdala Project.

"Hey, need some help?"

Amber looked up, and her eyes met with those of two kids, eyes that radiated friendliness and warmth.

One pair belonged to a boy. He stretched an arm toward her, nodding encouragingly.

"Thanks." Amber shyly took his hand and stood, regaining her balance.

"I'm Stanton," he said, pointing at himself. "And that's Haneul." He directed his gaze toward the girl at his side. "Nice to meet you."

31
HANDLER AND CREATURE

Amber woke to the sound of her alarm clock.

Another day of dealing with two dangerous creatures.

"One. Two. Three. Four. Five," she whispered. It was how she started each day. A reminder of the passing seconds being wasted. She stood groggily and rubbed her eyes to dissipate what remained of her sleepiness

Amber was proud of how she had arranged her room—from the bright, yellow walls to the couch and the bed and the bookshelves, everything looked so…perfect. No wonder Grecia had gaped in awe as soon as she had woken up from her long sleep and had laid eyes on her new surroundings—Amber's room.

Amber gazed at her alarm clock. *5:00 a.m.*

Plan the class. Eat breakfast. Teach Viktor. Go upstairs.

One. Two. Three. Four. Five.

She stood up to grab her *Nuntius.* With a touch, the gadget glowed, a few words rising from the screen.

22nd of January.

Amber Walsh, Viktor Collins' Teacher

Instructions for today's class:

-Vocabulary of the day

-Oral practice

-For today, an activity to enforce Viktor's trust in Nepenthe won't be needed, as the last one was successful.

From M. Jackson.

[More on the next page.]

The classes' plans weren't made by her, and it was the same for Stanton. The trained teachers in the Amygdala Project's team made a detailed blueprint for each day, and they were sent to her and Stanton. Classes were needed because the Amygdala Children needed something to remind them of home, and thus make them feel nostalgic. There was nothing better than classes to accomplish that.

In all honesty, the only thing Amber did in this project was teaching and making Grecia and Viktor trust in Nepenthe. She also needed to observe them while she was in the Observatory #31 with Stanton.

A plate of waffles materialized in front of her. Haneul had already sent breakfast to everyone on the third floor.

One. Two. Three…

Before she could reach five, Amber started eating the food.

Another full day of work was to come. A full day observing and staying with imperfect creatures.

A full day helping Nepenthe stay as a perfect city. Making dangerous creatures into loyal citizens.

"Hey," Grecia said.

"Salutations."

Amber watched Viktor and Grecia sit next to each other. Her Nuntius lay on her hands, a feed glowing out of it. It wasn't necessary for her to watch them at this time, as Haneul was in charge of observing the Amygdala Creatures as long as Amber and Stanton were on the third floor. However, for some reason, Amber had the urge to do so this morning. She was curious, after all that had happened last night.

Viktor blushed, probably shy because of last night's events.

"How are you?" Grecia asked. "We'll talk about lots of stuff at night, alright? Just see."

He nodded, the corners of his lips lifting ever so slightly.

Why is he smiling? Amber wondered. *What is it that makes a creature suddenly happy?*

"I hope today I can succeed in making a perfect crane," Viktor whispered.

"Yeah," Grecia said, lifting her spoon. "Good luck. Don't throw yours out the window, please."

With apparent difficulty, Viktor managed a laugh.

Guess last night's events affected his mood.

"I am lucky to have met you in such a difficult situation for me," he said.

Grecia blinked several times, probably not being able to believe her ears. "Nice to meet you too."

And for Amber, hearing Viktor saying such a thing was strange as well.

But the strangest thing was, the sad gleam she saw in Viktor every day wasn't present anymore.

"Amber?"

A voice squeaked next to Amber.

It was Grecia.

The girl with Louisiana's friendship necklace.

Amber gulped and turned around to meet Grecia's agitated eyes. The creature was biting her lips, which were going through an earthquake.

Amber wanted to do the same thing that moment, fear lurking from the depths of her mind. Truth was, she was scared of Grecia, no matter how harmless she looked.

What the mayor had told her about Grecia was frightening enough. Talking to her…that was another level.

Amber's fake, caring mode turned on. It was difficult to treat a creature like a child, but she had been trained to do so. "What's wrong?"

It was 3:01 p.m., right after class. Amber had been waiting for Stanton at the dining table, as her class with Viktor had finished. Just as she was going to transport herself to the Observatory #31, Grecia had spoken.

"I just…" the creature tapped her foot on the floor, "I just wanted to ask you something."

"Oh? What's that? You can trust me. Just ask." Amber might have as well puked.

Calm down. You're doing this for Nepenthe. You're standing up for the greater good. In a few weeks we'll have two very loyal citizens. Just see.

"It's about what you said when I came," Grecia said with a short, nervous laugh. "W-what did you mean when you said… doing things in the right way?"

Amber's heart started racing. She always got nervous whenever someone asked her that question. She would quickly come up with an excuse to not answer, but she had never met a creature who questioned it as many times as Grecia.

"Well, um…"

"Does it have to do with what Nepenthe wants? You know, like, what the government wants from citizens and stuff."

Amber felt as if a huge load had been thrown off her back. Until then, she hadn't noticed that her breathing had halted. She grinned. "Grecia?" she said. "You couldn't be any more correct."

"Really?" Grecia's eyes widened.

"You heard it," Amber continued.

"Thank you," she said, backing away. "Thank you, thank you, thank you, thank you, thank you. Thank you!" Grecia grabbed her head. "I feel like it's the happiest day in my life."

"Really?" Amber asked. "And why's that?"

Her heart accelerated. The anticipation might have killed her at that moment.

"Because… because I'll be free when I return to Nepenthe. And I like that idea. A lot. But, well. Thanks!" Grecia gave Amber a thumbs-up.

She'll be free when she goes to Nepenthe again.

If she wants to return to her home so much…then, maybe I'm succeeding. And Stanton, of course.

Amber let the satisfaction soak to her bones. The joy was quite infectious. It started as a tickle in her toes, much like the feeling she had when worried, but instead of bothersome, it was warm. Relaxing. Amber felt it pass through her like an ocean wave, washing away the stress of the day to leave her refreshed.

Just as Grecia spun to part towards her room, Amber grabbed her shoulders. There was a question she hadn't asked yet. A question that had been tickling her ever since Grecia arrived. A question that she had avoided asking, or even thinking about. But…it simply kept bothering her.

"Hey, I have a question."

"There are a lot of questions today," said Grecia as she crossed her arms. "Yeah?"

Amber took in a deep breath before opening her mouth once again.

"Where did you find that necklace?"

Grecia closed her eyes and looked down, scratching her back with unease.

Amber lifted her eyebrows expectantly.

A sigh escaped the creature's lips. "It didn't really have an owner. I found it in a house that had a bunch of blood on the walls."

As realization sunk into her, Amber's eyes widened. Blood. No owner.

Louisiana was dead. She was sure.

But she wasn't sure if she was supposed to jump up and down with excitement, excitement about the revenge she had eventually gotten, or if she was supposed to frown upon the news.

But someone she hated had died. An Amygdala Creature had died. Didn't she have to be happy?

32
THE CORE OF TRAINING

It was later that night, when Amber and Stanton were observing the Amygdala Creatures from the Observatory #31. As Amber rested her face on her right hand, eyes on the feed, a message popped out of her Nuntius.

She yawned, and then reached out to the gadget to read through the new message.

MAYOR NEVILLE

Dear Amber Walsh,

This message is of great importance, so I expect you to respond immediately.

The team and I believe that the time for the final phase has come—that is, making sure Viktor Collins and Grecia Rivera have become loyal to the city and its beliefs. This is what you have been training for. We have decided to have a meeting with you and your colleague, Stanton Carmichael, to explain some information regarding the blueprint.

"Um," Amber said, curiosity and surprise making her stammer. "I think you should read this." Her head spun as she read the words again.

The final phase.

This is what you have been training for.

"Mayor Neville?" Stanton asked. "We're here."

The governor was small, roundish, and moved with awkwardness, like a rodent trying to escape from a trash bag. His face was heavily creased, and the small amount of hair that poked from under his black fedora was thick, white, and had its own opinions on how it had to arrange itself.

Wonder how his voice can be so strong in such a state.

"I noticed." Mayor Neville said, smiling. "I knew you would come immediately."

"We feel nothing but gratitude for your compliments," Stanton said firmly. "Now, we must hear the plan, so that we can put it into action as soon as possible."

The mayor's smile becoming bigger must have been impossible. Nonetheless, it happened. He must have been pleased with the way Stanton spoke to him. With respect and reverence. "You are right." He glanced at the papers in front of him.

An awkward silence followed, as Mayor Neville closed his eyes. Amber, as still as she was, tapped her fingers on the table.

The circular meeting room was a small, yet impressive one. An oval table, the color of an arctic fox, stood in the middle, surrounded by chairs of the same color. They looked so comfortable that it was as if they were screaming, *come sit on me!* Thin lines were drawn across the ceiling and across the walls, light shining out of them. On the center of the table lay a small screen that was turned off. There were no windows—all that surrounded

Amber, Stanton and Mayor Neville was a circular wall closing in on them, and white, white and whiter. It felt like being trapped in a capsule.

"As I'm sure you have been waiting for this moment," Mayor Neville spoke with such conviction that it would've had anyone having the opposite belief turn against themselves. "I shall start speaking."

Amber gulped all the saliva she could manage, making her ears pop.

Her four years of full training, the time she spent studying about the Amygdala Creatures, all her efforts—it all came down to this.

"You have now spent a whole month with Viktor Collins," Mayor Neville started with a boom. "And with Grecia Rivera, who is a very special case."

Yes. It was a special case in so many ways.

So many ways.

"And so," the mayor continued. "I'm more than sure you know a lot about them. Spending time with those creatures and even staring at the feeds…how could you not know?"

"Sir," Stanton said. "You are right. I know these creatures as much as the articles in the Constitution of Nepenthe."

"I know you do. There's a reason the team chose you two for the job."

Amber couldn't help but grin, pride making her heart race. "We appreciate your kind words."

"Now." Mayor Neville coughed, as his face turned a tone darker. "What I need you to do these next few weeks is…special."

Amber tilted her head. "How's that?"

"Well," the mayor continued, "during these past days, you have been making these creatures trust in Nepenthe and its principles. However, that was only the process, the passageway to the result. During your final week with Grecia Rivera and Viktor

Collins, you'll need to test their faith, in the most personal of ways. Don't make it work on Amygdala Creatures in general, but for Grecia and Viktor personally. It has to mean *something* to them." He said the creatures' names with discomfort, as if they were cursed. Jinxed.

But that wasn't any of Amber's concerns. In fact, her heart fell into silence because of a different reason.

That's it?

Amber tried to grasp the mayor's words happily, tried to think of his orders as honorable. But she couldn't. No matter how hard she tried, it was impossible.

Disappointment sank in. She had been waiting to be told some crazy mission, some important and confidential secret to keep.

Not only that. Now, Amber had to *really* know these creatures. She had to dig deep into their feelings and thoughts. She had to know their fears. What they loved. And all to test their faith in Nepenthe, with something that would be meaningful to them.

"Don't worry about going to extremes," Mayor Neville said with contagious confidence. "Whatever it takes. We can't lose this opportunity. Each person counts in this city."

"I hear nothing but veracity," Stanton replied. "We shall do our best."

"I know." The mayor shook hands with him, as well as Amber. "I trust you."

Amber beamed at the governor, but deep inside raged a storm of dismay. There was also an eerie calm, however. A mysterious, eerie calm.

It's okay. There's a reason I've been ordered to do this. Like people say, Nepenthe is always right. Just stand up for the greater good.

This time, a genuine smile cracked on her face. "Stanton's

right. We shall do whatever we can to complete this mission successfully."

Mayor Neville coughed a few times before continuing. "Now, you should go back."

"Understood." Stanton moved his neck left and right as if to make the stiffness dissipate. "Tenth floor, Observatory #31."

He turned into a wisp of static.

It was now her turn.

But before she could go through teletransportation as well, Mayor Neville grasped Amber's shoulder at lightning's speed, holding it firmly.

She froze.

"Miss Walsh," he said. "I forgot about this. Stanton's already gone, but I don't think he needs this…um…warning."

"Warning?" Amber asked, stiffening. "What warning?"

The mayor closed his eyes, frowning. "If you don't achieve our goal, there will be consequences."

A chill went up her spine.

Consequences? What kind of consequences?

"Understood." Amber rubbed her arm, and with a gulp, she said, "Tenth floor, Observatory #31."

A tingle spread through her back, and the next thing she knew, her eyes were on the feed she was in charge of.

The feed that followed Grecia's every step.

That terrifying creature.

Calm down, Amber thought. *Calm down. She's just a kid who can make a whole society collapse.*

Just a kid.

She exhaled.

You'll succeed. There won't be any consequences. You'll accomplish your goals.

As Amber sat on her seat once more, she closed her eyes, trying to make every breath more even than the last.

She hated the fact that she was in charge of observing Grecia. Yes, Stanton was Grecia's teacher, but that was only for him to get to know her as well. Amber was Grecia's *personal* Handler.

She shivered, turning her head towards Stanton, who was sitting in front of the screen where his vision lay. Even Amber didn't know why she did that, but perhaps it was because she wanted some comfort.

Amber's cheeks heated up.

Whatever.

The mayor's words from a few days ago, still resonated in her head. A mere echo. But still enough to make Amber shudder. It had been while Grecia was still unconscious, a few hours after she crossed Nepenthe's borders.

"Grecia Rivera's father was the first adult to become an Amygdala Creature. Mr. Rivera...he tried to hack into the system to destroy our borders. He even got some of our confidential information, which I hope he didn't spread, including our plans regarding the Amygdala Project. With no other choice, we had to capture and send him to Alcatraz. So nobody could know about this; we, the government, told everyone his death was mysterious, and that he would be buried in the Nepenthe Cemetery. We kept a very close watch on his family, especially Grecia, because the team had a deep suspicion of the emotion being able to be passed down from generation to generation. At first, we thought Defiance hadn't been passed to her, but it had, just that it hadn't been strong enough to be detectable by our technology. When she was detected as an Amygdala Creature, we were quite surprised. Our initial plan was to send her directly to Alcatraz without giving her a second chance because the emotion was way too rooted into her.

"And then she crossed the border."

Mayor Neville had sighed, a weary look crossing his face.

"I thought we were finally free of the threat, but then, she came back. Nobody thought she would. But she did. And the fact that she

did *come back, is a sign that the emotion is withering inside of her, for which we have given her a second chance."*

Amber remembered the fear she'd felt while being told all of this. The mere thought of her having to deal with this kind of creature had been terrifying. And when she had seen Grecia with Louisiana's necklace around her neck, it had all become worse.

"Amber?"

Stanton's voice dragged her back to the present.

"Are you okay?"

It was when Amber touched her cheeks that she realized the sweat trickling down. "Yeah. Don't worry. I'm okay."

She directed her eyes toward the feed with one thought.

Just do what the government tells you to do. It all has a reason. And the reasons are good.

33

WHAT AMBER SAW IN THE FEED AFTERWARDS: GRECIA

For Grecia, a new friendship was the best gift someone could give to her.

But this particular boy, Viktor Collins…he was *different.*

Grecia plopped down on the boy's room's floor, ready for another of his classes, and ready to teach a class of her own.

"So," she started. "Hey."

"H-Hi," Viktor said with the hint of a smile. "How are you?"

How odd it was for Grecia to see him act in such a decent manner, regarding sociality.

"I'm fine. What about you?"

"I'm feeling relatively well. Great, actually." The boy coughed out a laugh. "Ignore that."

Grecia could tell Viktor was trying too hard to make himself seem as friendly as possible. But after hearing everything he'd been through, she couldn't blame the kid.

"Okay." Her eyes locked with Viktor's for a fraction of a second. Before then, Grecia hadn't realized that once, they had contained a sad gleam, as if he only had a few hours to live. That gloom was now gone, replaced by hope. Hope for what, she didn't know. But it was there, present, shining.

"So," Grecia started. "Wanna hear a joke? Okay? Okay."

Viktor didn't have the opportunity to respond before she spoke.

"What types of sandals do frogs wear?" she said, bursting out in laughter before she could finish telling the joke. "Sorry about that…Open-toad. Get it?"

Viktor raised his eyebrows. "Frogs can't wear sandals."

"It's a joke."

"Oh." Viktor lowered his head in embarrassment, his cheeks reddening. "I apologize for misunderstanding your phrase."

Grecia lost the fight against the giggles growing in her throat. They burst out like a waterfall, making Viktor blush even more.

He's weird. I like that. I like weird stuff. And people.

"It's fine," Grecia said after catching her breath. "Let's start with the origami."

But Viktor wasn't listening.

He stared at her with a blank gaze, and when his eyes cleared out, he doubled over with his hands on the floor. His hands shook.

"Viktor?" Grecia asked, concern filling her voice. "You okay?" She pursed her lips, frowning.

Viktor lifted his head, lips apart.

The noise that burst forth from him a second later was like a fusion of a snort and a laugh, unable to breathe between the giggles. He threw his head to the sky, another fit of laughter slipping through his windpipe.

Viktor is…laughing?

Grecia shook her head with a smile.

"I-I understand the joke," Viktor said, rubbing tears from his cheeks. "I understand." Another wave of giggles made him roll to his stomach.

So…my joke is that *funny? Nice.*

And what's more, Grecia was glad to see Viktor giggling like a maniac. Perhaps she *had* made a change in his life by hugging him, as she'd wanted. He *looked* happier. And that was what mattered to Grecia.

"Alright, calm down," she said with a smirk. "If today's origami crane is successful, we might start with actual drawings.

"That sounds interesting." By then, Viktor's chest had settled down, and the giggles' effects had vanished. "I look forward to this occasion."

"Let's get it then. Get a sheet of paper and start."

Viktor folded the paper so cautiously that even his hands looked as fragile as glass. They shook with every movement, as if his life depended on if he could make a perfect origami crane or not.

Well…in fact, it kind of does. Alcatraz still exists.

Nah, forget it. We're definitely doing the right thing *right now.*

"Viktor?" Grecia said. "You know it doesn't need to be perfect?"

"I know," he replied. "I have a certain appreciation for doing my best."

She shrugged to herself. Why Viktor was trying harder than normal, she had no idea, but at least he wasn't being careless or lazy. "Wanna talk about something? While you…work on the bird."

Viktor's face lit up.

…and then turned dark. The same cycle happened about three times, as if his face were being directed by an off and on switch.

In the end, Viktor's face settled on a single expression. It wasn't one of sadness or of happiness, however—but one of nervousness.

Yeah. He's definitely still having a hard time talking to people.

"I *do* believe that may help the final product," Viktor said, glancing at the semi-done piece of origami in his hands. "May help me relax. Or something."

He cringed. Grecia rolled her eyes at the gesture, a smile on her face.

"Okay then!" she exclaimed. "What can we talk about?"

"In fact, I have an idea in mind." Viktor slowly lifted his gaze. "Could you tell me about yourself?"

"Me?" Grecia tilted her chin in confusion, her thumb pointed at herself.

Strange.

But better than nothing.

"Well," she started. "I like painting. I *was* from the Artistic Sector. I feel a strange emotion, just like you. And my favorite drink is the cookies and cream milkshake."

Viktor shook his head. "I asked you to tell me facts about *yourself,"* He squeaked.

Grecia could tell he was trying to act strong and snappy. But for a person as shy as him, that was probably impossible.

"You're telling me facts about a random person. Tell me your story. Not some random facts," Viktor continued.

"Uh…"

What is he trying to say?

"I mean I guess, my story *is* kind of strange." Grecia shrugged.

Viktor grinned, as if encouraging her to go on.

"Well, first of all I have this strange emotion," she continued. "And a month ago, I failed the Exétasi for some reason…"

And so, Grecia told Viktor everything. From escaping, to

coming back. Sienna and Home, her classes with Stanton. Every detail, she spilled it out.

Every. Single. Detail.

With every word that came out of her mouth, Grecia's heart became lighter, and her mind relaxed. She felt…was it freedom that she felt?

Don't be silly, she thought to herself. *Last time you thought you were free…it didn't end up well. You'll be free when you return home.*

However, Grecia couldn't help but admit how marvelous it felt, to finally open up her heart and let out what had been locked in there for weeks.

"I-I," she stammered. "I just wish I had trusted the government earlier. I'd be having a happy life with Mom, y'know? It just sucks, thinking about that possibility."

Viktor nodded, stroking his chin. He looked thoughtful, wise even. "At least you did not die without knowing what awaits on the Outside. That was what you wanted, am I right?"

"Y-Yeah?"

"You know your life would not have been much better without getting your questions answered." He halted, rubbing his left arm. "Trust me. It is better to die with answers than to live with questions to remain forever unanswered. I am not sure about you, but I believe you went to the right direction. You discovered the truth by leaving Nepenthe."

"Okay," Grecia said after chuckling. "That's *deep*."

Her voice's tone wore some sarcasm, but deep inside, she knew that Viktor was right. And hearing those words, she could feel her soul dropping its remains into what was known as peace.

It felt nice to speak for herself for reasons other than survival or necessity.

I don't think I'm free just yet. But it feels like I've taken off a huge burden from my back.

"Thanks," Grecia voiced out. "A lot."

"You're welcome." Viktor held his hand in front of her eyes, showing a perfectly made origami crane.

34
THE SWEET BALCONY

"It's easier than I thought. You know, getting to know the creatures."

"Agreed."

Once again, Amber and Stanton lay on the balcony, a cozy blanket covering them both. This time, however, a *Nuntius* sat between her and Stanton, one of its most unusual functions in use.

Some people called this function a replacement for scented candles. The balcony was perfumed by the delicate smell of lilies, making Amber's nostrils flare in pleasure

"Do you think Haneul knows that we do balcony reunions without her?" Amber asked.

Because of Haneul's sometimes *too* upbeat personality, when she was around, having an intimate, serious conversation was difficult. At times, it was impossible. They still hung out on the balcony on Wednesdays, but sometimes, Amber wanted some private time with Stanton.

The thought stung.

"Don't worry," Stanton said. "She'll understand. Pretty sure she'll just brush it away and say it's okay. Because, well, she's Haneul."

Amber nodded. "Probably."

"By the way, I prepared something." Stanton turned his Nuntius on and said , "teleport the cinnamon cupcakes to the tenth floor's balcony, please."

Cinnamon cupcakes?

"What are you up to?" Amber asked, elbowing him.

The answer materialized in front of her.

Literally.

A seemingly invisible plate hovered in the air, and on it sat a dozen cinnamon cupcakes. Each one was as large as a tennis ball with syrupy cinnamon filling oozing out. Cream cheese icing engulfed the amber tops. It looked like it was going to be tough to take a bite without obtaining an icing mustache.

"What?" Amber asked, incredulous. "How? Where?" Her lips parted ever so slightly, and her eyebrows lifted.

"I prepared them all with the help of some friends." Stanton relaxed and crossed his arms, smiling.

"This is amazing."

"Thanks for the compliment," he said sheepishly. "Eating cupcakes after hard work sounded like a good idea."

Stanton stood from the floor and grabbed two cupcakes. He handed one to Amber, bowing exaggeratedly.

"I appreciate your gentlemanliness." Amber smirked and took a bite.

The sweet, juicy cinnamon flavor wasn't enough to distract her from Stanton's warm face.

"I like it when you smile so widely. It makes you look like an idiot," he said.

"Is that a compliment?" Amber raised her eyebrows teasingly. "Because I'm definitely taking that as a compliment."

"Yeah, right." Stanton wiped out the icing mustache Amber

had acquired. "You know you're like my little sister?"

Amber froze. Her face turned hot, and her cheeks turned into bright, red apples.

Of course she knew that. It was common knowledge.

But hearing those words with her own two ears, those words being spoken aloud by Stanton…it made her want to smile like, as he had said, an idiot. But at the same time, it stung. It stung that for him, she was nothing more than his little sister.

Nonetheless, Amber relaxed against Stanton's shoulder.

And though she didn't want to ruin the moment, she knew what she needed to say next. It was necessary. There were always a few priorities in life, after all.

"Regarding today's talk with Mayor Neville," she said. "We already have quite a lot of information about the two Amygdala Creatures. The only thing we need to do now is get closer to them. They need to trust us enough for the plan to work."

"Agreed," Stanton said. But there was some tiredness and disappointment in his voice, as if he wanted the past moments back.

Perhaps, there was another reason behind the gloominess.

Nah, I don't think so.

The plan was ready by the end of that night.

Every day after class, Amber and Stanton would spend one hour with the creatures. *Leisure Time*, they would call it.

This would help them to get to know Grecia and Viktor better, and that would allow them to make a solid plan to test their loyalty towards Nepenthe.

Now, they only needed to tell the creatures about this new period of their day, and make the plan work.

Amber couldn't have been more terrified.

35
THE CLOSER, THE BETTER

The next morning was fairly ordinary.

Amber receiving her breakfast and reading the plan of that day's class. And of course, a fair amount of her counting strategy.

One. Two. Three. Four. Five.

Five. Four. Three. Two. One.

"How are you feeling about this?" asked Stanton. He was standing in front of his desk, arms crossed, while Amber sat on a chair next to him.

She had gone to Stanton's room for a short reunion, just in case they wanted to change some details in the plan.

"I don't know, to be honest," she replied, fiddling with her fingers. "I mean, yes, I'm nervous and kind of scared. But I'm also proud of myself, you know? We're contributing to Nepenthe's goodness so much by doing this."

"I agree." There was a hint of a frown on Stanton's face. "Though I'm not as nervous as I thought I'd be."

By then, Amber could tell. Stanton had never quivered when interacting with the creatures, when she had been internally screaming the whole time. Neither did he show any uneasiness whenever he was physically close to them.

She still remembered his words, the ones he had said a few days ago on the balcony.

'I'm just kind of getting fond of them. It's hard to see them as... creatures. I mean, the training was necessary. I know it. There's a reason the mayor trained us. I just think I wouldn't have done bad without it.'

What had been going on inside Stanton's mind when he had said that?

Just think about it later.

Amber had enough going on, and one more problem would make her head explode.

Stanton was as loyal as she was, after all. The thought of him not believing in the danger Grecia and Viktor brought to the city was plain silly.

"Are you ready?" he asked.

"By all means," Amber said. She reached out to Stanton's hand and squeezed it.

"Now, at exactly 7:35 a.m., we'll stomp out of this room and tell Viktor and Grecia about our Leisure Time. Easy."

When it was time to put the first part of the plan into action, Amber forced herself to stand up and twist the doorknob, stepping into the living room. She gave Stanton a short nod as he placed his hand on her shoulder.

It was time, and they were as ready as ever.

They both walked up to the dining table, and soon enough, in front of her sat Grecia Rivera, whose father had been the first adult rebel, and Viktor Collins, the kid who had lost a dear brother. They turned their heads towards them, eyes wide in both confusion and curiosity.

Stop thinking about them like that, Amber chided herself. *They won't be rebels. Not if we work hard enough. Which we are doing, of course.*

"Hey, guys," Stanton said, pressing his lips into a thin line. "We know you've been through some crazy things."

Stanton's serious mode activated.

The creatures kept staring.

He gestured at Amber, which meant it was her turn to speak.

"Well," she said with forced yet realistic confidence. "We decided to add *Leisure Time* to your schedule.' She coughed and continued. "These will take place right after the afternoon classes and will be one hour long. We'll spend that time relaxing, and bonding with each other."

Grecia looked like she was being jingled by a puppeteer who was either crazy or drunk. That pretty much summed it up.

Guess *she* was excited. After all, from what Amber knew, Grecia loved socializing, no matter how old or young the counterpart was. Getting to become 'friends' with her teachers must have been exciting for her, that being a new experience.

Then there was Viktor.

That fake smile of his that almost seemed to be real. The fear in his eyes was as authentic as it could possibly be.

Viktor probably still hasn't forgiven his parents. And if he has, the mark they've left is permanent. Hanging out with the people who remind him of his parents must feel daunting.

Both Amber and Stanton knew his story. They'd seen him write dozens of words in his blue journal and had even seen him cross out a phrase.

Embrace your worst memories, so they never happen again.

"Now, let's go to class, shall we?" Stanton said, stretching his hands.

For once, Amber didn't think about the dangers Grecia and Viktor could bring to Nepenthe.

For once, the glasses that made her see them as creatures got snatched away from her. She thought of them as just kids. Which they weren't of course. But at least, it made Amber a little less afraid of what was to come.

"So, what are we doing in this…what do you call it?" Grecia said.

"Leisure time," Stanton replied with patience.

Part of the plan was to have *Leisure Times* take place in Stanton's room, as it had the most space out of all of the rooms because of its minimalistic style. The simpleness and faint smell of coffee also helped with the making of a more comfortable ambience for the creatures.

The four of them sat in a circle in the center of the room, legs crossed.

"Okay. Anyway, what are we going to do?" Grecia snapped her fingers. "Don't tell me we're going to hear some type of lecture. I hate those."

Amber awkwardly sat next to Viktor and Grecia, but she knew that she looked more than comfortable on the outside, thanks to her training.

"Let's play a game," Amber blurted out. "What ideas do you have?"

"What if we play the sentence memory game?" Stanton said, chin pointed at Grecia. "You go first."

Ah, the classic sentence memory game. It was a game teachers made kids play until they were eight years old and chose their Sector. It was used solely to make the children's memory level impeccable.

"Uh..." Grecia started. "Okay, I guess I'll go first. My sentence is...I believe in cookies and cream supremacy. But—"

"You believe in what?" Viktor asked. "That doesn't make any logical sense."

"Lemme finish." She glared at him.

Amber couldn't help but smile at their banter.

"Anyway," Grecia continued, "the sentence game isn't really all that entertaining. Let's play the chicken game instead. It's my childhood favorite." She gave everyone a thumbs-up.

"What's that?" Amber asked. This time, she was genuinely curious. That game sounded much more interesting than a memory game, in all honesty. It simply sounded bizarre.

And indeed, Grecia started explaining one of the strangest games Amber had ever heard.

Basically, the game consisted in everyone having to sit and wrap their arms around their knees, the opponents being all the players but yourself. You had to make the others tumble to win.

The weirdest thing? The chicken game was actually entertaining.

As all four of them went into their positions, the game began, and quite an affair of yells and laughs burst out in the room.

Suddenly, to Amber, the world looked colorful. Innocent. Joyful.

As Grecia pushed Stanton with her feet, making him collapse, he burst into a good laugh. He briefly gazed at Amber.

His eyes were drooping, surrounded by sadness. The same kind of eyes she had seen in Viktor only a few days ago.

Amber and Stanton spent the next few weeks sticking to the plan and their schedules. Eventually, everything began feeling ordinary.

And every time there was a Leisure Time, or whenever she had to teach Viktor, Amber's head drifted away from the thought that Grecia and Viktor were Amygdala Creatures. That they were not human.

That they were dangerous.

36
THE UNEXPECTED BIRTHDAY PARTY

It was the twenty-eighth of August.

Four days until the end of Amber's time with Grecia and Viktor.

She stood in front of her room's door, vision blank.

"Only four more days," she whispered to herself. "Four days. Four more classes to teach. Don't mess up."

She opened the door with a gulp and stepped outside, straightening her back. Her steps toward the dining table were evenly paced.

Amber almost felt like a robot as she reached the table.

On it sat a plate with a piece of bread, probably one from the sandwiches Grecia and Viktor were given. The bread was decorated to resemble an A with what seemed to be avocado sauce and nachos, all of which had been part of their breakfast.

A of abacus.

A of affable.

What could the *A* mean?

Amber fished through her brain, trying to catch a word that started with A. One that was relevant to the kids.

"Hey," Grecia said, waving her hand. "This bread thing is for you. Although it looks like it was chewed by a donkey, we did our best. Happy birthday." She extended her arms with a grin.

Happy birthday.

"Oh," Amber said, rubbing her arm. She looked away. "I forgot it was my birthday."

She remembered when everyone had shared their birthday dates in Leisure Time, though it was impossible to recall the exact dates. She vaguely remembered Grecia's birth month, but even that was fuzzy. Was it October? Or was it September?

But Grecia and Viktor…they had remembered the exact date of her birthday.

Amber's heart twisted into a knot.

"Happy birthday," Viktor whispered. A grateful smile spread through his face.

"Yeah. Thanks for helping us go back to our homes," Grecia said. "I mean, it isn't confirmed or anything like that, but it's still possible. And that's really cool. So, thank you. Here's the bread." She pushed the plate closer to Amber. "You don't need to thank us. *We* need to thank *you*."

"I-I," Amber stammered. Her heart twisted again. She chewed the insides of her mouth. "I don't know what to say."

Guilt plagued her mind.

They're creatures. Nothing more. Why am I feeling guilty?

As Amber stared at the floor, she wondered if Grecia's and Viktor's Exétasi results had been an error. Their actions were… too human. Too lovable and funny.

37
HOW MANY THINGS HAVE YOU BEEN HIDING FROM ME?

"What's with the glum faces?" Haneul asked as Stanton and Amber stepped on the balcony.

The tiled floor was the type of cold that was likable, like a pillow's cold surface.

"It's nothing." Amber shrugged, and then she hugged Haneul as she sat next to her. "How did stuff go today?"

Haneul's blonde hair spilled around her shoulders. "Seeing you guys play with the kids was hilarious. Like, Stanton, you looked so awkward. Grecia is seriously so annoying. She tries to make jokes, thinking she's funny. I mean, I make jokes as well, but at least mine are actually amusing." She leaned on the floor, stretching her arms at her sides. "You're very silent today, Stanton."

Stanton grunted as he sat down next to Haneul, hugging his knees. "I guess."

"We should go out to the city's center after all of this is over," Amber said after a chuckle. "I wanna spend some quality time with you guys. Because, y'know, I'm not in the best mood at 1:00 a.m. I'd say I'm kinda grumpy at that time." She glanced at the other two, searching for a smile on their faces. There wasn't any.

"Is this supposed to be the part where I say LOL?" Haneul elbowed her. "I can't believe kids used to think that cringey terms like that were cool." She smirked.

Amber smiled, but not for long. "So, Stanton. What did you think of today?" She folded her fingers against the floor.

"Haneul, what do you think of cinnamon cupcakes?" Stanton asked, ignoring Amber's question.

...What a random question. Is he avoiding me?

Amber frowned.

"Hmm." Haneul stroked her chin exaggeratedly. "First off, cinnamon cupcakes are rip-offs of cinnamon rolls, and that's unacceptable. And, for the one millionth time, it's pronounced *Hanul.* But like, the *u* is kind of combined with the *i* sound."

"Then why is it spelled like that?"

"I don't know dude, ask the creator of the Korean language."

"GUYS." Amber took a deep breath, and with closed eyes, she said, "we need to focus."

Stanton's brows furrowed, and his arms stiffened. "Focus on what?"

Haneul frowned. "What's up with you two today?"

"What's up with us today? Lots of things." Stanton glared at the sky.

Amber turned her head towards him, almost snapping her neck in the process. "What? What things?"

He sighed, waving her off. "I'll bring some cinnamon cupcakes, alright?"

Amber was about to ask *the ones from the other day?* when she realized Haneul was with them, listening to every word they spoke. She didn't want her friend to know she and Stanton were doing balcony reunions without her.

"Cinnamon roll rip-offs," Haneul muttered. Her sky-blue earrings dangled as she sat upright.

"Thanks." Amber grabbed a cupcake, the wrapping crinkling as she took it off. She smiled at Stanton, but he was already handing Haneul a cupcake.

"Mhm. No. Thank you for the offer but no. I've already made an alliance with team cinnamon rolls." She shook her head, eyes directly on Stanton. He pushed the cupcake to Haneul's mouth, his thundering laughs making the tip of Amber's lips go downwards.

She didn't want to admit it, but she was jealous. Why was Stanton acting so coldly to her all of a sudden, and was acting all fun with Haneul? She hadn't done anything wrong!

"Hey," Amber said, crossing her arms. Anything to grab their attention. "Let's talk about the Amygdala Project and make sure everything is going as planned."

Stanton glued his eyelids together and made a sound between a sigh and a groan. "Amber, please keep your mouth closed. We're trying to enjoy our time together and you're ruining it. I'm done. The other day, you ended our balcony reunion by talking about work."

Shocked, Amber's irises started quivering. "W-what?"

Never in her life had Stanton spoken to her in this way. He had always been the chill guy, the one always under control. He always thought before he spoke. Why was he suddenly acting out of character?

"What are you guys talking about?" Haneul stood, crossing her arms. "When did that happen? When was that balcony reunion you're talking about?

Amber couldn't take it anymore. This girl wasn't helping with her shallow questions. "The balcony reunions where we can talk in peace without hearing your stupid jokes, Haneul!" Her palms smashed onto the railing.

Amber immediately regretted saying what she had said. She bit her lips.

If only I could travel in time.

"The only thing you care about is work!" Stanton yelled, banging his foot onto the floor. "We just wanna have some fun, release ourselves from stress. Why is everything about the Amygdala Project for you, Amber?"

His words sliced her with no mercy.

"Well Stanton, you don't have any right to talk about what I'm doing wrong, okay?" Amber's cheeks went red, and this time, it wasn't love that was heating them up. "You're getting attached to the creatures...you, you maniac!"

"Well, I—"

"How many things have you been hiding from me?" Haneul's whisper was even more powerful than the maniatic yells coming from the other two. "Do you really see me as stupid, Amber?"

Amber turned towards her, and as their gazes met, she lowered her head. "I didn't mean—"

"You both don't trust me." Haneul backed up until her back touched the railing. "Why?"

"Haneul." Stanton placed a hand on her shoulder, but she slapped it off.

"Leave me alone. Have your private time or whatever." She whispered the teletransportation words—and then she was gone in a wisp.

Stanton swore under his breath. "Gosh, I really messed up." He spun to face Amber, and all of her anger dissipated.

They stood still, awkwardly staring at each other. Nothing like this had ever happened during their time as friends. Childish bickering? Yes. But yelling at each other with boiling anger? Not a chance.

"I'm sorry. I got carried away." Stanton stepped closer.

Amber's facial muscles relaxed.

"I forgive you."

Their uncomfortable gazes morphed into smiles. It would soon all be over. They would talk this through with Haneul. Tomorrow, everything would be normal again. Amber and Stanton had already partially forgiven each other. How hard would it be to be at peace with the most easy-going girl on the planet?

Tomorrow, it would be like the not-so old times. Because friendships are roads with bumps, right?

38
STRANGE CONDUCT, STRANGE CONCERN

The strange almost always starts with the normal.

The abnormality starts as something small and increases over time. Though it can also come in an immediate bang.

The day after the fight, the latter happened to Amber. And the experience wasn't pleasant at all.

"Hey," Amber said with enthusiasm as she teleported to Stanton's room. She was supposed to be there in ten minutes, but a surprise wasn't a bad idea. Besides, she felt like she needed to apologize for last night's events. True, Stanton was pretty chill and got over things easily, but an extra apology wouldn't hurt.

"Surprise!"

It was not he who was surprised, however.

Stanton wasn't there.

The bed covers were all disordered and crumpled. Even the smell of coffee was nowhere around.

"Uh…Stanton?" Amber scratched the back of her head in confusion, pacing around. "You here?"

No response.

That's strange. He never leaves his room when there's a reunion coming up.

Amber knew how organized Stanton was, even after a fight with his best friends. How he always stuck to his schedule. What had happened for him to not drink his usual mug of coffee, and to not make his bed?

A strong feeling of déjà vu washed through her.

Amber proceeded to send a message to Stanton. To the best of her luck, she always had her Nuntius tucked in her pocket, just in case.

Where are you? I went to your room, and you aren't here. What happened? She typed and with a click, sent the message.

It might have been about twenty minutes of staring at the ceiling in boredom before Stanton materialized right in front of her.

"Oh, hi," Amber exclaimed. She backed away in surprise. "Did something happen?"

According to Stanton's slight frown, something *had* happened. His limbs were stiff, as well as the muscles in his face. Not only that, but also, the edges of his nails were…deformed.

"It's nothing," Stanton said, his eyes on the left wall of his room. "I went to the balcony. The city was so beautiful this morning, and I forgot about our meeting. I just saw your message and—"

"It's still morning."

"Oh. Yeah. I didn't notice. Whatever. Let's talk about each other's ideas for the final phase."

It was Amber's turn to frown. Something was going on with him.

"By the way, I'm totally over with what happened yesterday, so you don't need to say sorry." Stanton smiled, but the edges of his lips twitched, struggling to keep the expression on his face.

Amber shrugged. It was normal for him to get over something so quickly. Nothing to worry about. "Okay, so," she started, "I was thinking about telling Viktor and Grecia that they are returning to their parents. This would make their hopes get higher and make them think that the rest of their lives are going to be perfect. When we finally get to test their loyalty, it'll hit them harder. We'll plan that test based on their responses to the announcement." She smiled at Stanton, expecting him to beam back.

Instead, he sighed. "Glad you made a plan. I didn't come up with anything."

What?

Stanton, of all people, hadn't come up with anything?

"Oh," Amber said. "It's fine. That can happen sometimes when your head is filled up with all these thoughts. Don't worry."

What thoughts were filling Stanton's head, exactly?

Amber's hair jiggled as she shook her head.

"Anyway," she said, "what about the classes today? Will we—"

"No," Stanton interrupted, "we want to observe them, remember? Observe their veracious reactions to returning to their parents. If there's class, their minds will be somewhere else. Knowing Viktor, if he were disappointed by the announcement, he might even pretend to be happy. They don't even know we're watching them. That would lead to their true reactions."

Where his sudden answer came from, Amber didn't know. But she wasn't going to complain.

"Well," Amber mumbled, "we have our plan."

"We do."

She let out a deep breath. "Let's do our best, you understand? This is the home stretch. The final phase. We're lucky enough to have been part of this in the first place."

"I know."

Stanton knew. For some reason, Amber's heart warmed up at that thought.

I've come a long way. I'm not giving up now.

"I have one request, though," Stanton said.

"Oh? What is it?"

"I don't want to be the one who announces that they'll return to their parents. Can you do it, please? I'll observe from the Observatory #31."

Even if it was an odd request, Amber saw nothing morally wrong with it. "Sure."

The door creaked. Amber stepped outside. Two steps. Two thuds.

When she approached Grecia and Viktor, they glanced at her without much interest but a "hi."

"Hello guys," Amber said. Her lungs filled up with oxygen. The last breath before the final part of the two long months with Grecia and Viktor.

"Yeah?" Grecia asked, sipping her orange juice.

Strangely, the moment wasn't as suspenseful as Amber thought it'd be. It didn't feel any different from other days. The words simply slipped out of her tongue. "You're returning to your parents."

And it was done.

It was that easy.

And that hard.

I did that…way too swiftly.

When Amber had announced the addition of Leisure time to the schedule, she'd been trembling, screaming inside. She had hated the idea of becoming 'friends' with creatures. She'd been terrified.

The creatures' trust had grown, but so had Amber's.

"There will also be no class today," she continued. "Because of this special occasion. You did things in the right way."

"You aren't joking, aren't you?" Grecia asked. The tears came before the smile did. Amber had never seen a smile as bright as that one.

"I'm not."

I'm going back home.

I'm going back home.

I'm going back home.

Is this real?

All the events Grecia had faced throughout the last two months passed through her vision. When she had stood right in front of Nepenthe's borders, after eating in the McDouglas Burger Shop. When she had crossed the borders, ran until she was out of breath. When she had met Sienna and Juniper, when she had run away. Waking up at the third floor of the NCG wasn't an exception.

All this time, she'd tried to find freedom, but failed. Over and over again. Now, Grecia was returning to her mother. The *real* freedom.

Her whole journey hadn't been in vain. If she hadn't crossed the border in the first place, she would have lived her whole life without knowing what real freedom was, even if it was right in front of her. She would have wandered around ignorantly.

Most importantly, she wouldn't have met Viktor.

I'm going back home. I really did *do things in the right way.*

The preoccupation of 'doing things in the wrong way' was now gone. She was finally going to be free, after twelve years of life.

Grecia rose from her seat and embraced Amber. The older girl, whose mouth parted in shock, patted her back.

"Thank you," Grecia exclaimed. "Thank you!"

"You're welcome, I guess," Amber said. "Now, I need to go to work upstairs, since we're not having class today."

"Okay." Another hug. "Bye!"

Viktor didn't know how he felt about returning to his parents.

Returning to the people who had caused his brother to be taken…that simply sounded scary. Truth was, Viktor still hadn't forgiven his parents. And he was sure he would take a long time to do so.

Now, however, Viktor had a friend. Grecia Rivera. That regrettable jokester. That hyperactive girl.

Different from him in so many aspects, yet the best friend he could ask for.

On the other hand, now that he knew some art, he could apply to the Governmental Sector. And even if he got rejected, which wasn't probable, he'd have Grecia. Viktor could even meet new friends.

He took a look at his friend, whose tears left a trail of dry liquid on her cheeks.

The edges of his lips couldn't help but lift.

To think that I have grown to be so close to her because of the shared emotion…

Right then, a realization hit him in the gut. Hard.

Viktor hadn't felt that strange emotion for weeks.

39
WHEN STANTON GOT DISTRACTED, AND THERE WERE CONSEQUENCES

Before she knew it, Amber had spoken the teletransportation words. Her particles landed right on her seat in the Observatory #31.

"I did it," she mumbled, combing her hair with bare hands. "I did it, Stanton!" She turned around to face his back. "That was such a wild ride, wasn't it?"

"I'm trying to concentrate," Stanton snapped. "Please. And yeah, we did it. But the work's still not done. After some hours of observation of their reactions, let's meet at the balcony, understand? To discuss ideas to test them."

Needles poked Amber's heart.

He's stressed. It's alright. You also have those kinds of days.

His voice's impatient, agitated tone had been unsettling, however.

It'll pass.

She faced the feed she was in charge of, where Grecia's face glimmered. Though Amber needed to focus on only Grecia, since the two kids spent most of their spare time together, it was inevitable to watch both of them. Viktor's voice could be heard clearly enough.

It was a joyful night for both Grecia and Viktor.

Like always, Grecia walked to Viktor's room, ready to have another boring yet vital lesson about weird words.

However, there was one difference: the combination of puffy, bloodshot eyes and a grin from ear to ear from both parts. Viktor was laying on his bed, and when he saw her, he stood up in a wobbly manner.

"I can't believe it," he murmured.

"Yeah." Grecia wrapped her arms around Viktor as she ran into him. "We're going back home. Sweet, right?"

She clutched his back, not planning to let go.

If only I could thank him in a greater way.

Grecia's eyes dripped with tears. Salty drops fell from her chin, drenching Viktor's shirt. She pressed her head against his shoulder.

"I-I," Grecia stammered, gathering as much air as possible. "I can't believe it. I really can't, Vik."

And then there was laughter. Kind of a hysterical one, yet instead of reflecting insanity, it reflected brightness.

Viktor joined with a much softer laugh,

"Viktor, I have tons of ideas," Grecia rubbed her palms together. "We'll have a picnic in the park, and then we'll go eat in the taco restaurant. I can't wait to introduce you to my other best friends. No offense. Their names are Cayenne and Liam. They're super cool. I can even help you with the Governmental Sector tasks that have to do with the artsy stuff."

"Seems fine to me," Viktor whispered, beaming.

"I know. I know, I know, I know."

"All of this is unbelievable."

"I know."

Viktor's focus, however, was somewhere else. His eyes were

locked with the pillow behind him, and Grecia could see the slight twitch of hesitation in his eyebrows.

"What is it?" she asked.

"Well." Viktor gulped. "Have you ever wondered where I get paper for the classes?"

In all honesty, Grecia never had. She'd been desperate, after all, but that moment, she wondered how no questions regarding the paper had popped up in her head. From what she knew, Amber and Stanton had never offered them paper.

"Nope. Why are you asking?"

Viktor reached for the pillow and pulled something out. A blue journal.

"My brother gave it to me a few years ago," Viktor said. "It's the only connection with him that I have left."

"Wow."

It was then that Grecia's eyes caught a small mark on the journal's cover.

Veronica & Co.

"I have, like, a very cool idea."

"What is it?" Viktor asked. "We are *not* doing the chicken game. I will not accept that." He spoke with such conviction that it made Grecia laugh aloud.

"You're weird."

"You've said that at least a few dozen times already." Viktor rolled his eyes, though he bore an evident smile.

"I know."

"You've said *that* at least a few dozen times today."

"Let me speak."

"Alright, alright. Go on."

We've come a long way," Grecia said matter-of-factly. "And

studying and teaching was part of the thing. What if we show what we learned throughout these weeks?"

"Uh—" Viktor started, "you just used the word *throughout?"*

"Not funny." She smirked, shouldering the boy. "What do you think of the idea?"

"Sounds fine to me."

"Good. Now, draw a face. It needs to be good, or else I'll have to teach the whole thing again."

"Right. What about you?" Viktor asked, pressing his ruffled hair.

"What about writing a poem with the weird words you taught me? Do you write poems in the Linguistic Sector?" Grecia asked.

"We do. I'm ready for this." Viktor unsuccessfully tried to crack his knuckles. "Uh, yes."

By then, Grecia had already grabbed a pen and sheet of paper and had started writing.

"I'm done," Viktor said after a while, raising his arms.

"Took long enough," Grecia chuckled. "Show me the sketch."

"Hope you do not see it as terrible," Viktor said. He flipped the paper in Grecia's direction.

It was more than decent.

The jaw had been perfectly drawn, and its sharpness was striking. The cracks on the small lips looked insanely realistic for someone who wasn't from the Artistic Sector. The person's hair lacked hair strands, but it was still acceptable.

Overall, it looked like a sketch drawn by a student in their first year in the Artistic Sector.

The person in the drawing looks familiar… Grecia narrowed her gaze.

Wait—

"Is that me?" she asked. Her voice went up and down, like a car speeding through the mountains.

"Yeah," Viktor said, blushing from embarrassment "That's you. S-Sorry if you couldn't recognize yourself—"

"Nah. You did an incredible job. Nobody has ever drawn me," Grecia said, wrapping an arm around his neck. She smiled, and tenderness surrounded her.

Out of all the people he could have drawn, Viktor drew me.

"Let me show you my poem." Grecia reached out to her sheet of paper and held it in her hands. "I hope it's not too cringey."

She then handed the sheet to Viktor.

I always knew about amity
But in the middle of a calamity
I found lots and lots of hope
That did more than help me cope
With the events I faced
The hope's name was Viktor.

Amber leaned on the balcony's railing. "Now that we've seen the creatures' reactions to the announcement, how do you think we should test their loyalty to Nepenthe?"

The night's warmth cradled her, as if saying, 'everything is fine.'

"I have quite a few ideas. But I'll give you the honor to speak first." She tapped her fingers on the rail at the rhythm of her heartbeats.

In reality, she wanted to hear whether Stanton had really been concentrating on his work, or if his head had been in the clouds, thinking about anything *but* work.

"I..." Stanton faltered. He took a deep breath and faced her. His lips were pursed, and his shoulders stiff. "Amber, I need to tell you something. And I don't know if you'll like it."

Dread creeped up Amber's spine, like a spider carefully making a trail of its spiderweb, and settled on her facial muscles. The air turned sharp, and it pierced her skin. The floor swayed beneath her.

He hadn't been stressed all this time. It had been something else this whole time.

"What is it?" she asked tentatively.

Please tell me it isn't anything out of ordinary. Please.

"Well, this thought has been developing in my head for some time," Stanton mumbled. He rubbed his neck furiously. "And..." He stared at Amber with pained eyes. The inner parts of his eyebrows were raised and pulled together, and a tremor shook his lips. "I hate it here. Nepenthe...Nepenthe is wrong. We're wrong," he stammered. "I feel like I deserve to die." He whispered the last words with an odd kind of care and gentleness.

I hate it here.

Nepenthe is wrong.

I feel like I deserve to die.

Stanton had just said those words? The one who trusted Nepenthe the most?

The words settled on Amber slowly. One second to hear them. Another second to analyze them. Another second to understand them. Still, Amber couldn't comprehend what she had heard.

But one thing was for sure. If one's heart can contain love, at that moment, her veins contained fury and wrath.

Stanton teleported to his room before Amber could speak.

She followed right after him.

"Third floor, room A7."

40
THERE WILL ALWAYS BE PRIORITIES IN LIFE

"What's wrong with you?" Amber asked. She wanted to yell at Stanton. To scream at him at the top of her lungs. But she couldn't let herself do so, not yet. "Why are you acting like this? What do you mean? Didn't you say you were over our fight from yesterday?"

Stanton paced around his room, eyes wild, muttering words to himself. It was as if he were seeing something beyond the walls. Every inch of his neck glistened with sweat.

His head turned to Amber and his eyes went even wider.

"Stanton?" Amber said, her fury turning off. "What's wrong? Are you okay?"

That was when Stanton exploded.

When everything changed.

He grabbed her shoulders and pushed her to a wall with such force that Amber grunted, a dull ache stinging her back. Blood trickled down Stanton's lips.

"You don't understand," he exclaimed, shaking Amber. "We're lying to them. They're not creatures. Nobody should be considered a creature in this place. *No one.* We're not good people, don't you understand? Our society is messed up. Those who go to Alcatraz…they're not creatures. They're us. *Like us.*" He took a shaky breath. "You know why I was acting so weirdly last night? I was freaking out, okay? I had some thoughts in my mind, and they were scary. They were so scary I thought I'd have a mental breakdown any second. But you know what? I didn't want to make you worry so I acted like nothing was happening, and just relaxing with you and Haneul felt so nice until you started asking questions about work. And you just reminded me of my thoughts, so I snapped. I snapped and I let it all out."

Amber covered her mouth with trembling hands. "What are you talking about?" she asked. Maybe it was because of her numb cheeks, but she couldn't feel the erupting tears. "What's wrong?"

"Please," he said. "Just, I can't. We're taking away what makes us human. Let me say it in another way. We are *all* animals. Creatures. Except for the Amygdala Creatures. They are the only ones that can be called people."

Stanton turned to glance at the open window.

"Don't," Amber said between sobs. "I can help you."

"I might as well leave Nepenthe." Suddenly, Stanton's face cleared. It was as if a raging storm had vanished at plain sight. "Amber. Listen to me."

"Y-Yeah?" Amber asked, sobbing even more.

"I'll die. But at least I'll die as a real human," he mumbled. "I-I'll try to do what Grecia's father did."

"What? You're joking, aren't you?" Her chest heaved in desperation. Is this all a prank or something? Please tell me it is."

This must be a nightmare.

This can't be real.

For a moment, the world froze around Amber. All motion around her was suspended in time. She imagined different scenarios of what could happen.

I need to do something. Should I hit him with a frypan?

"I know you'll know what I'm talking about. Someday.

Though I hope it's sooner rather than later." Stanton's hurt smile was what terrified her the most. "Don't worry about me. I want you to know that you mean the world to me. That's why I'm doing this." He closed his eyes. "Just promise me one thing."

Amber nodded. There was no hope. Stanton was now one of the creatures. He had joined their irrational cause. But for some reason, her mind refused to think about him in that way. For her, he was still her friend. That person who had brightened her world when she was in the dark.

This can't be happening.

Blood from Stanton's lips sprinkled the floor.

Drip. Drip. Drip.

"Whatever happens, don't tell Mayor Neville about what I'm going to do," he coughed out. "They're going to find out anyway. But…I don't want to die without knowing you did at least *one* thing a human would do."

His pleading, broken face was the last thing Amber wanted to see.

"I promise," she cried.

It might have been normal under different circumstances. It might have been heartwarming. But this time, when Stanton kissed her forehead, it only broke Amber's heart even more.

"Thank you," Stanton said, backing away, "and I'm sorry for smearing blood on your forehead." With a final breath, he spoke two last words. "Tenth floor."

Amber sat on her bed, a Nuntius in one hand, and two choices in the other.

She could send the message she had written to Mayor Neville and stand up for the greater good, preventing an imperfect world.

Or she could keep her promise.

Even though they were blurry because of her tears, Amber could read the words on her device.

Dear Mayor Neville,

Stanton and I made a plan that shall test the creatures' loyalty. We did this according to what Grecia Rivera and Viktor Collins love and care about, and also what they fear.

We decided to sacrifice one of us. In this situation, it's Stanton. He'll pretend to hack into the city's system and destroy Nepenthe's borders. This way it'll be more realistic and believable. When Stanton is put to sleep as 'a rebel', it will either make the Amygdala Creatures question our principles, or trust in them even more, because they care about him.

I ask you to be alert, as Stanton will soon be starting his act on the tenth floor, the NGC's control room. As soon as you catch him, proceed to what needs to happen.

Amber Walsh

"Stanton, I'm doing this for the greater good, okay? Because I care about you." Because she wanted Nepenthe to remember him as a hero. As a loyal Handler. Because she didn't want to live the rest of her life knowing that everyone around her knew he had been a rebel.

A traitor.

Why? Amber bit her lips. *I already lost one person to those creatures. I already lost Louisiana. Why now Stanton? Out of all people, why the two most important ones to me?*

With a final sob, Amber clicked a button.

And sent the message.

41
BETRAYAL AND HURT

Stanton didn't know what he was doing.

Standing in the room of the NGC dedicated to the surveillance system, the control room, he stared at the glitching screen in front of him. It casted an unnatural, blue color onto his skin, making him look like something inhuman—which, as funny as it seemed, was technically true at the moment.

Stanton shook his head, gripping at his braids. What was he even supposed to do now? Never in his life had he done something so reckless, something so unplanned. And it terrified him. What kind of person had he become? Yes, he believed in what he had told Amber — the creatures were the real humans. But there should have been a better way to reveal his new beliefs to her.

Stanton had no idea why he was following the steps of Grecia's father. He had simply...exploded. It was as if his brain had shortcutted, leaving him with nothing but raw emotion. Emotion that made him do whatever came to mind first, which happened to be Mr. Rivera's failed plan of rebellion.

He had always been praised for his ability to act logically, always having a second thought before acting. Why had that ability failed now, of all moments? Why in such a dangerous situation?

But as Stanton leaned on the cold, metallic wall next to him, and sunk into the ground, a new feeling positioned itself in him. He could now feel adrenaline pulsing through his body, and it was exhilarating.

Yes, perhaps he hadn't made the best decision in his life. Maybe his emotions had taken control of his actions. And yes, these were probably going to be his last minutes breathing. It was only a matter of time until the mayor caught him red-handed.

Stanton smiled.

But at least, the last decision he had made had been a little more human than the last.

He had not fully grasped the idea of dying until this moment. Strangely, it was more calming than nerve-wracking.

Stanton nodded. The past was past. From now on, he would calculate his every step.

He grabbed his Nuntius and moved his slender fingers across the screen's keyboard. Stanton already had a new idea to make a change in Nepenthe. Sure, it was a risky plan and kind of a leap of faith, but it was worth the risk. Especially considering how it involved Haneul. He knew how Haneul valued people more than anything—even her own job and future.

Stanton tapped on the flat surface a few more times before crumpling on the floor with exhaustion. The message was scheduled to be sent to Haneul on the next Regulation Day, and if everything went according to plan—if Haneul trusted him as much as he trusted her in this moment—he was sure Nepenthe's future would change.

He had done what he needed to.

Stanton heard loud chatters outside the door and crashing footsteps. Probably some guards, ready to arrest him for being a rebel.

And he was ready to accept his fate.

Or maybe not.

A familiar face popped in his head.

Amber…

Stanton sprang to his feet. Amber. What was she doing? Was she okay? Had she done what he had ordered her to do? He needed to see her one last time.

He *needed* to.

The man punched the glitching screen and slid both of his hands with rapidness. He switched from one security footage to the other, desperation clawing at his throat and reddening his eyes.

He paused when he found the security footage of Amber's room on the third floor.

She wasn't there.

Stanton continued his search, the footsteps getting closer and closer, the chatters louder and louder. He increased his pace. How had the guards caught him so soon anyway?

It was then that it dawned on him.

Stanton's forehead broke into a sweat, and he started gasping for air, for some logical explanation to this nonsense.

Amber had probably reported him to the authorities.

No. That couldn't be possible. Amber was more likely to quit her job than to betray him. They had been colleagues and friends for ages. He had helped her cope with the loss of her closest friend. She had been with him during the hardest of times.

Their story couldn't end like this.

However, as Stanton's eyes lay on Mayor's Neville's office's security footage, all his hopes tumbled into the darkest pits of his mind.

Their story really had ended like this.

"I have no words I could use to describe how proud I am of

both of you," Mayor Neville was saying, his back as straight as a wooden stick.

"I appreciate your compliments," Amber said with a slight bow.

The blood in Stanton's veins roared and his head thumped. He glanced at the electronic clock on the wall. It was 2:00 a.m.

Nepenthe was as dark as a night without any stars. Without any galaxy. And so was his heart. Empty. Confused. Disoriented. The only thing Stanton could do was stare at one of his two closest friends giving out the information he needed to finally realize that she truly had betrayed him.

"We'll talk more about this later," Mayor Neville said. "First of all, I wanted you to explain in what ways this…situation tests the creatures' loyalty. Not that I distrust you, but there is a need for me to obtain a general knowledge about the reasoning behind this plan."

Amber clenched her hands into fists. For some reason, this calmed the roaring in Stanton's veins.

"You see…" she said with a pinch of nervousness in her voice. "Well, you see, Mayor, what Grecia Rivera is the most scared of is losing her loved ones. Not being able to see them again. During these past few weeks, she became pretty close to Stanton. If she…lost him because of not trusting in Nepenthe's beliefs…" she halted, "it would definitely test her. If she is loyal, Grecia will stay firm, because she will know what he did was wrong. You know what would happen on the contrary."

Stanton frowned. Had that girl really made up such a weak excuse?

"Excellent," Mayor Neville acknowledged, clapping. "I can see you did the best you could."

"I appreciate your compliments...and about Viktor Collins," Amber continued, "he isn't the type of Amygdala Creature who likes..." As she was about to tell another stupid lie, Mayor Neville cut her short.

"Oh, no need to give voice to the rest of your reasoning." He chuckled. "From what I hear, I doubt there are any errors in your plan. Now, let's advance to the other topic."

Stanton's throat closed.

"It's about Stanton," Mayor Neville declared. He closed his eyes, as if he wanted to block his tears from coming out.

Instead, he started laughing.

Laughing.

Stanton turned off the screen with a violent click.

Stanton's hands dropped to his sides, trembling in disbelief.

Why would Amber do this? He had asked her to do one thing. Just *one* thing.

What saddened him the most was not the fact that Amber had affected the outcome of his rebellion. It was the fact that he would wave goodbye to this world without having seen Amber make a single human choice.

"Just tell me why!" Stanton yelled at the top of his lungs, his voice piercing the air. His emotions took control of him all over again, and he didn't care who heard him. He would die soon. In a few minutes, or perhaps in a few *seconds.*

Stanton knew that he was losing control once again. But this time, he didn't mind.

His thoughts traveled to when he had first met Amber, at the time a frightened fourteen-year-old who could only squeak when approached by someone.

She surely had changed.

Or perhaps, she had always been that way, and *he* had been the one to change.

All Stanton could hear was the bumping of his heart as rough hands grabbed his arms and pulled him away, away from a starry night called life.

PART THREE
WHEN THE SHATTERED GLASS GLEAMS

42
NOT SO STUPID ASSUMPTIONS

Grecia woke to the muffled sound of someone sobbing.

Whose voice is that? She rubbed her eyes. Ugh. She hated waking up earlier than necessary.

Considering how dark it was, Grecia guessed it was early morning. The lack of noise was also a clue to the time. She stretched her legs and arms, cracking a few joints.

Should I go see who it is?

Nah. Grecia wanted some sleep. She deserved some rest after having written a darn poem.

Yet her eyes kept gravitating towards the door, and her curiosity couldn't be kept any longer. She grunted and got off her bed, reaching out her hand to the doorknob.

By then, the sobbing had become a tiny bit more muffled, and the volume was lower than before. The voice though—it was the same one.

After opening the door, Grecia carefully tip-toed around the lobby.

The crying became louder, clearer, when she approached Amber's room.

Two words reached Grecia's ears.

"Why, Stanton?"

She frowned.

What happened? Why is she crying? Grecia thought with sudden horror. A thousand possible scenarios flashed through her eyes, and they made her heart race.

It's fine. Don't make stupid assumptions out of two words.

Even when Grecia returned to her room, the blankets as warm as ever, she didn't sleep for what remained of her schedule's sleep time. Not a minute. Not a blink.

"You seem to be down today," Viktor said, wrapping his fingers around his fork.

"What? Oh. Yeah. It's nothing." Grecia shifted on her seat. She tried to smile, but instead, her face came up with a grimace. "Why are you staring? I'm fine."

Viktor nodded and proceeded to eat breakfast. Pancakes once more.

Why, Stanton?

Those words attacked Grecia and her appetite over and over. All she could manage was a sip of milk, and even *that* made her want to puke.

A few minutes later, Amber emerged from her room.

The way her hair stuck up from her head made Grecia remember Sienna and Juniper. Huge eye bags surrounded her eyes. And…was that blood, smeared on her forehead?

What the heck was going on?

Grecia couldn't help but stare.

When Amber reached the table, she suspired. "Hey guys."

Apparently, Viktor had also noticed something was off, as he only managed a short wave before lowering his gaze to the floor.

Grecia kept staring, and staring, and staring.

Amber gasped several times. Was she…trying to contain tears?

After composing herself, she straightened her posture and looked right into Grecia's eyes. "Do you know what happened?"

Grecia hesitated, glancing at Viktor for guidance. He shook his head, and so did she.

"What happened?" Viktor asked.

Amber's gaze now bore into him. She bit her lips, eyes turning red.

Grecia could feel the panic squeezing her lungs. "What happened?" she asked firmly. Fear crawled up to her mind.

And then, Amber dropped the news.

The terrible, *terrible* news.

"Stanton rebelled."

Grecia's brain took some time to process the words. A few minutes, at least.

There was no need for Amber to say, 'he died.' It was clear enough. A bit too clear for Grecia to bear.

Her heart tumbled and fell into the endless abyss.

No. It wasn't true. It couldn't be true.

It can't.

It isn't.

43
GRIEF

One may have thought what hung in the air for the rest of the day and the day after that was desperate, confused misery and grief. One may have thought the only thing that Viktor and Grecia could think about was memories, hitting them like waves, not knowing how to swim.

But in reality, inside their brain was nothing. That eerie, utter nothingness. Their souls had been shattered into tiny glassy shards. Sharp as a knife, as weak as a feather.

These three days were timeless, with neither thoughts nor emotions. Everything blank.

Nothing.

Desolate.

Aimless.

Until a thought broke the surface from the depths inside of Grecia during the ghostly night of August twenty-ninth. A night that showed no light, no exit.

It's my fault, she thought. *It's all my fault. I'm a stupid creature. The only thing I am is a creature who failed the Exétasi. I must...I must have influenced Stanton. I must have gotten him killed.*

It's my fault.

I should have kept myself away from them.

I deserve to go to Alcatraz.

Grecia couldn't help but let the tears flow, and she threw whatever she could find and grab. She even hauled the desk so hard it fell.

"Why did I have to be myself in the first place?" she screamed. "Why did I have to be born this way? The emotion. Why?" She punched the walls, the chair, whatever she could find. Grecia yelled as her face went red in pain.

It's all my fault.

August thirtieth. It was two days before returning home. Before returning to his past life, two days before applying to the Governmental Sector. Making some friends. Talking to those he left when Elliot was taken.

It all crashed down after what happened to Stanton. To Viktor.

It happened again.

It happened again.

Viktor felt as if he was once again inside his closet, sobbing, shoulders shaking. He felt as if he were once again overwhelmed by the fact that Elliot was gone. His best friend, soulmate…gone.

Now, Stanton.

That one person who helped him make a friend. The one who helped him break through his fears. He was gone as well.

Forever.

I could have avoided this, Viktor shouted in his head. *I* should *have avoided this. I should have listened to that voice that told me that I shouldn't get close to anyone ever again.*

The metallic flavor of blood stung his tongue as he bit the inside of his mouth.

Viktor lost track of time. For him, an hour felt like a second, a second like an hour. Tucked under his bed covers, he could only stare at the ceiling, eyes as dry as a desert.

Twenty hours could have passed. Maybe one. He didn't eat. Didn't drink.

At a snail's pace, Viktor fell into the black hole of slumber.

Viktor was standing in Stanton's room once again. It looked emptier, however, though he didn't know why. Everything was in place, and the coffee machine lay where it had always been.

"Here."

Stanton's voice sounded next to him, startling Viktor. His mind fell silent as he turned around to meet the man's gaze.

"Stanton?"

Stanton pushed something to Viktor's chest, and the boy took a hold of the object.

A mug.

Viktor peeked to see what was inside.

Hot chocolate.

"I wanted to give you coffee," Stanton said, "but you're too young for that."

It was more like melted swiss truffle cake than the beverage Viktor normally saw in cafeterias. It coated the boy's tongue like a scarf before flowing down his throat, warming up everything in its path. The top swirled with milk foam, which was sprinkled with cocoa powder. It looked like a cheek with freckles. Viktor wrapped his fingers around the mug and let it soothe the pain. He was torn between savoring the beverage and inhaling the smell.

"Oh," Viktor said, sniffing. "Thank you."

"You're welcome, kid." Stanton crossed his arms and stared at the coffee machine on his desk, sighing.

Viktor couldn't take it anymore. "Why did you do it?" he blurted out. "I wasn't even too close to you. But it still hurts."

Stanton quizzically focused on the boy. "What are you talking about?"

"You are a rebel now. They killed you. W-why?" Viktor mumbled under his breath.

Stanton frowned. "Did you have a nightmare?"

"No. No. No," Viktor said. "No!"

"Are you okay?"

Viktor lowered his head, shutting his eyes. "It's nothing."

Stanton nodded. "Alright. I just want you to know one thing."

"What is it?" Viktor looked up to the man's face once more, eyes sparkling with hope.

"I'm in a better place now."

He's in a better place now.

Viktor gasped, sitting up. He looked around as his head spun. Cold sweat trickled down his spine. It wasn't even past early morning yet. Maybe 3 a.m., and even *that* was a maybe. His eyes could only catch darkness.

"W-what?" He slid a hand across his face. It was wet.

Viktor had been crying in his sleep.

There was an odd peace in him, however.

He stared at his hands, and then closed them. Viktor knew what he had to do.

He wouldn't commit the same mistake he did when Elliot was taken. He wouldn't let this experience prevent him from living his life to the fullest, make him drown in grief.

Viktor would live with the beautiful memories he was given.

"Thank you, Stanton. I-I will miss you."

44
HOPE BURIED IN SNOW

"Grecia?"

Though Grecia had lost track of the time, she could tell it was sometime in the afternoon, probably August thirty-first. The only hints were the golden rays coming from the window.

She lifted her head to face whoever had entered her room.

It was Amber. And she looked even more terrible now. She looked as if she hadn't showered for weeks, and her lips were an ugly shade of purple. Only a fraction of her eyes were visible.

"I was ...thinking about taking you outside," Amber mumbled under her breath. What startled Grecia was her voice. It was scratchy like broken rocks in a sack, rasping against each other. "It'd be good for you. It's been a while since you've been on the streets."

Grecia spoke. "I—" Her own voice startled herself, as she hadn't heard it in so long. She blinked several times before recovering and opening her mouth once again. "I don't know."

She didn't have much to say, but the simple act of using her vocal cords was satisfying.

"Hey," Amber rasped. "I'm trying to do you a favor." She

strained her voice, doing her best to act as if she was okay, and that there was nothing to worry about.

Why does she sound so angry? Grecia thought, unsettled, but brushed the thought away soon after. *Why am I even asking that? She was closer to Stanton than anyone. Of course she'll feel like this.*

"I'll go," Grecia mumbled. "A walk could be nice."

A few days ago, she would have rejoiced at the thought of taking her feet off the building. Now, it was as exciting as hearing *today we'll go to the graveyard.*

In front of Nepenthe's borders, all that revealed itself in front of Grecia's eyes was white, white and whiter. Nothing else to see. It was the type of weather between a blizzard and mild snowfall.

She'd come here through teleportation, but Grecia was so numb that even *that* didn't surprise her.

"Hey, Sienna. And Juniper. Maya." Grecia stared into the white, whispering so quietly even she couldn't hear herself. "Brink." She gulped. "Washington…and the person from the cottage. Louisiana."

She paused to let herself imagine the wind blowing at her hair, the cold anesthetizing her skin.

"Lots of things have happened since I left you. I don't even know what kind of life I want to live now."

What life do I even want to live by this point? Why don't I just follow the rules?

Grecia sniffled. It would only take five steps to experience a day of snowfall. Cold.

Freezing cold.

But inside Nepenthe's borders, those things didn't exist.

As Grecia stared at the never-ending white, she thought back to the decision that had started it all. The decision that had her end up in Home.

Leaving Nepenthe.

But the question arised. Had that really been a decision? What if she hadn't only run towards what she thought was freedom, but had run *away* from something?

It was then that it hit her.

She had run away from making a decision by herself.

Grecia had never really decided to take action. Back when she had the opportunity to run away after having lunch with Cayenne and Liam, she hadn't seized the chance. Because she was too afraid of what would change in her life, of what turn it would take. She was scared of the uncertainty of it all.

She didn't trust herself.

It took the force of her mother for Grecia to finally do what she had longed to do for months, and even then she didn't take immediate action. Of course, she ran, but did that really count? She'd woken up, found herself with a few strangers, and instead of digging deeper into the situation, she had gone where the wind blew. Where life took her.

She had followed Sienna and Juniper. And that hadn't ended well. This time, it had taken a wolf for her to finally decide on the situation. She hadn't even started questioning the Outside until she read Louisiana's journal and heard Maya's words, regardless of the many signs she'd seen that the place wasn't much better than Nepenthe. And she had ended up returning to this city.

Her lack of decisions had caught her in a cage, a cage that kept getting smaller without her noticing until it was too late.

The first real decision she had made was to talk to Viktor and to act upon this opportunity to return to Veronica. And that had ended with her discovering someone else who felt the emotion, and a friendship that now meant the universe to her.

Would she choose her life's direction this time as well? Or would she wither in the cage once again?

When asked what her story was by Washington, she had said that she didn't have one. Thinking about it now, she hadn't been wrong. Because this hadn't been her story. This had been someone else's story in her perspective. Someone else had been driving her life.

I need to know what's behind all of this.

I need to know what Nepenthe has been hiding from us.

I need to know what really happened to Stanton.

Once, Veronica told Grecia that snow marks a new beginning. Winter comes at the end of the year for a reason. All the mistakes that were made, all the regrets of the year are covered. Engulfed. And the next year, the snow melts to make way for new goals, new thoughts, new triumphs, and of course, new inevitable mistakes. Snow is physical proof that we should be able to move on from our pasts to be better people in the future.

After all, white is the color of hope.

Sometimes, however, the snow never melts.

45

IN WHICH GRECIA AND VIKTOR READ A CRUMPLED LETTER

Grecia hesitated, motionless in front of Viktor's room. She extended her arm but pulled it back not even a second later.

After gathering her courage, she finally gently tapped on the wooden door. Once. Twice. Thrice.

Around fifteen hours had passed since Grecia went outside and stared into the threatening white. The remains of her tears had vanished by then, replaced by dry skin.

Sleeping couldn't have been any harder. Each time Grecia closed her eyes, Stanton's face, with a lightly serious expression, came to her mind.

Two empty, brown eyes peeked out of the doorway. "Who is it?" A sigh. "Leave, please. I'm not in the mood."

It was then that the cord Grecia had been hanging from snapped.

She rushed towards him and burst the door open, wrapping her arms around the boy. Tears rolled down and soaked Viktor's shirt. She cried and cried, holding on to him. Grecia absorbed everything around her. Viktor hugging her back, his soothing voice, and her own wails.

It's all my fault.

More whimpers broke free from Grecia.

Viktor patted her, and then spoke a simple sentence that made an odd kind of calmness settle on her.

"He's in a better place now."

Her breathing almost halted.

"W-what?"

"Calm down."

Grecia's grip loosened, and her breathing returned to its normal pace. She rubbed her cheeks in an attempt to wipe her tears away.

"What did you come here for?" Viktor leaned on the entryway, arms crossed.

She looked away in hesitation, and then spoke. "Why do you think he did it?"

Viktor's vision landed on Grecia. "What?"

"Why do you think Stanton suddenly rebelled?" Grecia gulped with a frown.

He gritted his teeth. "I don't care," Viktor said abruptly. "I truly don't. Leave me alone."

"Don't you wanna know?" Grecia stepped closer, her frown deepening. "Why…Stanton…he…"

"I said I don't care." Viktor stepped away from her, grabbing the door's edge. "We're going back home. Stanton is in a better place now. I don't want to ruin my chances. *Our* chances. I don't want to ruin my life again."

Grecia's teeth dug into her lips. "Oh, for real?" Her hands clenched into fists. "Good job. Congratulations. You ruined your life again. I didn't know you were so selfish." She stumbled away in anger. "I'm going to Stanton's room, and I'm going to find out why he rebelled. Was it four weeks ago? Whatever, I don't care about time right now. You were the one who told me it was better to die with answers than to live with questions. So stupid of you to give that kind of advice and not follow it yourself."

Viktor kicked the door, making it swing outwards. It hit the wall with a *bang*. "Fine!" he yelled.

The boy's angered face melted as soon as he saw Grecia's shocked face.

"Sorry. I'm just…I'm too scared of what could happen." The tears he had been containing broke through once in for all. Nonetheless, not a peep came from his tongue.

She stared with a blank expression. When she finally took in everything, her anger turning off, she spoke. "I-I'm also sorry," Grecia stammered. "You're not the only one who's scared."

They stood in front of each other, head down.

They had both wanted to look brave in front of each other. They both had wanted to protect each other from what they feared the most.

"I'll do it." Viktor glanced at Grecia, a determined smile forming on his face. "I do want to have knowledge about…his intentions."

Grecia grinned, rubbing her nose. "And so do I. Follow me."

Grecia rummaged through Stanton's bed covers.

"There must be something here," Her movements were quick and agile, yet desperate. "H-he isn't the type of person who would just do that. Like, without leaving something. *Something.*" She groaned, ruffling her hair.

"He used the coffee machine often."

"What?" Grecia faced Viktor. "This isn't the time for random facts. Help me find something at least!" she said, exasperated. Tears formed in her eyes yet again. This time she threw the whole blanket off the bed, grumbling.

"Be patient," the boy said.

"Be patient?" Grecia asked. "What? You want me to be this patient, calm girl in a situation like *this*? Stanton's *dead*, don't you understand?"

Dead.

Gone.

Forever.

Her own words hit her like a thousand bombs. It was what Grecia had always feared. Hurting her loved ones because of the way she acted. Because of the way she was.

"Ugh!" Grecia threw her fist into a cushion. Then again. And again. "No. No!"

Tears dripped down her face.

"Grecia?"

"What?" she growled.

For the first time in weeks, the emotion erupted in her.

The emotion. She gasped as she grasped her neck. *When did I feel it for the last time?*

It felt so strange. So distant. Nevertheless, it had never been any stronger. What she'd felt in Nepenthe, in the Exétasi days, had been nothing compared to this. It erupted through her veins, and her heart dashed a mile per second.

"Grecia." On Viktor's hand lay a crumpled piece of paper.

"W-what?" Grecia grabbed the paper and carefully weighed it on her hand. "Is this…"

"I found it in the coffee machine. That was the reason I told you this 'random fact' you call." His face, however, showed fear instead of annoyance. His forehead was creased and his lips quivered. "Once, Stanton told me he used the coffee machine for things other than making coffee. I didn't know what it meant, until now. You can read it first if you want to."

"Okay," Grecia replied, a nervous laughter leaving her tongue.

"Okay, okay. I'm opening it." However, she couldn't make herself do it.

She didn't have the willpower to do this.

These are the last remains of Stanton. Someone I technically killed.

Should I really open it?

Viktor's urging expression made Grecia tighten her grip on the crumpled paper. Even though her arms trembled, along with the rest of her limbs and her chin, her heart was as strong and rooted to its place as ever. Beads of sweat trickled down the side of her head.

I'll do it. I need to do it.

She'd do it. She'd discover the reason Stanton became a rebel before going back home. Back to Veronica. To Cayenne. To Liam. To all of her loved ones.

After all, as Viktor had said, if Grecia wanted answers, she had to seek them.

With a final breath, she carefully unfolded the letter.

Dear Rivera and Collins,

First of all, you may be asking yourselves, why didn't I simply write a note on my Nuntius, and sent it to someone who could show you my last words (written, at least)? You see, I am afraid of the government. I am afraid of them reading these words. Which brings me to my next point.

Nepenthe isn't right. We aren't right.

We were lying to you. Tricking you. *We* are the creatures, Amber and I. The whole government. The whole city of Nepenthe. We've been watching you all along.

We aren't doing this for your good. We're turning you kids into people we want you to be. That emotion you feel

—we call it *Defiance.* It's when you're able to formulate opinions on Nepenthe's beliefs that differ from what you're taught.

"Don't complain."

"Nepenthe is always right."

"We need to be perfect."

We're trying to make humans things they're not made for.

I cannot explain everything. Time is running out.

But I just wanted to tell you that if there's one thing I learned from being a Handler—it's that I have never really done things in the right way.

Viktor...when we took Elliot, it wasn't your parents' fault. It was *our* fault. The government and Nepenthe's fault. Hate us. We deserve to be hated. And please. *Please.* Forgive your parents. They haven't done anything wrong.

You know, sometimes people use hate as a drug to ease grief.

And Grecia, Nepenthe isn't freedom. It has been the opposite of freedom since the beginning.

I need to leave. Amber is coming any second now.

If you need answers, all that happened has to do with the fact that you're not just "creatures." We call you *Amygdala Creatures*, if you need answers.

Thank you for everything. For making me laugh. Smile.

And let me ask you one more thing before I leave. Before I leave.

Are you living the life you want to live, or the one the others want you to?

From Stanton Carmichael.

Nepenthe Governmental Center

Handler from the Amygdala Team

Grecia stood, motionless.

"What's going on?" Viktor asked. There was a combination of panic and fear in his voice. "Won't you tell me?"

"They—" Grecia spat, dread building up in her throat. "They were lying to us all along. They were *lying*. Amber—she promised me. She promised I would return to my mother someday. She *promised*." She didn't blink, didn't stop to breathe.

"Hey. HEY." Viktor grabbed Grecia by the shoulders and then her face was in front of his. "Tell me what you read. Or at least give me that letter, so I can read the words myself," he said.

"We don't have time," Grecia cried out. "They'll find us before we have the chance to leave this place. I-I need to find her. Mom. I failed her. I failed everyone. The kids from Home…" She stopped the sob from bursting out of her. She shuddered, trying to not make a sound.

"Don't panic," Viktor said soothingly this time. "Give me the letter." He lowered his voice. "It'll be okay."

Grecia nodded with a shaky sigh and handed him the letter.

As soon as the boy's eyes made contact with the yellow, creased letter. his eyes grew wide. And wider. And wider.

Viktor shut his eyes down, blocking the tears' path to freedom.

"We have to go," he whispered. "Now."

How can we even leave? Grecia thought. *All this time, I thought returning would be freedom.*

It was hard to believe that after all these hardships, Grecia had been going through the wrong path. The wrong way.

Was it all going to end like this?

What was she even going to do now?

Grecia gritted her teeth. *What have I done?*

"What do we do?" she mumbled under her breath. "What do we need to do now?"

I did the right thing. I'm sure of it now.

Amber's thoughts were now firm and steady. There was no doubt now.

She would stick to the plan.

She nodded at Mayor Neville, who stood beside her. His eyes were locked with the screen in front of him.

How long had it been, since Amber had told Grecia that the door that led to this room was *employees-only*? She didn't know, but the creature hadn't been curious or suspicious about that fact ever since. Maybe once or twice, but not more.

"They've read the letter," Amber said. "I didn't know the creatures would fall for it without hesitation."

"Good," Mayor Neville replied. "Having similar handwriting to your partner has its positive points, doesn't it?"

Only a few hours ago, falsely personifying Stanton might have been heart wrenching. Now, it was as refreshing as a cold, fresh lemonade on a hot summer afternoon.

"I agree. Now, we shall see if their faith in Nepenthe is strong enough to get over the letter." She smiled at the mayor.

"I am impressed by your cleverness."

"I appreciate your compliments." Her eyes fixated on the screen.

The room was identical to the Observatory #31, the only difference being the color. It was the same yellow as the rest of the third floor, but brighter.

It suited the occasion, at least in Amber's opinion.

Yellow represents enlightenment.

I won't fall for those animals like Stanton did. I'm not as weak minded as he was. I'll make Mayor Neville proud, she thought. *I'll make the whole city proud. The greatest Handler of Nepenthe. Sounds good.*

"Amber," the mayor said with hastiness. "Listen to their conversation. There's some interesting stuff going on."

"Oh?" Amber directed her attention toward Viktor and Grecia.

"…the door!" Grecia was saying. "There's a door. A-Amber told me I wasn't allowed to go there. Should we go?" Her face lit up. "It might be the exit. Let's go." She extended her arm to Viktor.

Viktor didn't take Grecia's hand. He looked around, and then out the window, where Nepenthe stood in its brilliance.

He seems to be loyal even after reading the letter, Amber thought with satisfaction. But her hope collapsed when Viktor took off first.

"Let's go," he said.

Amber blankly stared at the screen.

W-what? she thought. *But, how?*

It was then that a thought hit her like a bullet to the heart.

I failed.

Thump. Thump. Thump. Her heart thumped like crazy.

I failed.

Thud. Thud. Thud. Not her heart this time.

Someone was trying to break into the room.

I failed.

There will be consequences.

"First we'll get rid of the Amygdala Creatures," Mayor Neville whispered into her ear. "Then we'll see about you."

46

THE LAST BITS OF TIME

"Let us go," Grecia yelled, flailing her legs. "Don't touch us."

"Haneul?" Mayor Neville said. "You'll be in charge of the creatures along with two of your colleagues, understood? You'll inject them with the Sleep Serum after fifteen minutes."

"Understood," a girl with amber hair said, hands in her pockets.

Sleep Serum? What was going on?

"Explain," Grecia halted in place and spoke firmly. "I need an explanation. I'm not going anywhere if you don't tell me what's going on."

What she said even surprised herself.

Everyone around her—Amber (whom she couldn't help but glare fiercely at), Mayor Neville (who looked stunned, as if he'd witnessed a murder), and Haneul with two other people, whom Grecia supposed were more of Amber's colleagues—stared at her, eyes wide.

"Ahem…" Mayor Neville started. "Amber, you might want to explain the situation to them. You're the only one who can safely speak to them."

Grecia hated it. How she was talked about as if she were a wild animal. She hated how she was being dragged about like a prisoner, without an explanation, as if she didn't need one.

All the things Grecia hated about Nepenthe flooded in. She remembered how innocent children were taken to Alcatraz. She remembered how angry she had gotten when Cayenne and Liam spoke so uncompassionately about them.

How had everything changed so quickly for Grecia, so many times?

"Grecia," Amber said, "and you too, Viktor. You're too dangerous for Nepenthe. That emotion you feel? That's what makes a rebel, well, *rebels*. Sorry, but we can't let you live among the citizens. You didn't fail the test because your brain wasn't developed enough..."

"That's what makes a rebel, well, rebels... You didn't fail the test because your brain wasn't developed enough."

Piece by piece, each sentence clicked into the bigger puzzle. The reason everything happened to her in the first place.

But there was one phrase that made her heart fully sink.

"Sorry, but we can't let you live among the citizens."

Please tell me I'm not dying, Grecia thought. *Please tell me I interpreted it in the wrong way.*

No matter how hard she tried to form a new reality from the words she had heard, everything remained the same. They weren't going to be sent to Alcatraz. She was going to die from what the mayor had called the Sleep Serum.

"But," Grecia yelled, "you said we were going to be sent to Alcatraz if we failed! You never said we were going to *die*!"

"Grecia..." Amber shook her head. "Alcatraz is a code word. It doesn't exist. All those who fail the Exétasi get injected with the Sleep Serum as well."

A wave of confusion washed over Grecia.

Alcatraz had always been a lie.

I see. Nepenthe has always been formed by a bunch of lies.

"Thank you for explaining," Mayor Neville said. "Now, Amber, come with me."

Grecia glared at Amber one more time. Anger burned through her. The worst thing was, there wasn't even a tiny bit of regret or repentance in Amber's eyes.

"I said come with me," Mayor Neville repeated.

"Okay, sir."

That was the last time Grecia ever saw Amber.

Grecia was stuck in a room. A black one, to be precise. It described her emotional state perfectly.

A bearded young man had thrown her in, along with Viktor. He had said they would stay there for fifteen minutes, until the Sleep Serum was ready for injection.

She sat in the corner of the room with Viktor at her side.

How had things crashed down so quickly? She had been supposed to see Veronica today…

Grecia was done. Done with being the weak one. Done with being controlled every second of her life.

"I'm scared," she mumbled. "I-I'm scared, Viktor."

"You're not the only one," he replied. Such a familiar conversation. He then squeezed her hand. "But remember, we're here for each other."

She gulped and squinted at the ceiling.

"How can you be so calm?" Grecia asked. "We're *dying*, Viktor. Dying."

Viktor looked down at the night-black floor. "If there's one thing I learned during my time here, it's that you need to clutch those good memories you have. That'll give you hope."

Grecia sniffed. "In a situation like this? I should be with Mom right now."

Viktor smiled wistfully at her. For the first time, she noticed how big his eyes were. How dark and shiny.

"Remember my first origami crane?" Viktor said with a dry laugh.

"Yeah. I do. It was pretty bad, not gonna lie." For once, she smirked. It hurt even to smile. "Do you remember," Grecia continued, taking a deep, shaky breath, "when we first met? It was so awkward, wasn't it? Like, super awkward. I kept talking to you and you'd ignore me. I thought you were some freaky boring nerd or something."

"People tell me that often."

Both of them cracked up in quiet, dry, yet genuine laughter. And so, began a retelling of old yet not so distant memories. Recent memories, yet hard to grasp.

And Grecia couldn't lie—it made her feel better.

At least all these events had happened.

Her mind surfed through all those sweet times in her life. When she'd made her own successful origami crane a few years ago. That time when Grecia had met Cayenne and Liam for the first time, in the McDouglas Burger Shop. Veronica's warm hugs and kisses. Those linguistic lessons with Viktor.

Even that time when Grecia swam in the cool water of the lake outside Nepenthe, with the kids of Home. Back when she thought she had succeeded in acquiring freedom into her life.

Freedom.

"Viktor? What do you think freedom is?"

But Grecia knew the answer before receiving it. Because now, she knew what being free was like.

Because now, she was free.

Stanton had written something in that letter.

Are you living the life you want to live, or the one the others want you to?

For all her life, Grecia had been afraid to choose. She had always needed approval from someone else to act upon something. Veronica. A wolf. A diary entry.

For all her life, Grecia had been terrified of hurting her loved ones, just by being the person she was. Grecia Rivera. The girl with the strange emotion. The girl who thought there was something off with Nepenthe.

She had bottled herself up inside and had acted like the person she was expected to be throughout her whole life.

Grecia had been forced to be someone she didn't know—to survive.

Although only for a short time, Grecia had been the person she really was. The person she wanted to be. She'd fought back against what she thought was wrong by her own will.

She had felt true freedom.

Grecia now knew why Louisiana had regretted leaving Nepenthe. It wasn't because of the atrocities she had faced on the Outside. Louisiana had regretted leaving Nepenthe because she had not done something to change what she hated the most about her home city. She'd left her loved ones without unblinding them.

Louisiana. Whoever you were. I've done what you always wanted to do. Although I don't know if what I did is going to produce any change, I did something against what's wrong. I acted against Nepenthe's government. And none of this would've happened if not for your diary entries. So, thank you. And I hope you know that even if indirectly, you did contribute to fighting back.

"Viktor, I got what I wanted all this time."

"Oh," Viktor said. "Well, I think I got what I wanted after all too." He wrapped an arm around Grecia. "This isn't that bad, is it? At least we reached our goals before...leaving."

Grecia nodded, burying her face into her own knees. Finally, the tears let themselves escape.

She hadn't expected to achieve freedom in this way. And it wasn't much, of course. Just a bit of yelling and pushing for a short amount of time.

But the realization of what freedom was, *being* free…that was enough for her.

"I'm happy I met you," Viktor said, sniffing. "Fortunate."

"Me too. It's gonna be a long time before I forget the deformed beak of that crane of yours."

Grecia covered her arm as Viktor elbowed her, giggling.

The young girl knew she was soon going to die.

Did she care? Not a chance.

47
GOODBYE, WORLD

"Stay still," an unknown, masculine voice said.

A blinding light was all Viktor's eyes could catch.

I guess this is the end, he thought. *This is truly the end.*

Accepting his identity as an Amygdala Creature, a future rebel…that had been the easy part. He knew his conduct was abnormal ever since they took Elliot.

But who was this *they?*

Answering that question had been the hardest, impossible part.

But now, Viktor knew. It had never been his family's fault. It had never even been their ignorance's fault.

Finally, Viktor had forgiven his parents.

Because he didn't see them as the adults who accepted that Elliot was taken, that he was 'a creature.' He saw them as the caring parents who made him grow as a person, loved him, and cheered him up whenever he had a hard time studying. The mother who brought strawberry milk whenever he was sad. The father who worked hard for the whole family.

Thank you.

A pain spread through his veins, quite literally. His arms burned lightly, as if he had acquired a first-degree burn.

Black and red spots danced around, as slowly, his consciousness shut down.

Slowly…

S l o w l y….

The black spots overpowered the red ones and covered Viktor's entire vision.

He thought back to an interaction he'd have with his brother the day he entered the Linguistic Sector.

"It won't be long until you make a friend," Elliot had said.

"Well, can you describe what making a friend is like?" Viktor had asked.

"You'll find out someday," had been his brother's answer.

Oh, and Viktor surely now knew how it felt to make a friend. A friend as great as Elliot.

He didn't know how he looked to the man who'd euthanized him, but to himself, he was smiling from ear to ear.

Thank you, Father.

Thank you, Mother.

Thank you, Elliot.

Thank you, Stanton.

And thank you, Grecia.

With one final gasp, Viktor drifted into the unknown.

Grecia watched, immobile because of the restraints and mute because of the mouth cover, as a man looked down at her, holding a syringe. It glowed against the blue, fluorescent light from the ceiling.

"Oh shoot."

The sound of crashing glass erupted in the room, and pieces of what had fallen clattered on the floor.

"What was that?" an acute voice asked.

"Sorry about that. I accidentally dropped the syringe. There are a bunch of shards on the floor. Could you clean that up and give me another syringe?"

As the image of the shards of glass flashed through Grecia's mind, she smiled. One moment, one's life could be perfect. But with a single mistake, it could completely break down—just like how the syringe had once been in a perfect state and was now shattered on the floor.

But on those shards of glass, in that broken life, there was a tiny gleam. There was light, something to illuminate the darkness. There was hope during a broken time. Because even during the most difficult of days, there was hope for the future.

Funny how objects can describe one's life in such a bold way.

Grecia felt a sharp prick in her left arm, and she stiffened.

Soon, the world got covered by black, thick ink. Grecia took a breath. Or at least she tried to.

I hope I made a change in Nepenthe.

Goodbye, world.

48
THE HOLOGRAM

It was the early morning of January first, the day of the first Regulation Day of the year. About four months after killing Grecia and Viktor, the Amygdala Creatures.

No. Not killing. Putting to sleep.

Haneul ran a hand through her face as she watched the clip from the feed once again. Stanton slammed Amber into the wall, and the liquids dripped to the floor. The blood of the rebel. The tears of the loyal Handler. Yells and screams, promises and whispers. After Stanton's particles, going through the teletransportation, vanished from the screen, Haneul replayed the video. Over and over again.

This couldn't be true. It couldn't. The three of them had been best friends in the past, taken selfies in the park, and played cards in each others' houses. How could Amber do such a thing?

But she remembered Stanton's pained face, how his lips had been trembling, and how he had kept mumbling, *Amber*, while Haneul injected the Sleep Serum. While she was killing him.

No. I didn't kill him.

Certainly, Amber had something to do with his rebellion.

After having received a message Stanton had apparently

scheduled before his death, the message that told her to not trust Nepenthe, that detailed a plan of rebellion, Haneul had tried everything to get footage of that night. She'd spent hours in the Observatory #31, but the only videos she'd gotten had been of the Amygdala Creatures.

When she'd remembered that there were secret cameras on the third floor only Mayor Neville could access, she had gotten permission from him to 'just look for something.' Haneul had thought that her doubts would be released from her mind, and that only comfort would remain. The comfort that Stanton had really just been acting.

But the clip she had found didn't look like an act.

Haneul buried her head in her knees, embracing herself. She brushed a few hazel hair strands away from her eyes, and the tears broke through.

I lost both of my best friends for the wrong reasons.

When Haneul was nine years old, a kid whose name she didn't remember had mocked her monolids, saying that because of them, she looked like she was always crying. She had been both annoyed and offended by his comments but had soon learned to ignore him.

That moment, as Haneul recalled the kid's words, she realized that perhaps, she had really always been crying inside.

Perhaps deep down, all along she'd known that her life was messed up in so many ways. Her dreams of working in the government, helping destroy human rights.

And that moment, Haneul knew how she could cleanse away the dried tears from her heart.

She would do everything Stanton had instructed her to do in that scheduled message.

"Excuse me? Mrs. Rivera?"

Haneul knocked on what used to be the front door of Grecia's house. When nobody responded, she double-checked the address on her Nuntius. Yup. This was the right place.

She crossed her arms, leaning on the cold metallic surface of the door. Was she crazy? Was this plan even going to work?

Haneul thought back to one of the things Stanton had instructed her to do. Grecia's dream was getting her art displayed on her school's ceiling, and she'd make it become a reality.

This is going to work.

Just then, the door smashed open, and Haneul fell to the floor with a thump.

"Ah…" She swatted away her mayonnaise-yellow hoodie from her head and thumbed her back. It felt as if a huge chunk of wood had stuck into her skin.

"Um, who is this?"

"Who? Me?" Haneul looked above her shoulder and found herself staring into Veronica Rivera's eyes.

They were so broken.

They were beautiful, the color a merge of gray and blue. But what could have resembled a calm sea now looked like a sandy beach undergoing a mighty storm. Her pupils quivered every now and then.

"Get out," Mrs. Rivera said, pushing Haneul away.

Haneul's head hit the floor once again, and all the air was sucked from her lungs.

"I was already told what happened to…Grecia." Mrs. Rivera's pupils stopped quivering, now replaced with a frightening steadiness. "I said get out!"

"Um, Mrs. Rivera" Haneul took a deep breath, standing up with a hand on the house's outer walls. "I'm here to help you."

Mrs. Rivera scoffed.

"I wanna help Grecia fulfill her dreams." Haneul gulped. "At least in this state. Do you have a…a painting? One Grecia made. The best one, I mean."

Haneul stepped onto the marble floor of Nepenthe's only school, and her footsteps echoed through the hall.

Stares rained on her, but she was already used to that. Wearing the usual green shirt of someone who worked for the Nepenthe Government always attracted gazes. Everyone's eyes were compasses, and she was the north.

A canvas tucked under her arm, Haneul crossed a strip of land free of chattering students. As a worker of Nepenthe, she was given top priority to do whatever she wanted. So here she was, students leaving space for her.

Just when Haneul looked up, ready to stick the painting to the ceiling…

I forgot to bring a freakin ladder. Guess this is the part where I say bruh.

"Who cares?" Haneul said aloud. She smashed the canvas onto the marble wall. "At least I remembered to put on the sticky tape on the painting's edges, so here it is."

She wasn't even a little bit embarrassed by her confusing actions.

"What is that?" a boy from the hallway asked. "Why are there kids sitting on planet earth?"

Haneul grinned. "This is hope for Nepenthe. This is your future."

"Hello there!" Haneul said, approaching a child. "I know this is a weird question, but is your name Liam?"

She had been leaning against the alma mater's cold, cement entrance, waiting for an orange-haired boy to pass by. Several kids with that hair color had walked through the door and had cocked their heads hearing Haneul's question.

This time, however, she had caught the right person.

"Um, yeah?" the orange-haired boy said. He tucked his hands into the pockets of his black trousers. "Who do you think you are? A super cool spy who knows my name?"

Haneul chuckled at his words and raised an eyebrow, smiling. "Perhaps. Do you want me to show you my laser gun?"

"You're kidding, aren't you?"

"Of course I am."

"Aw." Liam pouted from disappointment. "Well, how do you know my name then?"

Haneul turned the steering wheel of the conversation to another direction. "Were you Grecia Rivera's friend?"

The boy looked away, and his hair flopped in the air.

Yes. This is the reaction I was waiting for.

Haneul leaned closer to the boy and whispered, "The mayor has a surprise prepared for this Ceremony. He wants all of you to hear some very true and important words. Don't tell anyone."

Of course, all that she said was a lie. And of course, she knew that teenagers were the worst at keeping secrets.

But that was part of the plan.

"May I tell just *one* friend?" Liam asked, flailing his arms with an owl-eyed expression. "Her name's Cayenne."

Great. Another kid who could spread the fake news.

"Of course," Haneul said with a smirk.

Haneul was in charge of turning on the hologram in that ceremony. Below the stage, she stood in front of the machine, which was directed straight above. The room was relatively bland and boring, with no colors except gray, and a few boxes and machines here and there.

She peaked through the narrow cracks on the ceiling next to the hologram machine and spotted Liam in the farthest corner of the wave of the audience. Next to him sat a girl who she supposed was Cayenne. Around those two there was more rustling than usual.

The news was spreading.

Haneul trembled as the principal uttered the last words of his speech.

It's now or never.

Am I going to dry those tears or not?

"...let's start the show!" the principal was saying when Haneul clicked the black button in front of her. The hologram shone through the ceiling, and throughout the stage.

But it wasn't the usual scene that materialized. It wasn't the *creatures* who had failed the last Exétasi.

"So, Stanton Carmichael actually rebelled."

Haneul could hear her own voice from above.

The plan had worked. Thousands were watching the video she had filmed only hours ago.

Haneul's heart warmed up, boiling away those tears.

Everything Stanton and the Amygdala Creatures had gone through wasn't going to be a waste.

Her voice continued echoing from above. "Yes, you heard me right. Stanton Carmichael rebelled. And he actually did the right thing. Let me explain why."

EPILOGUE

Sienna sunk her feet into the lake. Into the place she belonged. Water.

She took a deep breath, and then splashed into the deeper part of the lake. Soon, her torso was blanketed with calm water. A slight embrace.

Sienna closed her eyes and grimaced. She couldn't believe this was happening.

But it was in honor of Grecia. She didn't know all the details, but she was sure the girl had been attacked by a wild animal. Probably a wolf, considering how many howls she'd heard while searching for Grecia.

With that in mind, Sienna started swimming.

The memories of all her swim meets, of all her swim training sessions flooded in as she glided through the cold surface.

She remembered wrapping her toes around the edge of the starter. She remembered lowering her head, taking a last breath before the beep. The beep that would make the adrenaline turn on in her veins.

She'd push herself forwards and land, fingers first, with a

splash. Icy water would surround her, telling her that the faster she finished the race, the faster she'd get out of the freezing pool.

Sienna would move—bent arms, splashing legs. When her lungs started burning, her head would break from the surface, and she'd gulp down a mouthful of air. She'd put her head back into the chlorine, bubbles floating past her nose.

As Sienna approached the edge of the pool, the pool's black line would come to an end, merging with all that was blue. She'd push the water with all the force she could manage and flip her legs towards the wall. Then, impact. She'd propel herself from the wall and start over again. Then again. And then again.

Might sound like a dull repetitive process for some people, but for Sienna, it was a sensation that she ached to feel again.

But as she slid her hand through the water, eyesight blurry, she laughed. Sienna swallowed an unlikeable amount of liquid and rose to the air, coughing. She continued laughing.

"Coach!" she yelled to the air, "I told you I'd do my best to become a better swimmer whatever the circumstance! Can you see me now?" Tears of joy streamed down her jaw and plopped into the lake.

Sienna propelled herself from the wet ground and switched to breaststroke. Each time she raised her head, she could see water running down the edges of her hair strands.

Her kicks and strokes came to a halt, and Sienna's head poked out of the lake.

The sunset was beautiful. A red blanket lay on the very top of the sky. The gradient combination of red, orange, and yellow at the very center shone aggressively. At the bottom, a coating of yellow surrounded the radiant sun. Sienna stared right into it, without blinking. She didn't care if the light was blinding. She simply stared right into the sun and smiled.

"Grecia," Sienna said, "did you really die because of the wolf?

Or did you survive with the help of your stubbornness? And if you did survive, where are you?"

Somehow, she had a feeling that the answers to her questions weren't ones she could imagine at the moment. Or ones she'd ever be able to imagine, for that matter.

"Grecia Rivera, did you find the freedom you wanted?"

ACKNOWLEDGMENTS

Wow. So, my book is finally out.

I started writing *A Gleaming Shard of Glass* when I was thirteen years old, and nearly two years later, whether it be digitally or physically, my novel now lays on your hands.

Would I have been able to do this alone? Not a chance.

First of all, I'd like to thank Mel Torrefranca for...pretty much everything. Not only did she help me go through the editing process, but she was also the one who made this publication possible. In addition to that, it was one of her YouTube videos that motivated me to write a book. Basically, if not for her existence, none of this would have ever happened.

I'd also like to thank my family—Mom, Dad, and the best younger brother in the world, Samuel a.k.a skittle (ㅇㅅㅇ), as well as my grandparents, my aunts, my uncle, and my cousin. They were the ones who shaped me into the person I am today, and without them, I would have never stepped out of my comfort zone. They also always supported me along the way, and for that I'll be forever thankful.

I am grateful for the amazing team I worked with during the publication process. Rakit Roket, for the insanely beautiful cover, Ben Loft and Mel Torrefranca for copy editing, Katie Flanagan for her constructive criticism, Nora Sun for her marketing guidance, and Bérénice Hamza for proofreading.

These acknowledgements would be incomplete without a section dedicated to my incredible beta readers, who helped this novel reach its full potential: Abigail Hendrie, Mara Quinn,

Beka, Esly Marina, Gabi Souza, Ray C., Luis Rodrigues, Jaidah Wyatt, Lari Rehder, Saumya Babbar, Jane Callahan, C.C.Wen, and those who chose to remain anonymous. *A Gleaming Shard of Glass* wouldn't have been the same without their helpful feedback and encouraging words.

ARC readers, thank you so much for giving my book a chance, and for reading and reviewing it before release. You truly have no idea how much you have helped the publication of A Gleaming Shard of Glass become a reality.

I'd like to thank my amazing street team: Victor Thong, Wrigley Page, Liam, Amarnath, Farah, and those who chose to stay anonymous. You guys made promoting *A Gleaming Shard of Glass* more successful and fun than I could have ever imagined.

I would like to express my gratitude to the Casuarinas swim team as a whole, from coaches to fellow swimmers, for helping me grow as a person and being the best friends I could ever have. Special mention to Adriana Mantilla, Ariana Abanto, Meylan Loo, Luciano Salas, Mauricio Abanto, Yussef Conocc, Rodrigo Saavedra, Adriana Quispe and Dylan Espino.

Shoutout to Alex and Christina Choi, Andrés Castillo, Noelia Droguett (Viktor's biggest simp), Gastón Carpio, Hyunji Park, Fabiana Príncipe, Jimena Castillo, Daniela García, Joseph and Grace Kim, Halen Lock, and so many more people (you know who you are.)

Finally, thank *you*, reader, for giving this book a chance, and for helping a fifteen-year-old kid's dreams come true.

BONUS CONTENT

SPOILER ZONE

BLOOPERS

These are some embarrassing typos from drafts two and three that were fixed throughout the editing process—enjoy!

1. "What things were hidden in the Nutria for Stanton to act in that way?" I meant *Nuntius*. Because my keyboard is in Spanish, autocorrect thought I meant *nutria*, which means otter.

2. "But you don't understand." Elliot smiled, banging his fists into the pillows. "You've always been the stupid one." Sleep deprivation must have gotten the hang of me when I wrote this—

3. "Grecia had a few seconds to contemplate the beauty of the avocado before it barked once, and charged." …I meant animal.

4. "It wasn't long before Grecia got wrapped in profound salad." Autocorrect must really love food.

5. "A sudden drowsiness hit Grecia, as if someone had hit her with a pancake." Oh no! Someone hit me with a pancake! My head hurts!

6. "Before she knew it, ambrosia had spoken the teletransportation words." I have no idea how it went from Amber to ambrosia, but oh well.

7. "Twenty hours could have passed. Maybe just one. He didn't eat. Didn't get drunk." ...What? XD

8. After all, no matter what happens, life goes on. Teemo doesn't wait for anyone. Didn't know autocorrect was a *League of Legends* player.

9. Her voice continued echoing from above. "Yes, you heard me right. Stanton Carmichael actually rebelled. And he actually did the wrong thing. Let me explain why." I was so confused when I read this for the first time.

10. "The sunburn was beautiful." How did *sunset* end up being *sunburn*?

FUN FACTS

Originally, Grecia and Viktor were five year old kids, and Amber and Stanton were middle-aged adults and really minor characters.

I added Haneul to the story nearly at the end of the editing process.

Originally, there were supposed to be over ten kids at Home.

Viktor used to be a relatively minor character. Glad I made him one of the main characters…I just love him too much.

A major inspiration for the first draft of *A Gleaming Shard of Glass* was the movie *Lion*, but the plot has drastically changed since then.

Grecia's name was originally *Annalise*.

Few things remain the same from *A Gleaming Shard of Glass*'s first draft, but one thing that hasn't changed is Nepenthe's name. I don't know why, but it felt right from the beginning.

Talking about Nepenthe...The term *nepenthe* comes from ancient Greek literature and myths. It was thought to be a drug that induced forgetfulness of pain or sorrow. Ironic, huh?

Grecia means *Greece* in Spanish.

Until draft seven, Sienna and Juniper's names were Emma and Ella, respectively. There was a change because their names were too similar to each other.

These were some other alternatives titles I thought of for *A Gleaming Shard of Glass*:

- *When the Girl Fled*
- A *Girl, a Train, and a Ghost* (back when the plot was a whole other thing)
- *Gleaming Glass*

ALTERNATIVE CHAPTER
BITTERSWEET CONGRATULATIONS

Chapter 41: Betrayal and Hurt was originally in Amber's perspective. I decided to rewrite the chapter in Stanton's perspective because I thought it would be great if readers could explore his head and thoughts during his failed rebellion, as well as take a peek at the failed rebellion itself.

But writing the original version was so much fun, so I decided to share it with you all. Enjoy! :)

"I have no words I could use to describe how proud I am of both of you."

Amber didn't know how she felt about Mayor Neville's words.

"I appreciate your compliments," she said with a slight bow. The blood in her veins roared and her head thumped with distress.

It was 2:00 a.m. The world was as dark as a night

without any stars. Without any galaxy. And so was her heart. Empty. Confused. Disoriented.

Why am I feeling like this? I did the right thing, she thought, pounding her head.

The image of Stanton's warm, glad face didn't help.

The only thing Amber could do was stare at Mayor Neville, and fight back a few sobs.

"We'll talk more about this later," Mayor Neville said. "First of all, I wanted you to explain in what ways this…situation tests the children's loyalty. Not that I distrust you, but there is a need for me to obtain a general knowledge about this."

Amber gulped, and clenched her hands into fists.

Does he suspect me? Does he distrust me? What do I say? she thought.

Besides raising an eyebrow, Mayor Neville didn't look like he suspected her. That made the roaring in Amber's veins calmer. The panic didn't go away, however.

"I-I, you see…" Amber stammered.

Calm down. Think about it. Panicking won't help.

"Well, you see, Mayor," she started. "What Grecia Rivera is the most scared of is losing her loved ones. Not being able to see them again. During these past few weeks, she became pretty close to Stanton. If she…lost him because of not trusting in Nepenthe's beliefs…" she halted, and gulped down a yell. "It would definitely test her. If she is loyal, Grecia will stay firm, because she will know what he did was wrong. You know what would happen on the contrary."

This one was easy enough. Coincidence or not, it fitted Grecia's situation.

Now, Viktor…

"Excellent," Mayor Collins acknowledged, clapping. "I can see you did the best you could."

"I appreciate your compliments."

What about Viktor?

"And about Viktor Collins," Amber continued, trying to keep her voice from trembling. "He isn't the type of Amygdala child who likes…"

As she was about to say a stupid, irrelevant word, Mayor Neville cut her short.

"Oh, no need to give voice to your reasons," he chuckled. "From what I hear, I doubt there are any errors in your plan. Now, let's advance to the other topic."

Amber tried to sigh in relief. Her chest tightened, and her throat closed.

She couldn't make herself do it. She knew there was more trouble to come.

"It is about Stanton," Mayor Neville declared. He closed his eyes, as if he wanted to block his tears from coming out.

Instead, he started chuckling.

Chuckling.

"Oh, Miss Walsh," he said. "You know how proud I am. Of you. Of Stanton too, obviously. He was willing to sacrifice himself for the good of the city." He stared out the glass walls. "Though I am not sure why he is doing that. It might be a lot better for him, and for you of course, to you, if he just pretended to be put to sleep, instead of making it real."

He isn't pretending to hack into the system! Amber wanted to scream. *He's a* real *rebel! An animal! Grecia and Viktor affected him!* She wanted to push herself out of her seat, throw it to the ground. She wanted to go back in time, and stop Stanton when she should have done it.

Through all her life, as a child, as a teenager and in the present, Amber had wanted to obtain a few things. Ice cream. A Nuntius. A part in the Amygdala Project.

As people say, you can't live having all that you want. There are some things you need to sacrifice.

At that moment, Amber wished she had sacrificed all these solid objects. She wished that back then, she had known that those things were worth sacrificing.

But at least she had helped good. Amber had reported Stanton to the mayor.

Yes. Think about it in that way. Please do. Please.

She thought in the same way she had pleaded herself to during training.

"Stanton insisted," Amber coughed out. "Such a true-hearted worker. He wanted the experiment to be as successful as possible. We lost one life, for the exchange of two young ones."

"Most certainly." The mayor's smile now looked creepy and robotic. He didn't seem to be one bit sad about Stanton's death. A beep came out from his own device, and a message popped out, though Amber couldn't see it.

"I forwarded your message to everyone in this building as quickly as I could," Mayor Neville explained. "They are on high alert. Seems like they already caught him, and they're about to inject the Sleep Serum. They need my signal." Then, his eyes met hers with a charismatic grin. "Shall we?"

Amber gulped. With her heart falling from the cliff of her hope, she said, "Send the signal."

She as well might have been drinking poison slowly, little by little, for a long time.

"They injected it," Mayor Neville declared after a few seconds. His claps sounded like thunder, the echoes like rainfall. "You may go to sleep now. Tomorrow, tell the children about what happened. Then, transport yourself to the Observatory. I will send Haneul to assist you with Viktor, since Stanton will not be present."

"Understood." Amber's head bobbed in partial agreement. "I am honored to work in the Amygdala Project. I'm sure we are on our way to an excellent, beautiful future. Now, I shall leave. Third floor, room A5."

The same tingle, and she collapsed on her bed.

The tears didn't spill out. The screams didn't escape her throat.

Nothing.

Her brain was too confused to act. There were so many mixed feelings, so many happy thoughts, and miserable ones.

"What have I done?" she whispered. "Why?"

Her breathing quickened once again. They were shallow, yet quick breaths.

You did the right thing. Calm down, her brain thought.

But Stanton is dead *you idiot!* Her heart countered.

"Stanton."

Her heart countered her brain.

Her heart.

"Shut it," Amber mumbled, making her eyelids connect. "Just shut it!"

She kicked her bed covers with all the force she could manage, though they barely flew off the cushion. Expectedly, the tears flooded out.

Have I really done the right thing?

ORIGINAL FIRST CHAPTER

WHEN THE GIRL FLED

I have said a few times that the first draft of *A Gleaming Shard of Glass* was…quite different to its current version. To get a feel for how different it was, here's the first chapter.

WARNING: REALLY BAD WRITING AHEAD

There was a girl who lives in the nation of Elysian. She had black, long hair and porcelain skin. Her striking blue eyes made a great combination with her full, cherry-red lips.

Her name is Grecia.

She slowly opened her eyes, one by one, contemplating the morning light gleaming on the window. If not for her small stature, she would have bumped her head on the ceiling while getting off her mat.

"Mama," yelled Grecia. This was the word she used the most, being barely five years old.

Grecia slowly trudged towards Mama's mat. She had tons of plans in mind for today, and didn't want to waste a second. This child had quite a lot of imagination for her daily schedule, wanting to do adult things, as she called it, whenever possible.

"Mama, wake up!" She giggled.

If not for their stature and skin complex, people would actually confuse Grecia and her mother. They looked so alike sometimes they could also be confused as siblings.

"Mama, I have a plan for today!"

What makes any mother proud is a young daughter already speaking sentences. That's what Mama felt that moment while waking up.

"Good morning darling," she whispered, kissing Grecia's cheek. "What a fine day it is."

This statement was true indeed. The sun hadn't come out for weeks now, and today a shining ball of heat shows itself in the sky. There were no clouds at all, and as if the flowers were also in a good mood, they were as colorful as ever. The windows glinted, along with the glasses laid on a desk.

However, the cottage in which they lived in didn't look as cheerful. In reality, it never had. It was so simple it could be described in a few words, even for a girl as creative as Grecia. Its size wasn't even big enough to be called a cottage, and the ceiling was so low tiny Grecia could reach it without a struggle. There was nothing inside except two mats for sleeping and a crooked desk. However, the family's house couldn't be happier.

The father died even before Grecia was born. Mama went through an extremely arduous situation, both in the inside and in the outside. It was hard enough to work assiduously to get a fortune, but she was also pregnant and was constantly worn out. When Grecia was born, Mama's life was lit up. She no longer needed abundant money. Her child was more than enough for her.

"What do you have in mind today?" asked Mama.

"I-I think we could go to the train station and to the market together," announced Grecia.

Mama grinned. Grecia was such a bright child. Other kids just wanted to stay at home and play whatever they can, like board games. That was just not the case for Grecia. She was more curious about the outside world.

"More precisely, let's go walking to the market and return home with a train," Grecia remarked. Even though they could return walking, she had always wanted to ride any kind of transport. Also, there was a train station right in front of the market, so why not ride one?

Mama's grin turned into a small frown. "Sorry, but we can't go to the train station. It-It's just not for girls of your age."

Grecia pouted in disappointment.

"But you said I could go there when I grew up!" she retorted. "I'm a grown-up now!"

This business was so serious Mama didn't even smile hearing that statement. "A no is a no, and you know that. I really don't understand why you want to go there so much, but you can't."

Grecia muttered under her breath.

Mama's lips curled into a smile this time, amused. "I'll buy some paper and ink for you in the market today".

Grecia's head immediately snapped into attention, beaming. "Really?" she asked.

"Why not?" her mother said, hugging her daughter. "A great talent can't be wasted. Now, let's go."

When the front door closed, the mother and daughter's eyes were blinded by the morning light, making them have to slightly cover their eyes. Even though Mama was a bit uncomfortable, Grecia was in awe, because she hadn't seen sunlight a lot, since she was only five. Sunlight *is,* after all, a rare thing in Elysian.

While Mama and Grecia walked, everything became greener

and greener. Even the houses looked like they had been painted again several times.

However, the structure of the streets was obviously the same. Just a straight, wide line, with the houses in each of the farthest sides. Beside every house was a garden, full of colorful flowers. In the middle there was a plain, gray road for people to walk in (Of course, Grecia and Mama were walking in here).

They walked for at least an hour.

"Do you think we should have ridden a train?" asked Mama, panting. She had forgotten how tiring it was to move with the bright sun above.

"Maybe," said Grecia. She was wheezing and drops of liquid trickled on her wet forehead.

Finally, they reached the market.

"That was a long way," said Mama, breathless.

Grecia wasn't paying attention, as she was looking at the train station. How the trains moved, how the people came up and down. Then there was a waving hand in front of her.

"Grecia, I asked you a question," muttered her mother. "Let's buy some things already."

"M-may I stay here?" asked Grecia, pointing a bench.

Mama was thoughtful for a sec. Could she trust her daughter to stay there and not get lost? Should she trust her, or be strict? She didn't want Grecia to get lost, but she had surely asked for a reason.

"Yes dear, but promise me something," Mama ordered. "You are not to move unless you see me."

Grecia just nodded, and sat on the bench. Her mother entered the market.

Minute after minute, the child couldn't get her eyes off the train station. For some unknown reason, that place seemed so… irresistible. She had never been so obsessed with something so much. The mechanism of the trains fascinated her, as well as its speed.

However, she obediently didn't move, not even an inch.

Half an hour passed when a voice came from a few feet away.

"Good job, Grecia!" Mama exclaimed, patting her daughter's head. "Now let's go back home. And I bought your drawing tools, by the way." She waved a plastic bag in front of Grecia's face, as if giving proof.

"Okay," Grecia said hastily.

Choo choo

A train departed, and the only thing the little girl could do was stare. And stare. And stare.

For more bonus content, visit Sowon Kim's website:
sowonkim.com

ABOUT THE AUTHOR

Sowon Kim, born in South Korea, is an author, translator, and social entrepreneur. As the daughter of missionaries, she moved to Peru with her family when she was just three months old. She hopes to raise awareness about the diverse social issues happening around the world through her stories, as well as inspire fellow teenagers to raise their voices.

When she's not typing on her keyboard (whether it be because of writing or schoolwork), Sowon can be seen swimming, reading, surfing, learning foreign languages, or translating for Lost Island Press and non-profit organizations. She is also obsessed with her adorable cat, Lucky.

Sowon started writing her debut novel *A Gleaming Shard of Glass* at the age of thirteen. She also translated *Leaving Wishville* from English to Spanish when she was fourteen years old.

sowonkim.com

Made in United States
Orlando, FL
19 July 2022